NAKED HEART

by

Jennifer Fulton

2008

NAKED HEART

ISBN 10: 1-60282-011-2
ISBN 13: 978-1-60282-011-1

This Trade Paperback Original Is Published By
Bold Strokes Books, Inc.
New York, USA

First Edition: April 2008

CREDITS
Editor: Shelley Thrasher
Production Design: Stacia Seaman
Cover Design By Sheri (graphicartist2020@hotmail.com)

Acknowledgments

I doubt I could write my own name without the love and forbearance of my dear ones. Not only do they provide hot dinners, undeserved praise, and thoughtful advice, they also feed my sense of humor. For this new work, I owe special thanks to old friends Dell and Jacqui for inspiration and good times.

Shelley Thrasher copy edited this novel with her usual precision and exhibits remarkable patience with my sometimes whimsical approach to style and syntax. Thanks to her, my flaws are not exposed to all. Lastly, without the friendship and vision of my publisher Radclyffe, this job would be a lot less enjoyable. I thank her most sincerely for being someone to count on.

Dedication

In memory of a dear friend and accomplice in sin.

Luce Acland
1963-1998

CHAPTER ONE

"There should be a law against you," said the corn-silk blonde sharing Penn's table.

"For making women wet?" Penn asked.

The leg touching hers quivered. "Arrogant *and* hot. How can I resist?"

A concentrated whiff of scent engulfed Penn, as though driven by a sharply exhaled breath. Through a haze of powdery musk she smelled salt and desire. She could close out this deal right now, she thought, but the blonde wasn't really her type. Too much makeup, and too brittle. Or maybe just too hetero.

Penn was flirting with her anyway. She had time to kill.

She glanced around the low-lit bar, searching the crowd for the man she was supposed to meet. It wasn't her kind of place. Lobbyists. Bankers. Business execs. No sign of Colonel Gretsky. She returned her attention to the woman on her right and wondered what her real name was. Not that it mattered. If she wanted to called herself Roxy Delice, who was Penn to argue? In certain occupations, her own included, anonymity made sense.

She reached into the shadows under the small round table and ran her hand up Roxy's firm inner thigh. The ultrasheer stockings crackled beneath her palm. The faint static was the closest she'd come to a current of awareness. She continued past the lace stocking top to the naked band of flesh beyond, determined to give her flagging interest every opportunity. Slippery moisture coated her fingertips, flowing through the flimsy satin panties. She pushed her thumb against the hot flesh beneath the fabric barrier.

Roxy's breasts rose with a jolt. Her glossy pink lips spelled out her terms. "Normally it's a thousand for the whole evening, but for you, I'm negotiable."

Penn had already guessed she was chatting with a professional. That was okay. She was the last person alive to judge how anyone made their living. She held Roxy's seductive stare. "For you, I won't charge a dime, either."

The blonde laughed, revealing a glimpse of someone real beneath the makeup, a girl next door long forgotten. Penn decided she could go there, after all, even though she usually hunted a different type. Degrees of queerness always factored into her enthusiasm, or lack of it. Roxy was probably on the straight side of bisexual. Penn preferred to bed women who weren't settling for a consolation prize. She was far from second best and chose sexual partners who could appreciate that fact.

Still, Roxy was here and willing, and Penn wasn't always so picky. She eased her damp fingertips from their snug haven between Roxy's thighs. The reaction was instinctive, the body straining for renewed contact. Penn heard a swift, hungry intake of breath.

"I guess I could take the night off," Roxy said unevenly. "Are you worth it?"

"A question I ask myself daily."

"Somehow I doubt that."

"Well, you have other options." Angling a sideways look across the room, Penn noted, "Chunky and married at ten o'clock. He couldn't keep his eyes off that nice ass of yours when you were coming back from the restroom."

Roxy sized the executive up in a quick, fleeting glance. "Ninety seconds. And he'd expect a discount since he didn't use the full half hour."

Penn shifted her whiskey sour aside and wiped her juice-coated fingers on the cocktail napkin. "Who would you normally target?"

"You mean, if I hadn't decided to let you put your hand up my dress?"

"Out of curiosity, what made you so…receptive?" Penn could have paraphrased with *How bisexual are you?* But she really didn't care enough to be interested—another bad sign.

"If I have a drink with another woman, I don't get hit on by ten guys who think they can get laid for free." Roxy's jaded smile didn't reach her eyes. "I prefer to take my time and choose the right john."

Penn refrained from asking the obvious question. She wouldn't get a real answer and, besides, it was no business of hers how this woman had arrived at her career choice. She didn't want to know. Only one salient fact mattered: was she in the mood to have sex with a woman who'd sparked so little desire in her that she would only be going through the motions?

She sipped her drink pensively and thought about wandering through Inner Sanctum, breathing in the sexual fog, waiting for her senses to react. A walk. A quick, hot look. A mouth worth kissing. Once she spotted the ideal plaything, she would study her for a while before provoking a response. Women knew when they were being watched, and Penn liked to make their necks prickle. An ancient awareness always forced them to turn around eventually, seeking out the predatory gaze they sensed.

Aroused by the thought, she swirled the pale amber fluid in her glass. The chase, in all its incarnations, turned her on. After she quit the CIA, she'd expected her highly tuned instincts to fade, but the change of scenery wasn't a change of personality. Instead she found ways to compensate for the adrenaline rushes she missed—she worked with the colonel and she chased unattainable women. A shrink would have a lot to work with, if Penn ever felt the need to prostrate herself on a couch and pay money to be told she had issues. But life was short and, in her case, precarious. She refused to suffer guilt over her nature; indulging it was more fun.

"I'd probably choose *him*." Roxy indicated a middle-aged man in a brown suit. "Road warrior from Wisconsin. Check out the briefcase. He's got all the important stuff with him because he doesn't want to leave it in his hotel room. He won't tip housekeeping, either."

"Wisconsin?" Penn couldn't see where that detail came from. "Cabin luggage tag on the handle?"

"I'm good, but not that good." Roxy giggled. "I overheard him when I came in. Something about tickets for a Packers' game."

"Why him?" Penn scanned the other solo males. There were plenty to choose from. Several had been staring at Roxy's hard nipples for the past fifteen minutes.

"He won't score with anyone else in here. He tried already and struck out. But he won't call an escort service, either, because his wife reads the credit-card statements and she's not stupid. So he's desperate." She cocked her head thoughtfully. "He's also the undemanding type. And tired. That's always a plus."

"You could be a detective."

"Fidelity testing? Yeah, I'm a real expert."

"That's a profitable field these days. So I've heard."

"What's your line of work?"

"Security," Penn replied vaguely. "Between gigs, I help out at a friend's nightclub."

"Were you ever a cop?"

"No."

"I didn't think so. You seem kind of…lawless."

"This from a woman who flouts the legislation of our fine state on a daily basis."

"Don't get me started on why I'm supposed to *give* my services away, but men who make porn get to *sell* their product."

Penn stroked the professionally manicured hand resting on the table. "I've spoiled the mood. I'm sorry."

"Me, too." Again the girl next door surfaced in a soft, regretful smile.

Penn sighed inwardly. She had hoped to get beyond her lukewarm interest in Roxy, but the spark wasn't there. If they had sex, it would be a routine transaction. No challenge. No uncertainty. She would have appreciated that in her twenties, when she was all about instant gratification. But these days she seemed to need hurdles and risks to stay interested. She wondered if her change of job really was to blame for her listlessness. She had a weird loss of urgency around getting laid. Maybe, at thirty-six, she was slowing down. The thought made her cringe, and she was about to make an offer her new friend couldn't resist when Roxy reached into her purse and produced a business card.

With a mixture of puzzlement and invitation, she said, "Want to meet me some time when I'm not working? Grab a coffee, maybe?"

Penn took the card and mumbled something noncommittal. No wonder the woman was confused. Penn had been sending mixed messages since their first "hello." Embarrassed, she offered, "Can I walk you to your car."

"No need. The cheesehead's on the cell phone to his wife. Watch me make him dump the call." Roxy gave the guy a big, wet, pouting smile followed by a coy wave. She couldn't have been more obvious. Or phony.

Mr. Wisconsin flushed and grinned, instantly smitten. It was a Viagra moment.

"Jesus, they're such suckers." Penn laughed softly. She had counted on that fact when she had a real career. The CIA derived some of their best humint from sex sting operations.

"If they didn't think with their dicks I'd be out of a job," Roxy said with equanimity.

She stood and planted a quick kiss on Penn's cheek, as though they were friends who'd shared a Friday night drink. Watching them, the john shoved his cell phone in his breast pocket and smoothed his hair. Roxy sashayed toward him, flipping Penn a tiny farewell wave.

Penn strolled out of the bar without looking back. While she waited for the elevator, her beeper came alive and she read the text message she'd been expecting all evening. She dropped Roxy's card into a trash bin and keyed a reply once she was in the elevator, proposing a new time and place for her rendezvous with the colonel. With each letter she typed, she was aware of her own edginess. She'd just turned down a woman she didn't want, but she was restless anyway, her libido signaling that three weeks without sex was a drought that had to break soon. There had been plenty of opportunities. Some had even involved the risk of failure with women who were hard to get, usually an unbeatable recipe. But Penn had allowed every hot possibility to pass her by.

Puzzled that she could feel horny but disinterested at the same time, she crossed the parking garage toward her blue-black BMW M6. The car absorbed her paychecks like they were wax polish, but she had a weakness for classy vehicles. This one looked like a large luxury coupé but performed like a Formula One sports car. She pictured a woman sprawled naked across the hood, a regular fantasy. Her senses responded at full volume. If the October weather wasn't turning bitter she'd be tempted to park somewhere discreet and explore that idea with a Ms. Right-for-Tonight. Assuming she could find one. And also assuming she wouldn't just give up on the whole idea and go home to watch porn alone and jerk off like a loser.

The M6 unlocked itself as though it had heard her footsteps. In fact, it had simply responded to the plastic remote card in her side pocket. Before she could reach the driver's door she noticed a woman changing the tire on her white Lexus a few vehicles away. Penn hesitated, but her better angels delivered a swift kick to the seat of her pants and she marched over.

"Do you need help?"

A pair of startling sapphire eyes stared up at her from a pale semi-shrouded face. The woman wore a paisley muffler wrapped tightly over her mouth and around her head, tucked into a bulky camel coat. Her slender, beautiful hands were smeared with grime, which, Penn decided, was completely unacceptable.

"Sit in your car and get warm," she said. "I'll deal with this."

"You're very kind. Thank you."

Was she just cruised? Penn looked twice at the stranger and decided her imagination was running wild. Right now, the stranded babe was probably preparing to call hubby and explain why dinner was late. Penn waited for her to close the driver's door and completed the tire change with her teeth chattering. No good deed goes unpunished, so she broke the crystal lens of her favorite Chopard wristwatch as she removed the jack.

Mumbling, "Goddammit," she closed the trunk and slipped between the parked cars to tap the driver's window.

It rolled down and the woman thanked her again in a throaty voice with traces of a Baltimore accent. She was still bundled up like her next destination was a dogsled event. "Have a nice evening," she said, and this time Penn *knew* she was being cruised.

If she weren't freezing and disheartened, she might have done something about the unspoken invitation, but her mojo was inert. Smiling with genuine regret, she let this one go. "Enjoy yours, too."

She didn't wait for the woman to drive away. All she could think about was thawing out her hands. The M6's plush interior was chilly—Penn left the heat-at-rest function disabled, preferring the slight shock of cold before driving. She allowed the cool to sharpen her senses for a few seconds then hit the ignition button. Soothing heat infused the driver's seat and quickly transformed the frigid space into a warm, luxurious cocoon. She stared at the empty passenger side and felt another rush of dismay. If she planned to satisfy her needs anytime soon, she would have to deal with whatever was distracting her.

Maybe she was bored with being single. It had to happen

sometime. She wasn't aware of any latent nesting urges, but perhaps she was in denial and using sex as a cheap placebo for love. What a cliché: the lonely, emotionally stunted failure unable to commit to the hard work of a real relationship. A basket case addicted to meaningless encounters with strangers who made her feel briefly alive.

Most women her age were in some phase of an LTR. Newly in love, or thrilled and having babies, or disillusioned and moving out, or divorced and getting back in the game. They weren't creeping around strangers' apartments at three a.m., trolling for a missing sock so they wouldn't have to field phone calls the next day because they left clothing hanging off a sofa arm. No, none of them were having that kind of fun.

Fuck them. Penn didn't accuse happy couples of being tamed into the grind of suburban life, settling for boring sex with the same familiar women who took them for granted. She didn't respond to the condescending pity of nesters by pointing out that she wasn't missing out on a whole lot.

Irritated, she backed carelessly out of her parking space and followed the exit arrows into the night. No, she wasn't pining for a picket fence and a partner who wanted more "us" time. Work wasn't the issue, either. Gretsky had an assignment to discuss and, although he'd missed their meeting tonight, he would connect soon and her bank account would be replenished. There was plenty of well-paid freelance employment for disenchanted former CIA officers.

She headed automatically for Eighth Street and decided she was getting herself worked up over nothing. She could get a woman anytime she wanted, and if she were honest, she knew exactly what was affecting her game. Lila Sylvette. The problem with no answer.

❖

Penn left the M6 in one of the reserved parking spots at Inner Sanctum, strolled to the side entrance, and entered her pin in the biometric lock before inserting her thumb to be read. She was one of the few people authorized to open the side and rear doors from outside the building. She glanced up at the security camera, making sure it was operational. The feed was transmitted to Lila's penthouse on the top floor and to the security posts on each level. Lila had leased a single floor when she started her club a decade earlier, but as she progressively took over more space it made sense to buy the building. With her father as her silent partner, she'd rebuilt the interior, creating one of the hottest club atmospheres in DC.

"Ms. Harte?" One of the stewards nailed Penn as soon as she walked in the door. "Thank God you're here. I was on my knees, darling. I swear. Just *praying* for you to come in early."

"What's up, Felix?" she asked.

"A catastrophe in the making." Felix was prone to exaggeration, but he was one of the best stewards in the club. He tugged distractedly at one of the thick silver nipple rings that peeped through his mesh vest. "We have ourselves a chastity-cage drama."

"Christ, not again." Penn dropped her duffel bag on the floor in the staff area, opened a spare locker, and hung up her jacket.

"Things were going so well." Felix glumly handed her a tank with the club's logo emblazoned above glow-in-the-dark pink lettering that read "Management."

Penn unbuttoned her shirt. "Is Lila downstairs?" Her best friend had a way with the clientele and could usually defuse a situation with a few good-humored words and complimentary drinks.

"She's not having a good day so she went to bed."

Penn removed her broken watch. It was still functional and read ten o'clock. Inner Sanctum didn't come alive until midnight, and on work nights she usually arrived around that time so she would be present during the one-to-three-a.m. peak. When the club wasn't taken over for theme and fetish events, it made money as an upscale urban venue. Tonight, the place would be jammed with the perverati for Lila's monthly Hedonism party. There would also be a heavy sprinkling of tourists unfamiliar with the club's etiquette. With the demise of VelvetNation and several other Washington, DC nightspots, a broader range of clubbers had invaded Inner Sanctum over the past year. The regular kink crowd was tolerant of the newcomers but didn't welcome disrespectful opportunists. Security issues were the inevitable consequence.

"Have you dealt with the problem?" she asked.

"We thought we had, but she came back ten minutes ago. Just hideous. Straight out of Housewife Road and wearing *the* worst pleather pants. Hubby slapping her ass with a plastic quirt from God knows…Home Depot. They seem to think one of Mistress Adele's slaves is simply *dying* for a threesome."

"So they have good taste, but no brains?"

Felix tittered. "They tied something to his cage and tried to lead him around. I was about to fetch poor darling Lila when you arrived."

"Let her rest," Penn said. "How bad is it?" Mistress Adele didn't take kindly to her slaves being handled without her consent.

"The suburbanites are still walking upright." Felix sniffed disdainfully. "That won't last."

Penn set the tank top aside and yanked a pair of black combat pants from her duffel bag. "I'll finish changing here and meet you at the security station."

She had intended to take a shower in her upstairs room, then visit with Lila before starting her shift, but she always took care of business first. Now that the evening lines were starting to form, the head of security and his crew were busy. Lila preferred that her stewards handled minor problems on the dance floor and in the other public areas. Security was only called in if a clubber ignored diplomatic warnings.

Penn laced her boots and made sure the Smith & Wesson compact strapped to her left calf had the safety on. The stewards didn't carry. She and several trusted members of the security team were the only people armed. Lila hated the idea that guns were necessary at all and flatly refused to carry a weapon herself, a fact that made Penn uneasy. If religious whackjobs were willing to shoot doctors and bomb abortion clinics, queer and kink venues seemed like an obvious target.

She crammed the rest of her gear into the locker and took the narrow side exit to the coat check at the front of the building. Felix was waiting for her in the office next door, watching the dance-floor and dungeon monitors.

"How's the situation?" Penn asked.

"They've adjourned downstairs."

He pointed to a tall man standing behind a petite blonde, his arms draped over her shoulders. The heteronormatives were engrossed in a scene that made Penn squint at the small screen. Two pale, identically corseted beauties were involved in an intricate bondage-and-whipping ritual. Each was a mirror image of the other. Long, sleek limbs. Small hips. Straight dark hair almost to their narrow, confined waists. Penn could not imagine standing upright in stiletto heels like theirs, let alone moving with their steely grace.

Felix cupped his cheeks between his slender hands. He looked awestruck. "Aren't they *too* sublime." He was downright gushy, a change from his usual bitchiness. "Of course that vile little beast, Nariko, picked them up from the airport. Heaven forbid any of *us* give offence with our surly presences."

As he rambled, Penn stared at the monitor in dry-mouthed fascination. She wasn't surprised by much anymore, but the women transfixed her. There was something intuitive in the way they worked, as though they functioned as two halves of a whole.

Theirs was a perfectly conceived choreography that explored the boundaries of pain and pleasure. Each move was precise yet languidly unselfconscious.

The usual churning chaos around the fringes of the dungeon had given way to strange stillness. Penn had the impression that everyone present felt they had a role to play in the tableau before them, if only that of fortunate voyeurs. Even one of the regulars, a bondage master in dated chaps and leather cap, stood with his arms folded and his eyes riveted. The wind seemed to have been squeezed from the trouble-making tourists. Slack-faced, they too had surrendered to the moment.

"God," Penn breathed. "Are they twins?"

Chapter Two

Cops were tempting. The blond one was a stocky, firm-bodied type with square hands, thick biceps, and a determined jaw. If she noticed Unity's body beneath the flimsy wrap, her steely blue eyes gave no sign.

"That's the window." She pointed as another officer strode into the living room. "Looks like forced entry."

The slouching male colleague inspected the wood frame. "Any problems in the street, Ms. Vaughan? Peeping Toms? Vagrants? Individuals loitering?"

"It's a quiet neighborhood."

Which was why she'd sold her soul to the bank to keep the house when her relationship ended a year earlier. Having spent her childhood in West Baltimore, Unity understood the value of keeping desperate people at bay. Bethesda didn't see much crime.

"When did you say you noticed the suspicious vehicle?"

"Yesterday, and I saw it here when I got back from the city an hour ago. I think it's an Escalade." Unity watched the female cop's butt as she climbed onto a chair to inspect the security catch at the top of the tall double-hung window. The uniform was a nice touch, even if it was kind of down-home.

The Montgomery County Police wore beige shirts and tan pants. They were well-scrubbed, polite, and respectful, offering another stark contrast to the world Unity had left behind. In Baltimore, cops assumed everyone was a criminal and behaved accordingly.

Officer Reynes jumped down off the chair and paced around the large living room while her colleague shared his thoughts with Unity. "You might want to consider getting a dog." He rattled off the advantages. "Peace of mind. Good company. A deterrent. You live alone?"

"Yes." Unity knew she shouldn't be rubbed raw by this confession. She thought she glimpsed derision in the quick look the officers exchanged. Despising herself for caring what these nobodies thought about a woman living alone in a big, expensive house, she explained, "It was originally purchased as a family home."

Let them invent a tale of woe for her: Respectable woman abandoned by creep, her hopes of children dashed. Stuck with a home she couldn't afford to sell in the terrible real-estate market. Algae in her swimming pool. Unraked leaves blowing across her yard. Bad signs to send—burglars were always on the lookout for absent homeowners.

Unity had chosen the house off River Road for its seclusion and the leafy charm of its surroundings. Both advantages were now redefined as scary drawbacks. A determined felon could exploit any number of doors and windows, unseen by passing traffic. Her vulnerable situation was not lost on Officer Reynes.

The well-built cop pointed toward the French doors that led out onto the patio. "I don't know if you've noticed, but you have a rusted deadbolt on those doors."

"I just use the key in the handle," Unity said.

"Well, this is a safe neighborhood but you can't be too careful." Officer Reynes checked the other windows, her broad, muscular shoulders drawing her shirt taut as she craned to reach the highest catches. "Your security system isn't exactly state of the art."

"I've been meaning to do something about that," Unity said meekly.

"Most home-security companies offer a free review service." Reynes kept up the good advice. "You could get a couple of assessments and quotes."

"You're pretty sure nothing is missing?" the male officer asked.

"A few things were disturbed in my upstairs office and the master bedroom, that's all."

"Want to show us?"

As Unity led them up the curving wood staircase, Reynes asked, "Did you check your jewelry?"

"I don't have any." Unity turned the heavy gold ring on her right middle finger. "Just what I'm wearing. A watch. Earrings. Nothing valuable."

"Is there a safe in the house?"

"Yes, but I don't use it. I can't even remember the code." She showed them into the master bedroom.

A stranger would see a clean tidy space with nothing out of order, but Unity knew her drawers had been opened and closed, the clothing in her closet had been swept from one side to the other, and her camphor chest had been opened, along with every other container in the room. Several lids were not quite flush. Perhaps the burglar had been looking for diamond rings and costly art. In an up-market neighborhood filled with opulent homes, the least he would expect was some cash, but the emergency stash she kept in her trinket box was untouched. That fact more than any other bothered her. Why break into someone's home and steal nothing?

She showed the officers. "I keep five hundred dollars in here. The burglar didn't take it."

The cops stared at the cash. They seemed just as bemused as she was. Very reassuring.

"Does anyone else have a key to the house?" Reynes asked.

"Only my mom and the maid service. Mom lives in the cabana past the pool. She's away visiting with my aunt in Nashville at the moment." Unity opened the internal door to her office. "As you can see from the mess, someone was in here snooping around."

Bethesda's finest surveyed the disorder with an air of lame apology.

"Since nothing has been stolen we can't do much except file the report," Reynes said.

Her eyes strayed downward, lingering with lesbian intensity at the gaping front of Unity's robe. A pink hue deepened the bronze in her cheeks. She rested her hand on the holster at her side and her eyes darted elsewhere. Unity pictured her gun belt dropping to the floor, the beige shirt sliding down her deeply tanned arms, her white wife-beater tee clinging to a firmly contoured torso. How butch was she, really? Unity sighed. Some cops just gave that impression, part of the image.

"Oh, you have a cat." A smile softened Reynes's squarish face. She crouched and ran her hand along Duchess's back in a slow caress that made Unity feel desperately untouched.

"I have two, but you won't see Dandy. He hides when people visit."

She couldn't quite ignore the fabric straining across Officer Reynes's crotch and along her powerful thighs. She pictured the cop sprawled on her back, unzipped, sliding a lubed hand down the thick shaft of a strap-on dildo. Short of breath, Unity turned away from her carnal imaginings and took a few paces out into the hall. A moderately hot woman was in her bedroom, *doing her job*. But Unity couldn't ask intelligent questions about home invasion and keeping herself secure. No, she was too busy drowning in hormones.

"Well, thank you for coming by," she said, stoically enduring a succession of fantasies that streamed through her mind. Handcuffs. A voice in her ear talking dirty. Fingers prizing her open.

The cops followed her to the front door. Defiantly, she let the robe slip from her shoulder just so she could enjoy the predictable stares. Cold air made her nipples knot. Both cops noticed. The slouching male stood up straighter.

Officer Reynes looked hastily at the porch light high above them. "You've got a bulb out, up there."

Yes, it was the perfect opportunity to play the helpless female. Maybe Officer Reynes could swing by later, just to make sure no one was hanging around. Unity would offer her a drink. They would both understand why she was there with her gun and her badge and her competent hands.

"I must take care of that," Unity said, as if an unreachable light bulb was her biggest problem. She ran her tongue across her dry lips and drew her robe together. "Good night, Officers."

Shivering in the damp fall breeze, she watched the cops walk away. She had their number. Maybe she would call Reynes and ask what she was doing when she got off her shift. They were grown-ups. It was okay to be direct. She locked the door and leaned back against the solid oak panels, weirdly disabled by her desires. What in hell was wrong with her?

Okay, she hadn't had good sex for more than five years. But she'd coped just fine. In fact, she'd even developed a slight aversion to the whole idea of getting naked with another person. Why fall apart now?

❖

"French fashion-designer mother. British aristocrat father. Thrown out of Le Rosey. So, they're trouble."

"I hear you." Penn knew Le Rosey, an elite Swiss boarding school attended by European royals and the ultrarich.

She'd been stuck there for a week once during a combined CIA/MI6 operation to foil a kidnapping plot. The place was overrun with the progeny of Russian gangsters, many with their own bodyguards camped out in the village to supply drugs and prostitutes when called upon. Security was a nightmare. Roseans occupied an impenetrable bubble of privilege, and the school administrators were at pains to avoid causing ripples in their pupils' lifestyles-of-the-rich-and-shameless existence. Penn couldn't imagine what the twins must have done to earn expulsion from that moral vacuum.

"They're a fixture at Torture Garden events." Lila continued to list Chloe and Colette's accomplishments. "They've been on the cover of *Gothic Beauty*, and they did that cat-food commercial—the German one that was banned over here."

"So you're paying a fortune for them?" Penn concluded.

"If I'm serious about the European fetish market, I have to take it up a notch. They love them over there."

"Why are they acting in porn?" If they were Rosey students, they couldn't need the money.

"I think they fell out with their family." Lila exchanged a froufrou blond wig for a sleek dark copper, asking, "What do you think?"

Penn dug beneath the hair pile on the dressing table and extracted a gamine light brown piece with honeyed streaks. "This one is softer."

Lila pulled the wig over her pale, naked scalp and toyed with the wispy bangs. "You're right. I looked like a hag in those loud colors."

"Are you nuts? You're gorgeous."

"Liar." Lila smiled up at Penn, her baby blue eyes big and sunny in her gaunt face. Some people manage chemotherapy better than others. Lila wasn't one of them. "So, anyway, I can't afford to have the hottest twin dommes on the planet lying around watching wannabe slaves crawling on uncooked rice for the next month. We have to start filming."

"I said I'd help."

"You don't know anything about erotic films."

"I watch them."

Lila scoffed. "You watch *The Bourne Ultimatum* and war movies."

"I own some dyke porn."

"Oh, please. The same six Sappho's Girls DVDs?"

"They're hot." Penn knew her taste in erotica wasn't the most adventurous, but she had nothing to prove. "What are you worried about?" she asked. "All I have to do is make an appearance every now and then, and throw my weight around, right?"

She was already managing Lila's club for several nights each week. Could a few actors in a high-class porn movie be any more demanding than the performers and clientele at Inner Sanctum?

"Oh, I don't know." Lila wrung her hands. "Maybe I'm crazy going ahead with this. I was even thinking of shooting two films simultaneously, using the same sets but different talent."

"That makes sense."

"I'm just worried because I won't be there much and you can't possibly know what to look for. Our stuff is so…specialized."

Lila had carved out a niche at the premium end of the market, making artistically produced fetish porn for the discerning pervert. Last year she had won the Pied Amour Society's Diamond Pump award for best foot-fetish DVD. Her preference for quality fare restricted the hits to her Web site, but she made out okay on membership subscriptions. Enough to pay the medical bills.

"Hey, if it doesn't rock my world to watch a nude guy harnessed to a cart, dragging Miss Daisy around, who cares?" Penn said reasonably. "I don't have to be the ultimate pervert to organize the catering and make everyone think I have a clue. You've got a director. There's a script. And from what I saw down in the dungeon tonight, Chloe and Colette can improvise just fine."

"Creative talent has to be managed, darling. Egos require massage. I might have surgery soon, if it's shrunk enough. There's no way I can handle everything here, too."

"Of course you can't." Penn kissed her cheek. "And you don't have to. That's what I'm here for."

Lila gave her a sweet but dubious smile, then rang a delicate china bell and a narrow-hipped Japanese woman entered the room.

"Hey, Nariko." Penn surrendered her chair. "Good to see you."

This gallantry was rewarded with polite indifference. Nariko Amari thought butch lesbians were indelicate and Penn was a slacker who only attracted women who weren't picky. Penn's enduring friendship with Lila clearly mystified her.

"Tea, Lila?" Nariko stood with her back straight and her hands folded neatly in front of her. She never fidgeted. Or slouched. Or made a single graceless move.

Lila said, "Perhaps later, after Penn has left us." She knew how to warm Nariko's heart.

They'd been working together for five years. Nariko had started out performing at the club in a Japanese schoolgirl routine. After the resentful wife of a fan attacked her one evening and slashed her face, she abandoned her act to become Lila's accounts manager and personal assistant. Penn didn't think the scars were all that noticeable, especially under makeup, but Nariko was a perfectionist. According to Lila, she thought she was marred and could not endure her flaws being paraded before an audience.

"What are you doing here?" Nariko regarded Penn as she might a pimple in the bathroom mirror. "Felix is looking for you."

"He'll just have to cope," Lila said. "Good news. Penn's going to help us keep Chloe and Colette entertained."

Nariko responded with an impassive nod that made her high ponytail sway like a sheaf of satin fibers. "Certainly Penn will stand out among the mistresses' usual companions. I imagine one can tolerate only so much exquisite refinement before pining for a brief descent into coarseness. Penn will offer just that change of style."

"So long as I don't have to take them to the ballet." Penn knew better than to get hurt feelings over Nariko's barbs.

With a faint incline of her head, Nariko conceded. "As always, your resolve is bottomless."

The double meaning might have escaped a stranger, but Penn knew better. Nariko never missed a chance for a sly dig over her lack of a partner. *Bottom*-less indeed. Picking up on the blunt inference, she invited her, "Just come right out and say it, baby doll. You know how I hang on your every word."

After a sober up-and-down inspection of her attributes, Nariko informed her, "Violette finds herself uncollared again." The submissive in question was a lust-object of Penn's. "I mentioned you, but she says she is not in the mood for more training."

The prospect didn't excite Penn, either. "Violette doesn't need training."

Nariko smiled with saccharine disdain. "I was referring to *you*."

"Poor sweet Violette," Lila mused aloud. "She holds her dominants to such impossible standards, that's the problem."

"She wastes her energy on lazy egotists who take her for granted," Nariko declared. "She coached that apology-for-a-domme for over a year and what was the result? Top's disease."

Penn kept her opinion to herself. She knew enough from her friendship with Lila and her involvement in the club not to criticize anyone's D/s dynamics. She had no lifestyle aspirations, herself, a fact that Nariko saw as further proof of a weak character.

"Well, thanks for thinking of me," she said with irony. "But Violette seems to want a twenty-four seven situation, not just a—"

"Semi-top who can't go the distance," Nariko completed, finally accepting the chair Penn had given up.

"Oh, ouch." Penn knew she shouldn't allow herself to engage, but she couldn't resist crooning softly, "Hey, still not getting laid? It shows, Nariko."

"Is that the best you can do?"

Penn moved a little closer and rested her butt on the edge of the dressing table. "Why suffer? Anytime you want that itch taken care of, all you have to do is ask."

She was kidding, but not entirely. Nariko had a beauty that was hard to ignore. Her face was captivating, with its flat planes and small mouth. Her nose was long and elegant, and her strong chin seemed at odds with her demure body language. She was easily dismissed by strangers as a neutral presence, but she drew attention like a cool, still statue in the midst of clamor, a soothing distraction to the messy human traffic around her. Penn often had an urge to shake her up, just to see the warm, real woman inside that marble calm.

Nariko sighed, her patience sorely tried. Without bothering to reply, she took Lila's hand between both of her own and said, "It's late and you should not be tiring yourself." Her tone was gentle and she spoke with a lilting emphasis on certain syllables. "I'll escort Chloe and Colette to the guest apartment and make sure they have everything they need. If Penn manages to come on set tomorrow, I'll introduce her and explain what is expected."

If she was waiting for Penn to get annoyed about being discussed like she wasn't in the room, she would be disappointed. "Sure, I can do that," Penn volunteered.

Without so much as a glance in her direction, Nariko said, "We'll start at two in the afternoon. Try to be punctual."

"Hey, Nariko," Penn responded softly. "Did I tell you how sexy you are when you take charge?"

A pair of nutmeg brown eyes flitted her way. "Did I tell you how bored I am by your insolence?"

"Frequently." Penn bent close enough to fan the compact delicacy of Nariko's ear with her breath. "But I know what you're really thinking. You want me, you just can't admit it."

"Who knew your fantasy life was so richly embroidered?" Mistress of the charming insult, Nariko smiled daggers. "I suppose you find it necessary to compensate for everyday shortcomings."

"You're the expert." Penn parted the few fine hairs that had drifted free of Nariko's ponytail and kissed the back of her neck.

"Get off me, you oaf," came the encouraging response.

Penn suspected Nariko enjoyed their games, not that she ever showed signs of weakening. "I love when you play hard-to-get." She toyed idly with her belt buckle, at arm's length from Nariko's face. "One day…"

With an eloquent eye roll, Nariko replied, "In your dreams." But her gaze dropped to Penn's crotch for a tell-tale second.

"Gotcha," Penn said wickedly.

Nariko reached out and plucked a tiny pink marabou feather off Penn's fly. "When will you learn that you are not irresistible? *And,* that it is imperative to inspect black clothing for lint?"

"Why bother when I can have you groom me?" Penn stepped in toward her. "Anything else you want to feel?"

"Go find someone who'll appreciate your…assets," Nariko advised. "This place is full of bimbos with low expectations."

"Darlings," Lila cut across their bickering with equanimity, "I need to vomit, so if you don't mind…"

Nariko was instantly on her feet, shoving Penn aside with her sharp little elbows. "Make yourself useful for a change," she commanded imperiously. "Open that bathroom door. Then leave us."

Placing her arm around Lila's waist, she walked her across the bedroom, her narrow face pinched with emotion. Penn had never seen her cry, but in her eyes she glimpsed a wounded inner creature hidden from the world, naked and writhing in its solitary hell.

"I'm sorry," she said, not really knowing who her platitude was for—Lila or all of them.

Her best friend's pricey fake hair clung to her damp forehead as she looked up. "Go party for me, darling. I want to hear every sordid detail tomorrow."

"You got it," Penn promised. She left the apartment before her own tears started to fall.

CHAPTER THREE

B ecause Lila hated the music that was flavor of the day in some clubs, the sound at Inner Sanctum varied from retro-house to disco, techno, and rock remixes. As Penn squeezed her way across the dance floor, the pounding backbeat worked her chest and groin. Hands brushed her, by accident or intent. Feathers tickled her face. A stifling cocktail of perfume, sweat, and hormones swamped her senses.

She exchanged shouted greetings with regulars and complimented guests whose spectacular costumes screamed for attention. The Hedonism party attracted everyone from the serious kink crowd to transgendered kids from the ballroom community who competed for trophies in the catwalk cabaret event upstairs. One of the housefathers tapped Penn's shoulder as she went by and asked how Lila was doing. People were noticing her absence, a fact that worried every club employee. No one wanted Lila to feel she had to be there all the time, but the atmosphere wasn't the same without her.

Penn gave an optimistic version of Lila's prognosis, trying to sound upbeat and positive. She'd always been able to compartmentalize, but her concerns about Lila's health refused to occupy a solitary corner of her mind, instead infiltrating her thoughts like a virus. Lung cancer that had spread to her liver— the diagnosis had seemed impossible at first. Lila wasn't even a smoker. A year later, there was no denying that, short of a miracle, her best friend would toast her last New Year in a few weeks' time. Normally Penn avoided drinking while she was overseeing the club, but she needed something to take the edge off. Beer and a woman, in that order.

She hung out at the bar while she knocked back a Bud. Across the expanse in front of her, clubbers strutted and vogued in the climax of a day-long transformation ritual, peeling back the masks of next-door neighbor and co-worker to reveal their erotic alter egos.

Exquisite, Penn thought as a tight, sweet body summoned her roving eyes. By club standards the young woman was conservatively dressed. She wore black Lolita chic, a short open-back skirt and ruffled petticoat teamed with a skintight strapless, nipple-high satin-and-leather bodice. Without the platform shoes she would easily be six inches shorter than Penn, but she was leggy for her height. Her small-breasted build made her seem almost too young. Penn couldn't get interested in the early twenties, but the self-aware gaze that trapped hers immediately suggested someone closer to thirty. Like she'd lost interest, the girl turned away with a swish of her blunt-cut pink-and-silver hair. She knew she had Penn's attention.

Their paths converged in the mezzanine lounge on the next level, where exhausted dancers gravitated to watch the display below. Those who wanted to chill out farther from the music could abscond to a cocktail bar in the middle of the same level.

Penn had a better idea. "I have a place upstairs. Shall we?"

Lila's Cabaret occupied most of the third floor, along with an invitation-only private club and several small meeting rooms. Penn had converted one of these to a bedroom so she could retreat somewhere private and catch a few hours' sleep if she wanted. Her house was an hour away, and with Lila's illness she spent most nights at the club.

The gothic princess hung over the mezzanine balcony far

enough so the back of her skirt rode up. "I like it here. It's cool watching everyone."

Penn stepped in directly behind her. A fraction closer and her crotch would brush the perky little ass beneath the skirt. The girl raised one foot at an angle, ostensibly to check the strap of her shoe. Penn moved even closer and steadied her hips, placing a hand lightly on either side. The brush of the firm butt against her zipper teased her clit to attention. When the hottie repositioned her foot, her legs were a little wider apart.

She leaned back, speaking over her shoulder. "You're Penn, aren't you?"

"Guilty as charged." Had she slept with so many of Lila's clientele that her reputation preceded her? Penn bent in so she could be heard. "You?"

"I'm Thalia." Her cheek brushed Penn's lips as she tilted her head to reply. She smelled of cinnamon. Her skin was very soft. "My older sister, Violette, comes here."

"Sure, I know Violette." Now that she thought about it, Penn could see the family resemblance.

"I've only been here a couple of times," Thalia continued. "Violette said if anyone hassles me you're the one to talk to."

Penn wasn't sure how she felt about Violette entrusting her with an alluring younger sister. Nice consolation prize, but also a signal that she'd been relegated to the sidelines before she could make a move. Not that she was in the running. What would she have suggested if she hit on Violette: *Hey, baby, want to take a walk on the tame side?*

She planted her hands on the railing at either side of Thalia, bringing them almost into full contact. Thalia arched her spine suggestively. She started to turn but Penn caught her around the waist and drew her back hard, aligning the length of their bodies. In her ear, she murmured, "You're making me horny. Is that deliberate? Are you a tease?"

"Why don't you find out?"

Screened by the mezzanine surround and the constantly shifting lights, Thalia took one of Penn's hands and drew it beneath her hitched skirt, letting it rest where her damp thighs gapped.

Penn clamped down over the hot mound. "Sure you don't want to see my bedroom?"

She pouted. "What's wrong with this place? I'm having fun."

Her breasts were beautiful, crushed against her bodice as they rose and fell. Penn thought about freeing them, spreading this babe out and making her beg. She hooked Thalia's panties aside and slid a finger along the wet crease of her flesh. "I suppose I could fuck you right here, with all these people. But having sex on the mezzanine is against club rules."

Thalia rocked into Penn's cupped palm. "No one's watching," she teased with sluttish innocence.

Her back was hot and damp against Penn's torso. Around them, voices and faces blurred. The air felt thick as honey. Penn withdrew slightly and turned Thalia so their faces were inches apart. She raised her wet fingers to Thalia's rosebud mouth and smeared the lips with her juices. Breathing each other in, they kissed slowly. Thalia tasted of mint and sex. Her slippery tongue coated Penn's with salty residue. The muscles of Penn's stomach tightened, and she gave herself over to the thrill of a new body responding to hers, the strangled sighs and cravings. She needed so much more. Flesh on flesh. The intersection of soft and hard. A hot, strenuous fuck that would leave her wrung out and happy.

A hand tugged at her belt. The seam of her pants was jerked against her clit. Groaning, she seized the hand trying to unzip her. In that moment, she looked past Thalia's shoulder and met a haughty stare. Nariko stood talking with one of the stewards, but observing Penn at the same time. She swept Thalia with a single, fault-finding glance. Before bored fortitude claimed her expression once more, Penn caught a flash of some other emotion. Anger?

She wasn't sure. A part of her was tempted to forget Thalia and forcefully persuade Nariko to come upstairs with her. Hadn't they danced around each other long enough? But hitting on Lila's staff was not her style, and it would be even dumber to have a one-nighter with the cranky assistant. Lila needed Nariko more than anyone and would never forgive Penn if she did something to compromise the situation. Besides, Nariko had made it clear that she'd rather have her eyeballs pierced than sleep with Penn. Five years of flirting hadn't gotten her to first base. Not even close.

Trying to refocus, she shifted her attention back where it belonged. Thalia was hot and right in front of her, just waiting to be fucked. They would have a good time even if there was no real challenge involved. Predictably, she didn't argue as Penn led her upstairs past the cabaret and through the private club. Penn paused to check in with security, letting them know she wanted no interruptions for the next two hours, then ushered Thalia into a narrow hallway accessible to pass holders only.

They walked with surreal composure to her room, no one tearing at clothing. When they got inside the door, they stood frozen for a moment, severed from the urgent beat of the music, the smell of perfume and recently groomed leather, and the thrust and heat of bodies close by. Like two kids on the brink of committing a minor crime, they stared glassy-eyed at each other.

Fidgety all of a sudden, Thalia said, "Nice room."

It was nothing special. When Penn began to spend more nights at the club, Lila had insisted on replacing the basic cot with a queen bed and closet. Felix had added what he thought were homey touches: red wallpaper, zebra-striped bedspread, light fixtures from the Ikea catalogue. Penn renovated the bathroom herself, with plain white tiles. After years in seedy foreign apartments, she appreciated clean surfaces.

She dimmed the lights, asking, "Drink?"

"Just water, if you have it." Thalia's eyes darted toward the bed.

"Second thoughts?" Penn took a couple of bottles from the bar fridge.

Thalia shook her head. In stark contrast to the modest flutter of her eyelids, her smile was a wicked little taunt. She reached behind herself and the black bodice fell away, followed by the skirt. Her red underwear was plain but looked sexy on her lithe curves. In the oblique cast of the lamplight, a down of soft fine hairs stood out along her arms. Goose bumps stippled her delectable breasts and thighs.

Penn dropped the water bottles on the bed and enfolded the small hand that moved unconsciously toward her own. "Let's go wash off the world." She led Thalia into the bathroom and turned on the shower. "Want to play with the temperature while I change?"

These preliminary moments could be awkward. Most people preferred to conduct their bathing routines in private. Having to share with a stranger could kill the mood just as easily as it could heighten arousal. Penn always looked for her partners' cues so she would know which way to play this warm-up phase. She dropped her clothes over the back of the small loveseat in the corner. Thalia had left the bathroom door open and was already in the shower when Penn returned.

"Come in." She opened the fogged glass door and slicked her hair back with both hands.

Penn had to stop herself from clutching a fistful of the damp pink-and-platinum tangle and pushing Thalia onto her knees on the hard tiles. *Slow down,* she thought. For some reason her usual control was suddenly tenuous. Her throat closed in on itself when she tried to speak. Wordlessly, she backed Thalia into the wall.

Hot jets of water rushed between them. Their limbs slid together. Penn added soap. The washing ritual was torture. She wanted to explore this body in all kinds of ways, but time would not permit.

Their breathing fell into ragged synchronicity. Jolts of arousal stabbed through Penn, calling every muscle into tense response. She would stay captive that way, drawn tight, aching for release, until satisfaction freed her. She loved losing herself in that feeling, the single-minded drive toward slaking her desires. No room for anything but the moment.

She squeezed the small up-tilted breasts and the hard nipples, dragging whimpers of need from Thalia. Rinsing the soap from her hands, she pinned the small woman more firmly and indulged in slow caresses. Thalia's pussy was dripping. Strands of silken arousal clung to the scallops of flesh. Her clit protruded, begging to be stroked. She pushed her hips forward in craving.

"Want something?" Penn asked.

Thalia strained closer. "Please. Touch me."

Penn ran her thumb up over the swollen shaft, rolling its fleshy hood back and forth, enticing throaty responses.

Thalia bit hard on her shoulder. "Mmn. That's so good."

"Tell me what you want," Penn growled from deep down where that familiar stalking creature had uncurled.

"Fuck me."

"That's what they all say."

Thalia's slippery folds pulsed and compressed. Penn circled her hot, tight entrance, toying with her slowly, enticing her to open wider.

"You think you're a stud, huh?" The question came out in a breathless rush.

"You tell me." Penn drove two fingers inside.

Thalia shuddered. Her hold on Penn tightened. Cupping her, Penn didn't move.

Thalia squirmed. "Please."

Penn wished she was wearing her strap. She wanted to lift Thalia and fill her full of cock. *Hold that thought.* A whimper broke across her shoulder. Thalia gyrated on her unmoving fingers. Penn responded with a short, sharp thrust.

"You haven't asked me what I want," she said, slowly withdrawing then sliding in once more.

Thalia blinked up at Penn, wet-faced. "What do you want?"

"To slam my big butch cock into you." Penn could feel Thalia sinking as her legs weakened. "To bend you over and fuck you until you can't take any more."

"Oh. God." Thalia's hips moved urgently. She clawed at Penn.

Crushing her firmly, supporting most of her weight, Penn pumped faster, drawing a scream of delight. Her sounds, the faint slurp of their wet bodies, the pounding of their hearts drew Penn's nipples even tighter. Her clit went out in sympathy, pulling at the surrounding flesh like a compacted knot. She savored the sensation, kissing and licking the hot skin sliding over hers.

"Deeper," Thalia begged, meeting each thrust with gasps and moans. She slid a hand between them, reaching for her own clit. "I can't wait."

"Yes, you can." Penn pushed the fingers aside and gently ground the ball of her thumb over the tiny head. "How bad do you want it?"

Thalia reached down with both hands, spreading herself so Penn could sink in deeper. "You're so fucking hot."

"And you're so wet and tight. You feel really good."

Her muscles closed around Penn. Their rhythm changed, their fucking suddenly becoming fierce. Head thrown back, Thalia murmured a steady stream of guttural demands. To fuck her harder. To haul her into the bedroom and hold her down. To make her sore.

"God," she moaned. "I can't stand up anymore." She started to shake. Her clit seemed to grow beneath Penn's thumb.

As her body keened and tensed, Penn said, "Let it go, baby."

With a startled whine of joy, Thalia shuddered through a violent orgasm, then her head dropped heavily against Penn's chest. They stood still in the wet steam, slow to separate until Penn turned off the water. Then they stumbled out and toweled off erratically. Still damp and panting, they made it to the bed without a word. Thalia crawled across, shoving back the covers, her cute round ass provocatively raised.

Penn flipped her onto her back and yanked her legs roughly apart. She liked easy access. "I'm not done with you."

Thalia's blue eyes swam with want. Her inner thighs were wet, the fluids glistening. She placed her hand over her pussy, feigning shyness. "I'm so afraid."

The hot throb at Penn's core was almost unbearable. She thought about having Thalia suck her off right now, but she wasn't ready to surrender this high-pitched intensity. She placed a hand over Thalia's. Her fingers were instantly drenched. The scent made Penn ache to get back inside her, but she wanted to taste her, too. She wanted to lick her and tease her until she was ready to give it up, then fuck her deep and hard. Releasing her hold, she moved off the bed.

"You have a great ass," Thalia said as Penn took her favorite harness from the dresser and dropped it on the bed.

She usually went through the requisite motions, conferring on size and shape preferences and having partners choose the dildo of their dreams from her collection. Tonight she wasn't in the mood, and she had a sense that Thalia was the accommodating type who preferred not to get detached by making design comparisons.

She slid a black, all-purpose toy into the harness. Not too long, but a decent girth, and the contrast always turned her on. Pink flesh wrapped around the dark shaft. Even with the lights down, she could see everything if she wanted to watch. And she did.

She pulled on the harness and adjusted the buckles, a little surprised when she had to move each one in past the usual notch. She'd lost weight. That explained the extra slack in her jeans. Dropping a few lube sachets on the night table, she sat down on the edge of the bed and turned the lamp to its lowest setting. Thalia moved behind her, reaching for one of the water bottles. She uncapped it and passed it to Penn first.

"No, go ahead," Penn said.

She enjoyed the sight of Thalia kneeling with her head back, a rivulet rolling down her throat and between her breasts. After taking a few gulps herself, she set the bottle aside and drew Thalia down onto the pillows with her.

"What's a sweet thing like you doing in a badass butch's bedroom?" she asked, trailing her index finger down the young woman's smooth, warm cheek.

Thalia answered with an oddly innocent kiss. She pressed her lips softly to Penn's like the final seal on a letter full of promises. The distant throb of the music reverberated up through the floor, adding ballast to the beat of Penn's heart. She was briefly overwhelmed with an urge to make love, not just have sex, and for several seconds she lay still, succumbing to a wistful wonder at the tenderness she felt.

The tip of Thalia's tongue curled beneath Penn's top lip and danced its way inside. Penn sank into the kiss, stroking the velvet curve of Thalia's spine. Her skin was a little cool in the aftermath of the shower. Penn closed her eyes, making room for her other senses. She let her hand wander over Thalia's ass, down her thigh, back up her supple flank and the dip of her waist, all the while listening for the sounds of pleasure. Thalia's breathing quickened and her mouth parted on a gasp as Penn found her nipple and clamped it between thumb and forefinger.

She stroked her tongue against Thalia's and inhaled the drift of scents in the room. The familiar citrus the cleaners used. The damp cotton smell left by their heads against the pillows. The salty tang of her own wetness and the sweeter tinge of Thalia's.

She released the nipple and cupped Thalia's breast, feeling goose bumps corrupt the patina of her skin. When Penn opened her eyes, Thalia was staring at her. They continued to kiss in sensual thrall. As she sucked Thalia's bottom lip, she felt the cool glide of a thigh over her own.

Thalia splayed her hand on Penn's back, inviting her closer. Her mouth whispered across Penn's, "I want you inside me."

She placed delicate kisses down Penn's neck and the slope of her shoulder. Her teeth sank in. She pushed Penn onto her back and straddled her. Not exactly what Penn had planned but the view was quite something. Thalia slid down until Penn's cock was sandwiched between them. Sitting forward, her hands flat on the bed, at either side, she moved back and forth, coating the shaft with her fluids. Penn rocked her hips and felt Thalia's weight shift.

"Yes, right there." Thalia writhed and moaned.

Penn placed her hands on Thalia's waist and drew her down hard. "Can you feel how I want you?"

Thalia answered a shaky "yes" and rocked back on her heels, closing one hand over the dark cock jutting between them. Watching Penn intently, she smeared moisture over the head and slowly worked down. Penn felt herself spilling and tightening at the sight of her small hand wrapped around the thick length. Something clawed at her insides, bursting up through her, demanding to be let loose.

With a knowing smile, Thalia rose and guided Penn to her dripping entrance. She lowered herself, taking an inch at a time until her body settled over Penn's and they were completely joined. With a low moan, she seemed to crumple forward then, bending over Penn and catching her breath.

"I didn't think I could take all of you," she whispered in her ear,

"I'll have to work on that." Penn gripped her more firmly and brought her down to meet the sharp upward thrust of her hips, drawing a harsh cry.

Thalia drew herself upright again, riding Penn with her legs spread wide and her breasts bouncing. Her nipples stood out, darker and harder than before. She tilted back, her legs spread wider, inviting Penn to watch. With each long, deep stroke Penn felt herself nearing explosion. The sight of her cock disappearing into the glistening cleft made her weak. Juices ran beneath her harness and dribbled between her thighs, her own mixed with Thalia's. Her clit pounded painfully with each change in weight and tug of the harness.

She wanted a different position, where she had more control, but that could come later. From Thalia's sharp cries and glazed unfocus, Penn knew she was close. Breathing harshly, trying to delay her own climax, she dropped a hand to the fair-haired mound, working the swollen flesh against the flat of her palm as she rubbed her thumb past Thalia's clit. She could feel her spiraling higher and higher as they fucked harder and faster, gasping, groaning, drenched in perspiration.

Penn dug her feet in and raised up so she could drive deeper. "Come for me," she urged, burning for release.

She felt Thalia's clit rise and peak against the ball of her thumb, quivering with the rest of her body until she screamed through her teeth, "Oh, God. Oh, God," and a hot gush of fluid soaked Penn's crotch.

Crazy with need, Penn angled herself just enough for a change in pressure and jerked hard, then fell back as her body spasmed in release. Thalia collapsed over her, a deadweight, panting and sighing.

They lay still and sweaty, glued together in the aftermath of their mindless union. Eventually, Penn glanced at the digital clock on the night table. She would have to get back to the club pretty soon. But first...

"Get on your knees," she said, sliding out from beneath Thalia. "I want to fuck you from behind."

CHAPTER FOUR

I miss going down on you. I miss skin.
Unity stared blindly at her notes, horrified to be dragged back in time to the silent self-talk of her disintegrating relationship. She could still feel her ex sleeping next to her, each breath scraping her nerves like a dripping faucet. She could hear her own noisy heartbeat as she lay awake gazing into the shifting shadows, marking time till morning. Looking back, she could track the death of her feelings less in the single, crushing blows that sped disillusion and more in the passage of those long, empty nights. Love could survive too long on crumbs. Dreams were slow to disintegrate in the face of hope. Doubts were filtered through love's forbearing rationalizations until the simple truth could no longer be denied.

Unity had learned something painful from that process: you can't make someone want you if they don't.

And Merrill Walker didn't.

Unity stared cautiously across the conference table at her ex and saw a competent, well-dressed CEO with two governing passions: her corporation and her schnauzers. Right now the three show dogs would be in a warm, well-equipped playroom with animal-loving kennel supervisors whose background checks Merrill conducted herself. She left nothing to chance when it came to the creatures she loved.

Her eyes lost their softness, then, and what Unity observed in their muted gray depths was not regret, or embarrassment, or even the same intensity of focus she'd once mistaken for desire. Merrill regarded her with a mixture of disappointment and irritation, as though let down in some crucial way. Unity guessed she still hadn't found a replacement wife. Merrill couldn't tolerate loose ends of that kind in her personal life. Being single implied inadequacy. She needed the right kind of partner, just as she needed the right kind of car and comfortable furniture for her home. From the look on her face, Unity could tell nothing had changed. Merrill still blamed her for the failure of their relationship.

They'd first met seven years ago when Merrill was in takeover negotiations with the small company Unity worked for back then. Merrill had fascinated her. She was articulate, ethical, honest and very young, at forty-one, to be a senior executive at a huge company like Fortis Biosystems. Unity was intrigued. Confidence was sexy, and Merrill had tons of it. Their rapport was instant—the attraction of an egotist and an admirer. At least, that was how Unity finally saw it once she could distance herself enough for an honest postmortem.

At the time she'd mistaken their effortless simpatico for a sign of destiny. Foolishly, she'd read into Merrill's interest a reflection of her own heady passion. If any proof was needed that love was blind, she was the ultimate control experiment.

They didn't start dating right away. Merrill lived in Chicago and had returned there once the negotiations were over. A year later they ran into each other at a conference and the same magic was still present. Unity wasn't willing to walk away without exploring what those powerful feelings meant, so she stayed in touch with Merrill after the event. After a few weeks of e-mails and phone calls they started traveling to see each other. Merrill moved to DC six months later so they could live together.

Unity had her own company by then. After the takeover, she'd resigned with enough cash for a start-up, from the sale of her stock and options. Vaughan Biotech focused on an area of research that fascinated her, surfactant chaperone technology. Her ultimate goal was a new protocol for treating spinal-cord injuries. Early on, she'd secured several research grants, then an investment from the Department of Defense. The DoD wanted to create supersoldiers, so the prospect of an injection that would halve recovery time for burns and traumatic injuries, and possibly end paralysis, excited them. They'd been pouring millions into regenerative medicine, including adult stem-cell research, and the injection of funds allowed Unity to employ a team and expand her company.

Over time some unexpected findings in protein folding had taken her along a new path. She'd kept quiet about her digression and did not involve any of her team. The DoD was not funding work in this additional field beyond its applications to surfactant chaperones, and Unity preferred to keep it that way. She knew the military well enough to know they'd divert funding from the therapeutic field to warfare in a heartbeat.

She wasn't sure how the information eventually leaked out that she'd made a breakthrough with major ramifications for fusion toxins, but she suddenly found herself fielding awkward questions from her principal investor and takeover bids from several large corporations, one of them Merrill's employer.

"Have you read the offer in its entirety?" Merrill asked.

Unity perused the document in front of her, wanting to appear respectful if not convinced. "Yes, it's very generous, but as I said in my e-mail, Vaughan Biotech is not for sale."

"We're willing to discuss a higher figure if you can provide the concrete data we've requested."

Merrill consulted her BlackBerry and a tender smile disturbed the nerveless calm of her face, suggesting a more complex human being than one might expect, a person with hidden emotional depths. But Unity knew the expression well. Her ex was reacting to endearing canine antics; she kept her browser on the doggie daycare Web site so she could watch schnauzer-cam. No fellow human could hope to inspire such naked adoration. For a start, people talked back.

"Let me be clear about something," Unity said. "My refusal to sell isn't a negotiation tactic. I'm not asking for more money. I'm simply saying no."

The thin, older man seated next to Merrill steepled his hands and peered over his rimless eyeglasses. Sullivan Brady, the chairman of Fortis Biosystems, seemed puzzled by her reluctance.

"Dr. Vaughan, with respect, if the rumors we've heard are true you're in an awkward position. You don't have the resources to advance your protein-engineering research unless you cut a deal with Defense, but you don't want to have to divert your primary focus to biochemical warfare in order to do so. I can understand that. With the backing of a parent company, you wouldn't have to make such a choice. You would, in effect, have your frosting and your cake."

"I don't know what rumors you've heard, but perhaps they're overstated," Unity said carefully.

"Come, now." Brady spoke like a benevolent grandparent. "Did you really think no one would find out about your meeting with Gustafson? According to the Duke rumor factory, you're a month away from the holy grail."

Unity laughed. "Oh, sure. And they've just patented the pill for eternal life."

Merrill rolled her fountain pen between her thumb and forefinger. Unity had given the silver Waterman to her on their first anniversary. "We know you discussed predictive folding-pattern algorithms."

So, bite me. "Well, that *is* the professor's field," Unity said blandly.

"The impression is that you're extremely close to the *de novo* design of an artificial protein," Merrill responded. "Are we way off base?"

"I haven't filed for a patent."

Unity glanced sideways at her attorney. He looked uncomfortable, perhaps because he had her application to the US Patent and Trademark Office in his briefcase. She hadn't completed her work, but she'd advanced far enough to file a claim to protect several key discoveries. If she was successful she could add her final claims to the same patent later.

Sullivan Brady interrupted again. "Contacts of ours in the DoD have expressed certain concerns." Ignoring a frown from Merrill, he continued. "Being a scientist, you can't be expected to be familiar with the political nuances, but it's only right that you should know exactly what you're dealing with."

He didn't intend to patronize her, Unity thought. In fact there was something vaguely gallant about his disclosure. A certain kind of researcher would have rushed straight to the military with preliminary discoveries like hers and tried to shake loose a big injection of capital, regardless of the consequences. But Unity wanted to buy time. Her discovery frightened her. The weapons conventions that governed toxin research were well-intentioned but open to broad interpretation, especially in her field where the potential for good brought with it a terrifying risk for evil. She didn't want to be propelled into a reckless drive toward the latter. Money was not the only consideration.

Wondering exactly what Sullivan Brady knew, she asked, "Can you be more specific, sir?"

"The world is changing quickly. We're in a cold war with Europe, not that most people have noticed. Having an isolationist foreign policy means we must rely on our military strength more than ever, and that means—"

"Staying ahead at all costs?" Unity completed.

"You understand me."

"No one can make me divulge my ideas."

"They don't have to," Mr. Brady said. "You'll file for a patent sooner or later, because you have no choice. And you may be surprised what the federal government is willing to do in the interests of national security."

"You're saying if they think I might sell to a foreign firm I can expect negative consequences?"

"Are you so naïve you have to ask that question?" A trace of contempt filtered into Merrill's tone. "They could shut you out of your own company if they wanted."

"How would they do that?

Merrill shrugged. "Let me count the ways. For starters, you have a Top Secret clearance, don't you?"

"Of course." The clearance was mandatory for Defense contractors, and Unity accessed classified information for some of her research.

"Imagine if it were revoked." Merrill's smile was grave and sympathetic. She always adopted a soothing expression when she thought she was winning an argument.

"Is that some kind of threat?"

"Not at all, Dr. Vaughan." Sullivan Brady frowned at Merrill as though she'd crossed a line that affronted him. "We don't wish to harm your company, we want to buy it."

Merrill backed down grudgingly. "Still, it's fair warning. Not everyone is as honorable as Mr. Brady. If I were you, I'd be careful."

"Your concern is touching." Unity's voice came out evenly, leaking only a trace of irony. She knew how to hide her feelings. For that skill, she had Merrill to thank.

Merrill moved on briskly, apparently certain that an acceptance of their offer was inevitable. "With us, you will still set your own personal research goals. Of course, we'll expect team priorities to support company objectives. You have to be realistic."

Unity almost laughed. She had wondered how long it would take for Merrill to deliver one of her typical end-run pronouncements. *You have to be realistic*—implying that she normally wasn't. Merrill was a master of preemptive invalidation.

Unity forced herself to relax. This was not one of their

bedroom showdowns. Merrill was not the one holding all the cards and refusing to make compromises. Unity had left that unhealthy dynamic behind the day she finally fell out of love. She no longer had to endure subtle put-downs and patronizing remarks every time they had a discussion.

Watching Merrill's expression closely, she said, "Naturally I see the advantages in accepting Fortis's bid. However, I plan to remain independent in the foreseeable future."

"You're making a mistake," Merrill said flatly.

"Quite possibly."

A rare hesitance delayed Merrill's response. "If I were you, I'd take some time. Emotion can cloud one's judgment."

Unity looked her dead in the eye. "As can the lack of it."

Ignoring Merrill's seething anger, she stood and shook hands with Mr. Brady, exchanging farewell pleasantries. "Thank you for meeting with me. Have a safe trip back to San Jose, Mr. Brady."

"If you have a change of heart, my door is open," the older man said.

As he and his team filed from the conference room, Merrill hung back. "Dr. Vaughan, a quick word if you don't mind."

"Actually, I do." Unity sidestepped, trying to move around her, but Merrill shoved the door closed. She took opposition badly.

"Is this personal?" Merrill's question was more of an accusation.

Unity made an effort to breathe slowly. "Not at all. I have nothing against Mr. Brady."

They both knew that wasn't what Merrill meant.

"You won't get a better offer," Merrill responded impatiently. "So if you're simply being contrary, I would advise you to rethink."

"And I would advise you to take a different tone with me." Unity reached for the door handle. "Not that it really matters. This discussion is over."

Merrill didn't like being challenged on her behavior. Obstructing the door so that it couldn't be opened, she said, "I'm trying to do you a favor. Can't you see you'll be completely fucked once you go public with your findings?"

"Well, that'll be a change," Unity said with an acid smile.

Merrill seemed confounded. "I can't believe you're throwing this opportunity away because of a grudge about *us*."

"Not everything is about *you*, Merrill." Unity was surprised that she felt no anger as she spoke; in fact, she felt nothing at all. It didn't matter what Merrill said, or thought, or felt. She truly didn't care.

Shame clawed at her. She could not reconcile her weak-kneed behavior in their relationship with the strong-willed, assertive person she was now. If she were completely honest, she owed Merrill a debt of gratitude. She'd learned a lot about herself during their relationship. Loyalty, single-mindedness, and a refusal to accept defeat had made her a fool in love, but the same traits were ideal in a research scientist.

She took in Merrill's neatly cut salt-and-pepper hair and her firm, clean features. She looked ten years younger than forty-eight, fit and perfectly groomed. The only thing different about her was her mouth. It was a little thinner, and Unity no longer yearned for those lips against her own. She no longer imagined passionate dialogue spilling from them.

She wondered if Merrill had already tried to find another ideal wife. Maybe this time she would choose someone who valued material possessions more than intimacy, the right kind of woman for her. Unity doubted it. She would probably be drawn to another starry-eyed idiot whose emotions she could drain dry.

"How are things for you, Merrill?" she asked, giving in to her curiosity.

"Same as ever." Merrill's face was hard to read. "It's been a good year for the company, so my bonus is going to be worth having. The dogs are doing great."

"So are the cats."

"You cut your hair," Merrill noted.

Unity didn't explain herself. She simply said, "Yes."

Merrill wasn't prone to giving compliments. If she ever remarked on Unity's appearance, somehow she conveyed disapproval.

"Are you dating anyone?" Merrill's question sounded casual but her jaw was stiff.

Unity considered inventing an imaginary lover, but she wasn't willing to tell lies just to watch her ex squirm. "I don't have time right now."

She could read Merrill's relief in a softening of her mouth. She'd always been absurdly possessive; apparently that hadn't changed.

Merrill sighed. "I wish things had turned out differently for us."

Unity detected an unspoken nuance—Merrill was dropping a hint, opening a door, waiting for her to rush eagerly back. She would have, once. But there was no point stating the obvious, that choices had consequences. Merrill's choices had inflicted hurt and distress during their relationship, but knowing that, she'd made them anyway. And Unity still hadn't forgiven her. More painfully, she hadn't forgiven herself. She had made choices, too—and paid for them in unhappiness.

On a sharp, indrawn breath, she said, "Well, it's all in the past, and we both have work to do. Since this conversation is going nowhere, let's move on."

Merrill regarded her with unusual emotion. "Unity...I'm sorry."

"So you've said."

Unity returned to the table to collect her stuff. If Merrill wasn't going to take the cue and leave, she could remain in the conference room by herself. There was another exit. Unity headed for it briskly.

"Wait. Please." Merrill gripped her arm. "I think we should talk."

Unity wished she'd just kept quiet. The last thing she needed was one of *these* conversations. She shook Merrill loose. "I have to go."

She pushed out through the exit at the rear of the room and strode down the narrow beige hallway.

Merrill came after her. "Listen to me, please." A note of desperation altered her smooth tone.

Unity stopped walking and faced her. "There's nothing left to talk about. What's done is done. We both made mistakes so let's not beat ourselves up. I'll speak with my attorney about the offer and if—"

"I want another chance," Merrill broke in flatly.

Unity couldn't even form a reply. Another chance? Did Merrill really think that was an option? Dumbfounded, she said, "You had a thousand days with me. That's a lot of chances."

"Let's not get into tit-for-tat recriminations. I'm serious. And this time, we'll do things differently. I can see that our priorities weren't always in step, and I'm willing to re-examine mine."

As she continued her pitch, Unity pictured them on the sofa in the early months of their relationship, Merrill next to her, absorbed in paperwork. So close, yet so distant. Ignoring her physical cues, her seductive hints. Claiming tiredness when Unity kissed her. Fobbing her off with promises she would never keep: *Let's go upstairs early tomorrow and make love.* Unity's needs and desires were irrelevant. Merrill didn't share them, so they were sidestepped as an inconvenience. Her strategy was simple. She withheld. Affection and sex were bargaining chips. Merrill's special knack was to get what she wanted without having to deliver in exchange.

"What do we have to lose?" Merrill insisted. As always, she was convinced by her own logic. "We're both single. We could start out dating. If you don't want me to move back in right away, that's fine. Give it some time and—"

"No."

"That's it? Just 'no'?"

"What do you want me to say?" Unity felt like slapping her. "We're incompatible. No amount of wishing can change that."

"I disagree. You're always so black-and-white about everything."

In the past, Unity would have responded to that ludicrous assertion, pointing out that she was a scientist. Nothing was ever black-and-white until she had proof. Even then she questioned her interpretation of the data. Refusing to fall into her old defensive pattern, she stayed calm and said, "You're a good-looking, financially successful woman, Merrill. Just go out there and be who you are. Find someone who can appreciate the real you."

"I don't have time for that." Merrill snorted. "And to be quite honest, the right kind of woman isn't easy to find. I'm too old for bars and clubs, so it's online dating, and people are so deceptive."

"Yes, it's hard to get to know someone from e-mails and phone conversations," Unity said coldly. "I mean, before we lived together, I had a certain impression of you, based on your letters. Romantic. Considerate. Sexually adventurous..."

A serious, reflective expression moved across Merrill's face. "Well, that was part of courtship."

Unity knew she should end the discussion, but she had always been mystified by the intimacy of their earliest communications. The person revealed in Merrill's phone calls and letters was the one she'd fallen for, yet as soon as they started living together that romantic, sexy woman was nowhere to be found.

"What do you mean 'part of courtship'?" Unity asked.

"We were in different cities," Merrill said. "How else could I compete with women you could see any day of the week?"

Astonished, Unity said, "There were no *women*. There was only you."

She felt sick. Merrill's letters had spoken to everything she'd ever yearned for. The stark contrast between those paper promises and Merrill's actions once they were together had bewildered her. At first, she blamed the stress of the house move and the demands of a new live-in relationship. Then she blamed herself for somehow alienating the woman she was in love with. Then, as things got worse, she challenged Merrill on her behavior and they ended up in a classic blame cycle. Now, if she'd heard correctly, Merrill had just said those letters were contrived. All being fair in love and war, she'd simply told Unity what she wanted to hear.

Since their breakup Unity had been clinging to a kinder truth: that Merrill had presented herself as the lover she wished to be, but then couldn't live up to that vision. Like all unhappy couples, they'd built lousy communication patterns. Each time Unity's disillusionment reached a crisis and she decided to leave, Merrill would promise to do things differently. Unity kept giving their relationship another chance because she truly believed the woman who wrote those letters was there, somewhere, and she wanted to be with her. It took almost three years for her to abandon that hope.

Trying to sound detached, she asked, "Are you saying you pretended to be romantic to keep my interest? Everything was… calculated?"

"I wanted to marry you, not seduce you." Merrill's tone was defensive. "I bought us a beautiful home. You had everything a woman could possibly want."

Except a lover. Unity supposed she wasn't the only woman who'd ever fallen for a mirage and allowed herself to be manipulated. She wasn't sure why it shocked her so much that Merrill had engineered a "romance" to get what she wanted. If she wasn't cunning, how else could she have become what she was now, one of the youngest CEOs of a Fortune 500 company?

Unity's heart felt leaden. She had thought nothing else Merrill ever did or said could hurt her. "There's something I don't understand. Why did you choose me and not someone more like you?"

Merrill gave this question thought, her brow creasing slightly.

"It's not that easy. Most femmes are emotional and needy. But you're a scientist. I suppose I thought you'd be rational once we settled down."

"I'm very rational when I'm not in love," Unity said.

"And that's why we should talk." Merrill looked pleased with herself. "Now that you're not taking everything personally, I think there's an opportunity for us. We were always good company for each other, and we have a lot in common. The animals. Politics. Taste in music."

"You're suggesting we live together as platonic companions because we have shared interests?"

"Why not? We could do worse." As if she were making a generous concession, Merrill said, "It doesn't have to be platonic."

"We weren't sleeping together when we broke up," Unity pointed out.

"That's not true."

Unity wasn't going to be trapped into an argument. They hadn't had sex for three months when she told Merrill it was over. They never kissed or made out. But Merrill thought so long as she made an appointment for sex occasionally, they were still a couple regardless of follow-through. Unity couldn't think of a single promise ever made about their intimate life that Merrill had kept, and that would never change. She could never again harbor the illusion that Merrill wanted her as anything but an outward stamp of success in a part of her life she neglected. It was time to end the discussion.

Most people would be elated to receive a bid like Fortis's for their business, but Unity felt dispirited. She hadn't intended to have this conversation—she knew better. Yet here she was, picking open the wounds of her past. Aggravated with herself, she said, "It's a moot point, anyway. We're not getting back together."

She started walking again, heading for the restrooms.

Merrill caught her by the wrist. "I love you," she blurted out. "My life is empty without you." Her voice rang with bitter sincerity.

Unity waited a few seconds for this declaration to register in the stony terrain of her heart. A familiar cotton-wool numbness descended. Borrowing a phrase from Merrill's playbook, she said, "It's not my responsibility to make you feel good. You have to do that for yourself."

"I'm not asking for adoration."

"Really? I had the impression it was like water for you."

"I should have expected this," Merrill muttered. "I reach out to you, and all I get is attitude."

Unity kept her temper in check. Merrill knew exactly how to push her buttons, but she wasn't going to react this time. With a disinterested shrug, she said, "If you need a new wife, maybe you should consider an executive dating service."

She met Merrill's incredulous stare without flinching.

"Pay a fee for blind dates? That's nuts."

"You've had four long-term relationships go south." Unity kept up a mild, dispassionate tone. "Maybe it's time for a new strategy."

Merrill was silent for several seconds before biting out, "I guess you think this is funny, me crawling back."

"Actually, I think it's sad." Unity turned away, pushing open the restroom door.

"I won't ask again," Merrill warned.

The crack in her voice was real. In their entire history, Unity had never felt powerful in any of their interactions. Even when she walked away a year ago, the emotional wrench had torn her apart. There was no sense of triumph, no satisfaction at finally discarding Merrill instead of feeling discarded herself. But everything was different now. She held all the cards. Not only did Merrill want to take over her company, she wanted *her*.

Unity hesitated, her back propped against the door. She'd begged for them to work together to breathe life into their relationship before it withered completely. Now, Merrill was belatedly asking her to do just that, and Unity sensed she really meant it. Part of her wanted to say yes, if only to acknowledge the bruised self who'd thrown everything at love and walked away bereft. But that would be the worst kind of betrayal. She couldn't do that to herself.

An uneasy turmoil wiped the self-assurance from Merrill's face. She took a step forward and reached for Unity, a kiss on offer.

Unity drew back instinctively and felt the last vestiges of Merrill's hold on her falling away. "It's too late," she said with a finality that shook her.

Without waiting for a response, she slipped past Merrill and almost fell into the pungent sterility of the restroom. Her knees trembled and she felt nauseous. She went to the hand basin and splashed her face with cold water. Between her splayed fingers, she stared at her changed self with a survivor's calm.

The spell was broken. She was free.

CHAPTER FIVE

Penn noticed the eyes first, glowing neon sapphires against the lily hue of her skin. Her features were finely wrought, the brow high, the nose slightly long. The lips were unexpected, a full, smudged bloom that seemed too hothouse for the cool reserve of her expression. Chin-length ash blond hair framed her face. The cut was slightly ragged, the effect almost a rebellion against her striking beauty. If she lightened her hair and wore it in shoulder-length waves, she would look like a movie star. Apparently, that wasn't her goal.

"Who's the babe?" she asked, sliding the head-and-shoulders photograph back across the table. There was something familiar about the face, but Penn couldn't match it to anyone she knew.

"Unity Vaughan," Colonel Troy Gretsky replied in his clipped commander-of-the-realm manner. "Your new case."

"Who's she fucking?" That was the usual deal. Gorgeous woman fucks politician. Can't shut up. Has to be dealt with. No blowback.

"No one," Gretsky said.

In other words, the dupe in question was not just your average moron ruled by his dick, but a big shot whose name could not be spoken. Penn wondered which "family-values" slimeball it was this time.

"Same shit, bigger fan?" she remarked.

"Wrong. We got ourselves a nerdfest." This was Gretsky's term for industrial espionage.

Penn tapped the photo in disbelief. "Are you trying to tell me *this* is a nerd?"

"Founder and chairwoman of an outfit called Vaughan Biotech," Gretsky replied. "Some kind of genius is what I hear."

So this babe had something other people wanted, either data on a hard drive or a hazardous biological agent.

"Okay, what am I stealing?" Penn asked.

"Nothing. The client wants Dr. Vaughan's cooperation in a business matter. She's been intractable so far. Your job is to obtain biographic leverage."

"Biographic leverage" was intel-speak for blackmail material. Penn glanced back down at Vaughan's beautiful face. Everyone had secrets. She wondered what this woman was hiding that could be used against her. "Who's our contact?"

"KR."

Penn was surprised. Kyle Roth was in the business of political damage control for his masters. He sent the sleaziest jobs to Gretsky, who paid various freelancers to deliver the necessary results. Penn had been working with the colonel ever since he recruited her for the CIA while she was still a student at Georgetown University. His retirement had coincided with Porter Goss's takeover. Like many seasoned veterans, he'd kept his head down in the acrimonious post 9/11 climate, but Goss brought in a squad of arrogant know-nothings who alienated anyone who still gave a damn about ethics or doing their jobs, Gretsky included.

He'd taken early retirement. Penn had just walked away, like many of the best officers. Careers weren't the only thing destroyed during Goss's partisan purge. Inconvenient evidence, like detainee-torture videotapes, were another casualty of the faithful Bushies. But the Gosslings had departed now, and word was out that Michael Hayden, the new director, wanted disgruntled exiles like herself to come in from the proverbial cold. Gretsky said he was too old, and he was making too much money in the private sector; these days a lot of counterintelligence work was being outsourced. But Penn was seriously considering the idea. Her life had been a mess ever since she left. Working as a stringer wasn't her style.

"Somehow I don't see KR running a nerd shakedown," she said, refocusing on her next paycheck. "Is there something you're not telling me?"

"Of course."

"Yeah, I had a feeling about that. So what kind of leverage are we talking about? Does she have a husband with a temper? Am I supposed to get pictures of her flirting with some guy and threaten to hand them over, or something?"

"More or less."

Straight-out blackmail. Penn could work a scam like that with both hands tied behind her back. "What's my end?"

"Twenty-five up front. All costs. Bonus upon satisfactory completion." Gretsky placed a key on the table.

Back in the glory days, when they were both undercover, she and Gretsky had used a locker at Union Station for drops in DC. But Amtrak had ceased that service after 9/11, causing vast inconvenience to numerous spooks and felons. In the changed world they now inhabited, Gretsky left her cash bundled inside an envelope in a lockbox at the Bank of America on Dupont Circle, along with a dossier on the target and all the usual need-to-know crap about each assignment.

"Well?" he asked.

"I'll have to think about it. I'm kind of busy right now." Penn didn't want to seem too keen. If Gretsky thought she was on the ropes she'd end up with the kinds of shitty interim assignments no one wanted to take. Poodle bodyguard-cum-dog walker. Driver of getaway vehicles. The usual pavement-artist crap—shadowing and surveillance.

"KR asked for you by name."

"I'm flattered, but like I said…I'm short on time, and twenty-five isn't raising my blood pressure."

"How does fifty sound?"

"Like there's a catch."

"I doubt you're going to see it that way." Troy Gretsky's face showed signs of life for the first time since they'd been talking. He was probably close to sixty but was one of those tanned George Hamilton types who never seemed to age. He kept himself in shape and had his hair dyed light brown. "If I were ten years younger and looked like Brad Pitt, I'd handle this one personally."

"You've lost me."

He pushed the photograph back across the table. "You're going to seduce this woman, film your sexual encounter, and provide a DVD."

Stupefied, Penn said, "KR wants a video of me fucking? Forget it."

"He doesn't want *you*. He wants Vaughan. And he's after the lesbian angle."

"I'll bet he is, the little perv." Penn's imagination ran wild for a few enjoyable seconds before she got serious again. Something about this job didn't make sense. "I'm not seeing how a porn video is biographical leverage in a business scenario. What's the threat? Embarrassment?"

"Embarrassment isn't the issue." Gretsky paused. He always chose his words carefully during their discussions, trying not to give away more information than she needed. "Fortis Biosystems has made an offer for Vaughan Biotech, but Unity Vaughan says her company is not for sale. The client worries that she'll accept an offer from elsewhere."

"They want her to make the deal with Fortis?"

"Yes."

"Why not increase the bid?" Business was business.

"They tried that. She won't sell."

"I still don't see the leverage." Penn was uneasy. This assignment felt off in some crucial way. If something was going to blow up in her face, she wanted to know before, not after.

"It's not our problem if KR is barking up the wrong tree. He's the guy writing the checks."

"No one wants to see themselves plastered all over XTube," Penn mused aloud. "But KR's nuts if he thinks anyone is going to sell a company to stop the public seeing her tits."

"Just make the video. Okay?"

"Sure…if I can film her with someone else."

"That could be a problem. There's no one else."

"Not even casually?" Penn found that hard to believe. "How do we know?"

"The client hired a private detective several months ago. He came up empty. Hence the handsome offer for your…er… services."

Penn tried to look as though there was nothing outlandish in being paid fifty large to have sex with a babe she'd happily fuck for free. "I'm interested but you're talking about my naked ass here. What's going to happen to the DVD once Vaughan caves? That's if she does."

Gretsky weighed in with his usual complaint. "You ask too many questions."

"That's how you trained me. Tell me why this is going to work and I'll think about doing it."

After a brief hesitation, Gretsky said, "People with TS clearances can't afford to have kinky sex videos of themselves all over the Internet."

Penn grinned. "It has to be kinky? That's going to cost extra."

Gretsky's response was more of a grimace than a smile. "That's what the fifty is for. Call it a hardship bonus. No pun intended."

"So, based on the porno tape, the client will threaten to compromise her clearance?"

The plan was starting to make sense. As well as conducting "periodic reinvestigations," the Defense Security Service could randomly review any clearance holder's status based on new information, such as a tip-off about someone's behavior. Nobody wanted a TS clearance revoked; it was impossible to work for certain branches of the federal government without one.

When she left the CIA, Penn's TS clearance was inactivated, adding insult to injury. She hadn't enjoyed being placed under a microscope for the routine PR every five years, but losing her clearance had shaken her more than she expected. She hadn't realized how completely her job defined her until she was suddenly a civilian. For about a year, she sucked up the freedom and lack of structure. Her life was a constant party. But the novelty had worn off, and instead of becoming a relaxed, rounded person, she was bored and restless. And without her clearance, there were definite limitations to her marketability.

"Is she a defense contractor?" Penn asked.

"In the broad sense. Her company has received DoD research funding."

"Which would dry up if she lost her clearance." A double whammy. Under the Project BioShield train wreck, billions of dollars were being diverted into biodefense research. Entrepreneurs were scrambling to tap into this river of federal largesse. No one in the field could afford to lose their meal ticket. "So, she's screwed either way. If she doesn't sell, she probably won't be able to keep her company going."

Gretsky nodded. "Simple. Effective. Clean."

From his self-congratulatory tone, Penn figured he'd probably dreamed up the idea himself. "And with the DVD, they'll have her where they want her even after the sale goes through."

"The gift that keeps on giving," Gretsky murmured happily.

"Just what I always dreamed of," Penn muttered. "KR gets to hang on to a video of me having sex for as long as he wants."

"Don't worry, he'll only drool over it alone."

"That's a huge consolation."

It crossed Penn's mind that if the client wanted Unity Vaughan's company simply to get their hands on sensitive information she could probably steal whatever they wanted and spare herself the fate she'd rather avoid—the thought of KR hitting replay on a porn video of her made her want to puke.

"What's the deal here?" she asked. "Her company owns some kind of proprietary technology, right?"

"Vaughan's an innovator," Gretsky said. "There's a rumor that she's made a discovery with defense ramifications. So far there's no sign of publication or patenting."

"The data is in her head?" Penn didn't buy that for a minute. Scientists always wrote their theories down.

"Some key components, at least. Her idea of an insurance policy, perhaps. If she doesn't write it down, no one can steal it."

"Want me to see if I can find something?"

"We've already searched her office and her home, but knock yourself out." Reflectively, Gretsky added, "I think the commodity they really want is her."

And who could blame them? All that and brains, too. Penn sipped her espresso. Soft target. Easy money. She could use an influx of unmarked bills. She'd been careless recently and the coffers were depleted. Again she was puzzled by KR's involvement. He was a grubby weasel of a man, but Penn wasn't aware of him dabbling in private-sector affairs like this one. The change of MO could only mean one thing. The client was either Defense or the NSA, in which case only an idiot would refuse to play ball.

Penn stifled a sigh. "How does KR know she's into women?" she asked.

"He doesn't for sure, but I sent in the guy who works the gigolo cases last month. He bombed."

"So maybe she's not interested in one-night stands. Kind of a fatal flaw in the plan, wouldn't you say?"

"Your impressive track record speaks for itself." Gretsky's grave approval was marred by a faint twitch of his lips.

Rolling her eyes, Penn asked, "What happens if we do this and she still won't agree to sell?"

"People who love someone can always be persuaded. She has a mother."

"Well, that's a relief," Penn said cynically. "It gets old kidnapping targets' children."

In the family department, she was thankful for her own invulnerability. She was the perfect recruit, Gretsky had told her after their initial meeting at Georgetown University. At twenty-two, with her parents and brother all dead after their yacht sank several years earlier, she had exactly the right background for the clandestine service. Patriotic middle-class family. Both parents working for the federal government. Three languages. A thirst for risk. The ability to pass polygraph tests.

"You have twenty-four hours to decide. If you decline, leave everything in the lockbox. If you accept, call me with your plan."

Penn picked up the key and slipped it into the front pocket of her jeans. She left Gretsky sitting at the table. They both knew she'd already made up her mind.

❖

At night, the Vaughan Biotech building ticked erratically, as though a faulty clock lay hidden in a wall somewhere. Time passed slowly in the small hours, marked by the faint whirr of the ventilation system and the drawing of breath. Once Unity sealed herself in her baby blue pressure suit in the change room, all external sounds were cancelled out. Her heart thumped in her ears and each exhalation emerged as a deafening whisper. She checked the gaskets around the tops of her boots and gloves, then passed through the airlock anteroom. A soft whoosh of suction tugged at her suit as the innermost door opened and she entered the Biosafety Level 4 area. The air pressure was kept low in BSL-4 maximum containment labs, so that it was easier to breathe inside the HEPA-filtered positive-pressure suits. The ventilation system pulled all the air inward toward the fully sealed space and filtered it out through the roof.

Vaughan Biotech leased its facility from a research institute that had moved to larger premises. Unity supposed she might not have been tempted to take her work in the direction she had if she'd been faced with building her own BSL-4 lab. The isolated zone, with its biological-safety cabinet rooms, chemical showers, and decontamination autoclaves, was a costly addition. She didn't have that kind of funding.

Working in the suit area was always slow and methodical. Process was everything. She made herself think of a calm blue sea as she took her equipment from the fumigation chamber and laid it out on the seamless bench top. Her companion, Dr. Neil Stambach, was on his own sleepless planet, a fact she appreciated. For safety reasons no one was permitted to work alone in the BSL-4 lab, so she usually teamed up with him on late-night stints.

She'd hired him to continue her surfactant-chaperones research while she sidetracked into fusion toxins and proteins. Normally his work would not be conducted in a maximum-containment environment, but she had him analyzing tissue samples from a group of Ebola victims, bread-and-butter vaccine research they carried out as a sideline. He had some idea of her progress, having spent more time around her than most of her staff, and he'd heard the same rumors as everyone else. But Neil had been the only colleague to state an interest in assisting her. He was nearing retirement and ached to have his name on something that would enthrall the scientific community for decades to come. Unity drew him in occasionally, testing his loyalty and discretion with tiny fillips of information. So far, nothing had come back to her, and she felt she could trust him.

Unity's work had propelled her into the middle of one of the huge moral challenges of the twenty-first century. She hadn't set out to create a bioweapon, but tangentially, unintentionally, she had done so. She wished her personal dilemma was black and white like Oppenheimer's. The Manhattan Project had been set up to create a weapon of mass destruction. No one pretended otherwise. Unity hadn't been asked to work on military applications, but she couldn't pretend she'd been blind to the ramifications of her research. No one in her field could claim naiveté. Her discovery had military significance, regardless of its therapeutic potential.

For the past two decades, scientists had faced the same dilemma, knowing where genetic research could lead. They'd asked politicians and legislators to look ahead and address the risks posed by emerging biotechnology. As usual, nothing had been done, perhaps because the subject opened a can of worms. Large numbers of American voters still thought evolution was open to question. They weren't ready for new laws that would implicitly make a lie of their beliefs. The battle lines between science and religion had moved over the centuries, but the war still raged. People needed their faith, and if that meant burying their heads in the sand while semihuman chimeras were bred and superviruses engineered, so be it.

Unity shivered with anticipation and nerves as she prepared her control, and then an incubated sample, for molecular electron microscopy. On their own, cryo-EM density maps were not enough for atomic-structure determination, but along with X-ray crystallography and her sequencing data she could arrive at fold assignment of the constituting domains and make progress on the underlying genetic algorithm. Simply put, she would have proof that she'd created a completely new protein by arranging amino acids in a manner unknown in nature. Because she had the key to building her de novo protein and understood why it folded as it did, she could map it and ultimately tailor it to carry out specific tasks inside a cell. It could be fused with a virus to make it weaker or stronger. It could target certain cells in a body and destroy them or enhance them.

She shouted to Neil, "Take a look at this."

He cocked his head. They couldn't hear clear sentences in the pressurized suits so she summoned him in sign language.

For a long while he stared at the images. Without reading her notes, he wouldn't know exactly what he was looking at, but he knew enough to step back with a stunned expression.

Unity pointed toward the airlock door and yelled, "Let's call it a night."

He nodded and they stored their samples and placed all their equipment in the fumigator. After they'd been through the chemical showers and the change rooms and finally emerged from the secured zone in the center of the building, they rode the elevator down to the parking level in silence.

"Is that what I think it is?" Neil finally asked, walking her to her Lexus.

"Yes."

"What are you going to do?"

"I filed the patent application last week."

"Jesus." He sounded short of breath. "When are you publishing?"

"That's my quandary." She found the remote in her jacket pocket and unlocked the car. "I've been procrastinating, and I have a lot more work to do. The peer-review process will be extensive. If you're agreeable, I'd like your help."

Neil's angular face flushed and he moved a few damp silver strands away from his forehead. His Adam's apple bobbed above his open collar. "You can count on my complete support." He sagged back against the car as though his legs had almost buckled.

Unity knew exactly how he felt. "I thought about throwing it all away," she said.

"Making supersoldiers wasn't enough for you?" He laughed weakly.

Unity sighed. The DoD could only dream of how many veterans they could return to duty if spinal-cord damage could be repaired. Vaughan Biotech had received a generous research grant after she sold the idea that this was a viable goal. Everything would change once she published her research. Defense wanted quicker recovery time for wounded troops, but they wanted ultimate weapons of mass destruction even more. She knew which priority they would support in the next round of funding.

If she still owned her company and her patents by then, she could negotiate a compromise. But if she sold out to Fortis or some other giant, she would be kissing good-bye to her focus on therapeutic applications, no matter what her new overlords promised. The major players in her field didn't make billions by being ethically squeamish.

A serious expression tightened Neil's face, making his nose seem beakish and his mouth invisible. "This is huge," he said with awe. "And, Jesus. What a dilemma."

Unity felt a sense of relief that made her almost light-headed. It was good to talk with someone who understood. "I've been worried."

He nodded. "Everyone's going to want this."

"I suppose that's what drove me," she admitted. "The inevitability of it all. If I didn't do it, someone else would."

"Better we own the technology than the North Koreans," Neil said.

"I hope that's true."

"You know it is, or you wouldn't have filed for the patent." He placed an arm awkwardly around her and bestowed a brief, big-brother hug. "Do you have the algorithm yet?"

"Almost. I'm working on it with Fred Gustafson at Duke. He's using the Jaguar supercomputer at Oak Ridge National Laboratory." Unity shivered. The air felt damp and bitter. One day soon it would snow. "Bizarre, isn't it? We're here talking in a parking lot on an ordinary night in America, but what we saw back there could change everything."

Neil chafed his hands. "Hah. The Nobel crowd will wish they hadn't been so fast thrusting the mantle upon Roger Kornberg. I suppose there was a certain dynastic flavor with his father getting it in the fifties, not to take anything away from Roger."

"Oh, God. I'm going to be on a permanent lecture tour," Unity muttered. "I hadn't even thought about that."

"Imagine…the Vaughan Protein…or even the Unity Protein—that's got a ring to it. Picture the cover of *Nature*." Neil's eyes shone. "Congratulations. I really mean it. What you've done is incredible."

He stuck out his hand and Unity clasped it, appreciating the old-fashioned formality of the gesture. They shook solemnly, peers acknowledging a moment bigger than them and a journey into the unknown still to come.

Neil opened the driver's door for her. "Go home and get some rest. We'll make a plan for the peer review tomorrow."

"I doubt I'll sleep," Unity said, more to herself than to him.

She hunkered into her seat, feeling overwhelmed. Her hands shook as she started the car. She had set in motion a chain reaction that would transform her life and had no idea if she would regret or rejoice in the outcome. Perhaps one day, reviewing the consequences, she would want to turn back time and choose a different path.

Hoping she would never have to face that dread realization, she backed out of her parking spot with a sense that she was spinning into a vortex with nothing to catch hold of. It was too late for second thoughts now. All she could do was brace herself.

Chapter Six

The target slept alone. Worked alone. Dined alone. Drank alone. Went to social events alone. It wasn't that she had no one around her. Penn's job would have been simpler if Unity Vaughan isolated herself. But she was surrounded by people most of the time. Sequestered with a team of lab rats at work or taking a few minutes after hours to shop at the supermarket. Her trick was to seem like part of a crowd, friendly and open, when she was really solitary and guarded.

Penn had been juggling work at the club with surveillance on Unity for almost a week, hoping to uncover a secret life involving a lover who could take her place on the blackmail DVD. She'd followed Unity from A to B, hidden a positioning device under her white Lexus, bugged the house in Bethesda, and set up hidden cameras, including a high-tech system in the bedroom. It was time to close in on her target, and she'd planned to do so tonight, but the state-of-the-art technology had suddenly stopped working yesterday. So instead of seducing Unity, she had to get into the house again and fix the problem. Her plan was to hang out here at the cocktail party until the crowd adjourned for the banquet. Once she was sure Unity was seated at a table and would be stuck here for the rest of the evening, she would go take care of business.

So far, the surveillance feed had been unimaginably boring.

Unity led the life of a nun. She worked late every night, came home and played with her two cats, read books on molecular biology, and sat at her computer. She showered twice a day, phoned her mother every morning as she got ready to leave for work, and had a maid service twice a week. The maid watched *The Bold and the Beautiful* on Unity's big-screen television during her break and sometimes had her husband come over to clear the kitchen drain.

Unity had several close friends from college. They exchanged e-mails, shooting the breeze. Penn had read everything after copying Unity's hard drive. The friends were all married with kids. Penn could see them slowly drifting away as their interests no longer intersected. Nostalgia had a half-life that could sustain such friendship for years, but people changed and eventually too much was unspoken and unshared. They became irrelevant to one another. She knew the pattern well. At a school reunion the previous year, she'd felt like an alien, her life shrink-wrapped into acceptable bites. She wondered if Unity had the same sense of not quite fitting.

Penn watched her moving around the ballroom, shaking hands and sipping the same drink someone had handed her an hour ago. Tonight's social event at the Marriott was a departure from her daily norms, a cocktails-and-banquet gig for a bioethics conference. She'd presented a paper the previous day and there was buzz in the room about an impending announcement. Penn had latched onto a nerd to get the lowdown. Rumors were flying that Vaughan Biotech had made a major breakthrough. The nerd wanted a job there and, failing that, a date with the boss. Unity had given him the brush-off.

He was one of many. In a room swarming with earnest, unfashionable men and their bored spouses, Unity seemed to exist in a radiant sphere of her own, exuding a force of attraction that altered the crowd patterns in her corner. Despite the allure of her looks, she had a shielded quality that made her seem remote.

The aura of aloofness was hard to resist, and a cluster of men fanned out around her. Those on the margins kept trying to close in, vying for position. Occasionally, Unity made an effort to push back the boundaries of her personal space, taking steps one way then another. Moving her arms. Waving casually as though she saw an old friend across the room.

She hadn't dressed to get attention. There was no expanse of naked flesh on display, no slutty designer fashion. Her simple, knee-length dress was cut to avoid clinging to her delicious curves. The gunmetal color shimmered discreetly, the perfect foil for her creamy skin and brilliant blue eyes. Her shoes were the one contradiction in what appeared to be a mission to downplay her looks. Black and scooped low over the foot, they were so sexy they could feature in one of Lila's films. Little white satin bows perched on top. The heels were high and the soles flashed red as she walked. The walk was quite something, too, a balancing act on heels too steep for a practical stroll. The result was a twitchy sashay that flaunted the firm domes of her ass. And that was one butt just crying out for a pair of hands.

Penn didn't want to draw Unity's attention, so she kept her distance and avoided staring for too long at a time. Originally, she'd planned to make her move tonight, but the technical issue with the cameras had changed her objectives. She would hit on Unity in the next few days. Tonight she would simply watch her and make a behavior assessment. Faced with days of conference boredom and meaningless chitchat, a woman who liked her space would want some time out. Penn had to tempt Unity at the right moment, and the more she watched her around other people the better she could gauge that exact moment.

Weaving among the crowd with a glass of whiskey in her hand, she made her way to fringes of another cluster, this one near the bar. The small crowd was gathered around an elderly man sitting on a chair. He wasn't saying much, but each pronouncement was received with reverent awe. Penn concluded she was in the presence of greatness and soaked it up for a few minutes, trying to understand the discussion. She recognized key phrases like "human genome" but the rest was a mystery. It was pretty funny to hear a conversation in English and barely understand a word. She'd always considered herself intelligent, but these people were in a league of their own.

With a faint smile, she stepped aside when a tall, spindly man jostled past her, eager to debate some esoteric point. A splash of liquid doused her hand as she collided with someone. Several ice cubes bounced around her feet.

A woman said, "Oh, I'm sorry."

The voice registered as one Penn knew. She turned awkwardly, hemmed in by suits. A flash of recognition brightened the lovely face upturned to hers, then faded as Penn didn't react. Up close, Unity Vaughan's eyes were even more riveting than the neon of the photo. The irises were a web of hues drawn from an Impressionist palette. Crystalline shards of light sapphire filtered through a deep blue ocean. Traces of platinum shimmered below the surface, forming a mercuric halo within the shadowed rims.

Before Penn could make a fool of herself by letting her jaw drop, Unity looked away, toward the bar. "I wanted to swap my drink for a glass of water, but it's so crowded."

In the glare of a chandelier directly above, her hair seemed lighter, feathered with fine snowy streaks. Her style was uneven at the tips, or maybe she just used mousse to create the tiny spikes. Penn was afraid to look at her mouth. She had a weakness for those old-fashioned bow-shaped lips, plush little cushions built for long, hot kisses. Unity wore her cherry-red lipstick like a dare: *Don't you wonder how it would feel—just you and me?* Somewhere beneath the cool, composed scientist exterior was a woman who refused to be dismissed as sexless.

Penn took the glass from Unity's fingers and said, "Let's get that water."

Working at the club had taught her how to clear a path

through a crowd. She escorted Unity on a rapid zigzag toward a corner of the room where some waiters had their staging area. Several tables had been pushed back into a curtained recess. Stacks of conference literature covered their surfaces.

Penn pulled out a chair. "Catch your breath for a minute, while I muscle in at the bar."

Unity looked embarrassed. "There's no need. Honestly. We'll be going in to dinner shortly, I imagine."

"It's no problem." Penn caught the eye of a waiter shoving bottles of Pellegrino into a large ice bucket. "Excuse me a moment."

She tipped him ten and was discreetly served out of sequence. When she returned, Unity said, "How come they never do that for me?"

"You don't have that look," Penn replied. "With me, it's either a tip or a black eye. They take the money." Setting the glass down, she offered her hand and the fake name she used on assignments. "Pat Hunter."

"Good to meet you, Pat. I'm Unity Vaughan."

"I know. They can't stop talking about you over there in the dateless-dweeb corner."

Unity laughed. The sound was so natural and infectious Penn joined her. They shook hands with the formality of strangers, but the moment their palms met, a spine-jolt of awareness cramped Penn's muscles. Her shoulders bunched and her lungs burned with a breath she couldn't release. Her eyes refused to budge from the curve of Unity's throat and the way the dress tugged across her breasts. She couldn't remember the last time she'd felt like this—maybe the very first time her eighth-grade crush planted a chaste kiss on her cheek.

Stunned, she scrutinized Unity's face, trying to quantify her effect. Yes, she was so effortlessly beautiful she could melt paint, but Penn had been with plenty of smart, hot women, some of them much more glamorous and seductive. Anticipation stirred deep down in her gut. The thought of getting naked with Unity Vaughan made her clit surge so powerfully she winced. Walking around for the rest of the evening was going to be a trip.

"You don't recall me, do you?" Unity said with mild amusement.

Penn's mouth went dry. What was she missing? Had they stood in the same line at the supermarket a year ago or something? Stalling as she searched her memory, she said, "Odd you should say that." She latched on to her first thought when they collided a few minutes ago. "Your voice seems familiar. I've been trying to find out why."

"You changed a tire for me recently."

She was definitely losing her edge, Penn thought. She'd shoved a tracking device under the chassis, for crying out loud, and still hadn't made the connection. "The white Lexus," she said with an unspoken *Duh!*

"I guess this is my chance to buy you a drink, as a thank-you."

"Oh, the pleasure was all mine. I get off on rescuing damsels in distress."

Very smooth. Rumor had it, the CIA chose undercover officers for their élan as well as their ability to cut the throats of enemy targets. What a credit she was to the agency. No wonder the NCS chief had let her resign without a protest.

Unity let her off with the patient smile of a woman who'd heard every corny pickup line and then some. "You should have told me you broke your watch."

Penn blinked. "How do you—"

"I took off my driving gloves when I undid the lug nuts. When I went to get them, I found the broken crystal. It wasn't there before, so I knew it had to be yours." She paused. "You'd already gone by then, of course." She lifted Penn's wrist and inspected the gold Chopard. "I see you had it repaired immediately. I'd be happy to reimburse you."

At the brush of her fingers, a ripple of tension scaled Penn's arm and settled between her shoulder blades. "There's no need. It was time I replaced it, anyway. The old one was scratched."

Penn didn't mention the rest of the repair job. It was weird enough that their paths had crossed before she ever took this assignment, let alone that her watch had stopped at that exact moment. The only other time the Chopard had stopped was the day she found out that her family was gone. The gold dress watch had belonged to her father; he'd given it to her for her high school graduation. Penn had been thrilled, but also puzzled. She'd assumed her older brother would receive this traditional father-son acknowledgment and was still not sure why she was chosen instead. The watch meant a lot to her.

She stared down at the hand resting in Unity's loose clasp, struck by the tanned breadth of her wrist against the streamlined ivory delicacy of Unity's palm and fingers. A rush of emotion took her by surprise, causing a lump in her throat. She didn't have the first idea what she was feeling and kept her head down, unwilling to have her confusion witnessed. A subtle fragrance compounded her distraction. Its layers were complex and hard to unravel. Penn recognized the scent of faded bergamot and orange swimming in a subtle tide of neroli.

"Your perfume," she said like a callow youth. "It's really something."

"Thank you." Unity let Penn take back her tingling wrist. "Mixing my own fragrances is a hobby."

Trying to sound more normal than she felt, Penn asked, "Does this one have a name?"

A puff of pink clouded each cheek. "Bliss."

Unity wrapped an arm around herself. Her long, dark eyelashes fanned down, veiling the innocent candor of her stare. Her smile was bittersweet, her expression remote and introspective. Whatever she was thinking, she would never share it. In that moment, Penn recognized a woman who inhabited her own internal landscape and did not allow others in. There was something elusive about her, a lot like the fragrance she'd distilled. She defied pigeonholing. It would be easy to make superficial assumptions. Penn suspected she invited them deliberately: the dispassionate professional woman who didn't have to exploit her looks.

Unity looked up again, all bland composure. "And you… you're wearing Ambre Narguilé?"

"You have quite a nose."

Again that smile and the downturned eyes. "It's a unique scent. A dreadful mistake for some people, but with the right body chemistry…very edible."

"Finally, an explanation for the bite marks." Penn felt crass as soon as she'd spoken. Making small talk with classy women brought out the worst in her.

"Are you normally devoured by a lover or by strangers?"

The deadpan question tampered with Penn's pulse. For the first time in about twenty years, she blushed. "I'm single." She winced over the unsophisticated comeback.

"Interesting." Unity didn't elucidate. Her dress hiked up a few inches as she crossed her legs. Slowly swinging her dangling foot, she asked, "What's your field, Pat?"

It was hard to ignore the strong, sleek calf and the dark nylon pattern on the underside of her thigh. Penn wanted to push her hem up and unfasten the garter she glimpsed. Who wore genuine stockings anymore? Unity's were the old-fashioned ultrasheer kind instead of the lace-top thigh-highs Penn encountered quite often. She lifted her gaze and knew she'd been caught looking. They stared at each other for far too long.

Freeze this frame, Penn thought irrationally. She had the strangest feeling that she was locked in a moment in time, freefalling into a future completely different from the one she had been heading for only ten minutes earlier.

Shaken, she said, "My field? I'm in security."

A small frown nagged at Unity's brow. "I heard Professor Maass had bodyguards these days." She glanced toward the white-haired elder still holding forth from his chair. "How dreadful that he has to deal with threats at this stage of his life. He's over ninety, for God's sake. Those so-called Christians should be ashamed of themselves."

Penn allowed the assumption to go unchallenged. When the perfect cover drops into one's lap, why contradict it with the official version?

"I thought you were just party-crashing," Unity continued. With sudden consternation, she said, "I guess I'm keeping you from your work."

"Not at all," Penn said smoothly. "Part of my job is to blend in."

Unity studied her with the same speculative hunger Penn had glimpsed that night in the parking lot. "Let me give you some advice." Her voice was husky. "If you want to blend in, think beige and get rid of the leather jacket.

"This doesn't work?" Penn swept a hand down her clothing.

Unity's laser blue stare burned a path straight to Penn's core. "It works fine." She paused. "Just not for this crowd."

Adrenaline rushed through Penn's veins. Something darkly wanton had entered Unity's expression, an explicit hunger that found its match in Penn. Her body responded down low in her gut with cramps of awareness that pierced even deeper, spilling desire into her briefs. It was all she could do not to gasp out loud and utter something bluntly sexual. Shocked by the stark force of her arousal, Penn looked away as though distracted by the clatter of glasses or the tide of conversation.

She felt disoriented. Nothing was working to plan. Here was the perfect opportunity to nail her assignment—so what if the bedroom cameras weren't acting right? There were others. She forced herself to process her options coldly, like the professional she was. They could get it on in the living room or the kitchen—assuming Unity would go for sex that didn't involve a bed—and Penn could cut something together from the lower-grade footage. She pictured Gretsky having a coronary and refusing to pay the rest of her fee. He'd hired her because she was one of the best. If he wanted grainy long shots and no close-ups he would have given the job to a PI.

Conscious of the seconds ticking by, she mentally regrouped and returned her attention to Unity. What she saw was a look she knew well, a quiet expectancy that left her in no doubt; Unity was simply waiting for her to take the initiative. Penn's thoughts careened away from logic and good planning. Maybe they could go back to Unity's, have sex, and Penn could make another date after the cameras were fixed.

She dismissed the idea immediately. Women who slept with strangers usually didn't repeat the encounter. And she'd already learned enough about Unity to know casual flings weren't her style. Tonight, if anything happened, it would be an aberration, so asking for a rain check was a delicate business. Whims passed. Conferences ended and everyday life resumed, along with status-quo patterns of behavior. Penn was only going to get one shot, and if she didn't take it sometime in the next couple of days, she would have to be pretty inventive to carve out another opportunity. The perfect solution presented itself. She would come on hot, but point out that she was stuck with the old professor for the rest of the night. Tomorrow, however...

Before she could speak, a hand landed on her knee. Unity must have decided she needed to drop a stronger hint. "These banquets can drag on for hours. I thought I'd slip away early. If you're not doing anything later, maybe we could meet up somewhere."

Even as she spoke, she seemed to be having second thoughts.

Hastily, Penn said, "I wish...but Professor Maass is going to need me later."

"Yes, of course."

It was hard to tell what was going on behind Unity's guarded expression but Penn's imagination filled in the blanks. She'd sent the wrong signal. Her hesitance could easily be mistaken for lack of interest. It seemed incredible that a woman as attractive as Unity would expect to be given the brush-off. Obviously she didn't make a habit of hitting on women or she'd know how unlikely that was.

Penn allowed herself a slow, hot appraisal that couldn't possibly be misinterpreted. "Trust me," she said. "I like your suggestion a whole lot better."

The response was so impassive, she almost choked in dismay. Unity uncrossed her legs and rose from her chair. Standing so close her thigh grazed Penn's, she said, "I see one of my colleagues."

She indicated a gangling, bespectacled stereotype of a scientist, all neck and bony wrists. Next to him stood a squat, chiffon-clad woman who could only be his wife.

Wonderful, Penn thought, she'd totally blown it. She could feel Unity's retreat as if it were physical. Was she only going to get a tiny window in which to make her move? Had that moment already passed her by? She could have kicked herself. Normally, if she wanted a woman she let her know, and she followed through. What in hell was wrong with her game tonight?

Unity gave the bony brainiac and his wife a bright little wave. Her shoulders seemed stiff. "It's been pleasant chatting with you, Pat. Thank you for the drink."

Her cool disinterest was gorgeously compelling, a glove thrown down in challenge.

Overwhelmed by an urge to kiss her, Penn said, "I'm free tomorrow evening. Maybe we could catch up then."

After only a fractional pause, Unity shook her head. "Unfortunately, I have a prior commitment."

Penn thought, *Liar.* "Duty calls?"

"Actually, I find my work a pleasure." With a distinct edge, Unity added, "One that endures."

"You're fortunate," Penn said softly. "I have to take my pleasure where I can find it."

Unity gave her an ironic little smile. "Well, good luck with that."

She walked away without a backward glance.

CHAPTER SEVEN

Rattled, but thankful she hadn't made a complete fool of herself, Unity drove west on Wilson Lane. What had she been thinking, hitting on Professor Maass's bodyguard? Did she want the entire planet to know she was not just desperate, but also queer? She never made a secret of her sexual orientation, but she didn't broadcast the fact on public radio, either.

Thankful to leave Woodmont behind, she took several calming breaths as she approached River Road. Occasionally she thought about buying a house with a view of the murky Potomac or moving to one of the condominium complexes in Wisconsin Avenue, close to the ritzy shops of downtown Bethesda. But she enjoyed the grove-like tranquility of her neighborhood. Nothing moved on the tree-lined streets, not even the dead leaves on the sidewalks. Like most upscale residential areas of Bethesda, hers was well-lit and silent, its residents slumbering in large, luxurious homes with garden settings.

Unity made a mental note of the few cars parked near her place as she approached. The SUV a few yards from her driveway was owned by her next-door neighbor's son. He left it out in the street when he came home late so his mother wouldn't hear the garage door open. Over the road, the Kershaws had guests again. They virtually needed their own valet parking. With six grown-up children and sundry college friends, spouses, and offspring, a mob seemed to descend on the place most weekends.

Their driveway was crowded with cars, and at least three unfamiliar vehicles were parked near the imposing front gates. An expensive-looking BMW was incongruously sandwiched between a beat-up Toyota and one of those ubiquitous white vans used by half the contractors who worked in the area. Unity recognized the Beemer as the same model owned by a divorce attorney a few houses away. He paid eleven-year-old Mitch, the Kershaws' afterthought son, to polish it every Saturday after sports practice. Unity hired Mitch to clean her Lexus when he was through with the lawyer's car. The kid was saving for a new bike. For every dollar saved, his father added a second dollar so long as Mitch donated fifty cents to charity.

In the spirit of things, the neighbors helped out by adding their donations to the money they forked out for chores after school. Last year Mitch had raised almost two thousand dollars for various causes. Unity often wondered what it must be like to have a childhood like his, surrounded by family who set an example and taught real values.

She killed her lights as she approached her garage doors. For a few seconds, she waited in watchful paranoia to see if any other vehicle passed by; then she hit the remote and pulled into her parking space alongside a neat stack of storage cartons, her mom's possessions. Unlike Unity, Ellen Vaughan was a packrat. Occasionally she managed to donate clothing she hadn't worn for a decade, but she still couldn't bring herself to sort through the boxes lining the garage and Unity had given up bugging her about them.

She sat in her locked car until the door closed behind her, then gathered her briefcase and dry cleaning and let herself into the house. Duchess and Dandy rolled on the floor at her feet, and Unity made kissy sounds as she dropped her stuff and headed for the kitchen. She always left food out and set the television to Animal Planet when she went to work, but her babies yowled as though they'd suffered shameful neglect. Unity opened a can of their favorite chicken dinner and filled their bowls. She contemplated the tub of ice cream in her freezer but couldn't get interested in a snack. The hollow feeling in her belly had nothing to do with hunger.

Her gaze drifted to the card Officer Reynes had left the night of the break-in. She tweaked it from beneath the fridge magnet. Would the nicely built cop be on duty? Unity dropped the card on the counter and walked away, irritated with herself. She had a perfectly adequate vibrator in her bottom drawer. If she needed physical release, that's what an electronic device and a good imagination were for. She didn't need to seduce law officers or the bodyguards of luminaries. Her thoughts strayed again to the woman at the cocktail party and a bolt of lust shot home between her legs. She'd been damp all evening, wriggling uncomfortably during the banquet and speeches, unable to stop her eyes from darting around the room, seeking her out.

A strange disappointment gripped her when she realized the bodyguard was no longer there. She had wanted to tease her for a little longer, buying herself time while she made up her mind whether to do something out of character. She'd considered having one-night stands when she was with Merrill, but had never acted on the urge. Her fidelity seemed absurd in hindsight. Merrill hadn't attempted to bridge the desire gap between them and seemed to take for granted that Unity wouldn't cheat.

Was that what tonight's impulse was about, some kind of belated recompense? The possibility made her blaze with anger. She was no longer in a relationship with Merrill. She could do whatever she liked with whomever she chose. Fiercely, she kicked off her Louboutin pumps and snatched her purse from the sofa. It slipped from her hand and landed on the floor a few feet away, disgorging its contents.

Unity let out a colorful curse. Tears stung as she slumped onto the sofa and picked up the remote. Leaving the sound on "mute," she surfed aimlessly through news channels and late-night shows. No, her attraction to the bodyguard had nothing to do with Merrill. The stranger was hot. Something about her sanguine self-awareness stirred deep, dangerous longings in Unity. It was impossible to be near her and not notice the sexual vibe. Some women were like that. One look and you knew exactly what they were thinking about.

Unity was still reeling from their handshake and that honeyed slap across the senses—Ambre Narguilé in all its elegant depravity. If she had to describe the ingredients, she could only call to mind something sweet crushed inside a leather glove that had once held a cigar. The hedonistic scent lingered so powerfully in her olfactory memory, she wondered if it had clung to her dress.

With a sharp, craving sigh, she switched off the television and reverted to her nightly routine. She checked all the first-floor windows and doors, shoveled the contents back into her purse, picked up her shoes, and went upstairs. Leaving the lights off in her bedroom, she drew the curtains back and opened the French doors onto her modest balcony. From her second-floor vantage point, she stared up at the stars, then swept a critical eye across her front yard.

When she had time, she enjoyed working in her garden. Lately she'd been too busy and it showed in the thick carpet of dead leaves, the unpruned roses and azaleas, the roaming wisteria weighing down the walkway arches. Moths beat against the walkway lanterns, reminding her that every outdoor light fixture needed cleaning. Her witch hazels looked clumpy, another job for the yard service her mom had forgotten to call.

When Ellen moved into the cabana she'd promised to take charge of home and garden so Unity didn't have to think about the usual maintenance. Her enthusiasm had lasted for about a month. Unity avoided raising the topic. She and Ellen resembled each other in their determination to leave the past behind. There would be no shouting anymore. Ellen was two years clean and sober, and so long as she stayed that way Unity wasn't going to risk their fragile truce.

She stepped back into her bedroom, leaving the doors open so she could be a part of the inscrutable night beyond. The chill air tickled her flesh as she undressed. Her perfume had faded and she could detect traces of chlorine and grated lemon rind on her skin, a lingering residue that seemed to hide in her pores and emerge when she perspired. At full antiseptic strength, the body wash would repel a shark. The disinfectant chemicals could not fully wrap their pungent residue in a citrus disguise. She'd been at work before setting off for the conference, and had showered several times after leaving her pressure suit and lab clothing in the autoclave. Normally she would shower again but she needed to get some sleep.

She moved around her room in the moonlight, discarding her clothes in the laundry basket, placing her watch and ear studs on the dressing table, pulling a thin chemise from her lingerie drawer. Again she noticed that someone had violated her privacy. Her nightgowns were kept identically folded in a neat stack. This one had been shaken out hastily and crammed back toward the wall of the drawer, scrunching the fabric. The matching kimono wraps were in disorder. Almost two weeks had passed since the break-in and she hadn't had time to refold everything.

With an apprehensive glance toward the open doors, Unity slid the chemise over her head and smoothed it down her prickling skin. She closed the French doors and got into bed with her heart suddenly racing. It was quite normal, she reasoned, for someone to feel heightened anxiety after a break-in. She'd behaved wisely and obtained quotes from two home-security firms. Soon her house would have new locks and a state-of-the-art alarm system. She wasn't going to get a dog. It wouldn't be fair. She didn't spend enough time at home and that situation wasn't going to improve anytime soon. But maybe she would talk to her mom. Ellen adored dogs.

The grandfather clock downstairs struck the quarter hour and Unity made an effort to let go of her mental To Do list. She was wide-awake when she should be sleeping, tense when she should be relaxed. Irritated, she let her thoughts lapse again to her pressing physical needs. If there was one thing an orgasm would guarantee, that was a sleep-inducing flood of oxytocin. She leaned over the side of the bed and dragged her magic wand from the bottom drawer. Normally, it took her about three minutes to come. Tonight she was so hormonal she'd probably get off in thirty seconds, even if there was no skin to enjoy or arms to lie in afterward.

Depending on a gadget for satisfaction was a mixed blessing. Yes, there was physical release, but with it came the reminder of all that was missing in her life. Sometimes she felt so desperately lonely after she came that she fell asleep crying instead of smiling. Which was fine, she rationalized as she plugged in the vibe—sleep was sleep. A few minutes of misery and alienation were a small price to pay to avoid popping Ambien. And there was nothing wrong with self-loving; most of the time she could frame her pragmatic masturbation in that positive light. By any measure, she was better off with her mechanical accomplice than a partner who made her feel unwanted. The magic wand was reliable. It didn't roll away from her with a loud sigh when she tried to get its motor running. It didn't mock her cravings. She didn't have to beg it to pay attention to her; all she had to do was hit the "on" switch.

Unity always delayed that moment until she could settle on a fantasy that would sweep aside her ambivalence. With that goal in mind, she slid the vibe under the covers and let her thoughts wander. Officer Reynes drifted into focus with her cute ass and tight muscles, but Unity couldn't get interested. The bodyguard at the cocktail party loomed in her mind's eye, wreaking havoc all over again. Unity's nipples tightened as she relived the long look they'd shared. There was a prowling intensity to the woman that should have signaled danger, but Unity had been drawn to her anyway. Even that night in the parking basement, she'd been blown away and had driven home thinking she'd just seen the sexiest woman alive.

The chemistry between them shook her. Tonight, in a single glance, the bodyguard had somehow conveyed that she wanted Unity naked in her arms. The mental picture was so vivid Unity had succumbed to it without a fight. Within seconds, she'd come close to abandoning both common sense and discretion, and had hit on her. She couldn't figure out what made the bodyguard so compelling. Nothing about her was exceptional. From her tousled dark sable hair to her jeans and leather jacket, and the well-kept matte black boots, she could be any good-looking butch Unity had ever seen. But none of those women made her instantly wet. None of them spoke so clearly to her desires before a word was exchanged.

The eyes were a factor, she decided. Shielded with short, straight lashes that would never curl, they were wise and strangely colored, a ghostly grayish-green spattered with ripe orange. Her mouth didn't part when she smiled, and her smile was cynical. She wore a thick gold earring on the helix of her left ear. There was a slight height difference between them. Without her Christian Louboutin pumps, Unity was probably shorter by several inches. Perfect for kissing.

A sinking sensation invaded the pit of her stomach and a fine sweat broke across her skin. Not for the first time, she wondered what would have happened if she'd brought the sexy stranger home. She rejected the idea immediately. If she were going to have a fling with anyone, she needed to be completely in control. And she knew instinctively that with this woman, she wouldn't be.

Next time they saw each other, she vowed she would be icily rational. If there was a next time. With any luck the bodyguard would be too busy doing her job to strike up a conversation again. Unity had no intention of revisiting the nightcap offer. She planned to keep her distance as the convention chugged along.

In the meantime, she could make good use of her lapse into lust. Drawing a deep breath and closing her eyes, she steered the paintbrush of fantasy to a familiar canvas. A dark shape leaned against the wall just inside her door, the faceless phantom who joined her when she yearned, more than anything, to feel loved. She parted her legs and stroked her breasts. Her nipples puckered, aching for a warm mouth and the soft compression of teeth. The clinging chemise felt harsh against her sensitive flesh. She removed the garment and threw it aside. Her fingers closed around the vibrator. She summoned sense memory, calling up the damp tingle of breath on her skin, the silken heat of fingertips tracing her hairline, followed by the soft brush of lips. Kisses. On her brow. Her cheeks. The corner of her mouth.

A voice. "You're beautiful."

Her reply. "I've been waiting for you."

A finger stroking her lips. A tongue teasing them open. A hot, sweet kiss. A hand opening her closed fist, taking each finger, one after the next, and slowly sucking it. Leaving them slippery and tingling, throbbing in time with her clit.

Again the voice, thick with passion and only for her. "I have to have you."

Another kiss. Deep and profound. Her thighs opening wide. Pressure building. The tantalizing promise of fingers. Her skin prickling with every touch, her senses drowning with the smell and feel and sounds of her lover. The weight of a body on hers. Warm skin. Smooth, firm muscles moving beneath her hands. Another heart pounding against the wall of flesh confining her own. The scent of herself. The hollow ache at her core, compelling her to arch her back and lift her knees. Hot breath in her ear. A tongue on her neck, tracing the tendon. Teeth at the base of her throat. The sliding pressure of a lover's body rising over her. Thighs gliding together. Her clit straining. Her body heaving. Tiny moans escaping.

And finally, breasts brushing her torso. The sleek sweep of

dark hair. A hot mouth traveling down. The faintest sensation of warmth enveloping her clit. So sensuous. So giving.

"Please," she whispers as she pushes into the mouth exploring her. Losing herself in the tug and suck of tongue and lips and the piercing thrill of being spread wide and filled. Wanting more. Legs stiff. Tension climbing. Her fingers clamping down on a pair of hard shoulders.

Unity gasped. She mustn't open her eyes. Or let herself think. Or hear anything but her own noisy breaths and sharp moans, and the wet cadence of her imaginary lover lapping and sucking and kissing and groaning. Her clit was hard and sensitive. Every lick summoned her closer to the edge. She wanted an orgasm squeezed from her by tongue and teeth and hands. She wanted the irresistible demand of body over mind. Ruthless possession. Blind surrender.

She hit the low speed on her vibe and cried, "Yes. Oh, God."

She wanted to hear a lover's hoarse insistence, "Come on, baby. I need this from you. Do it for me."

Words rushed from her, "Yes. Yes. Love me," as everything fell away and she convulsed into shudders.

Quivering and pulsing, she killed the vibe and dropped it over the side of the bed. Then she lay there, sucking in shallow breaths, letting herself float. She rolled onto her side and imagined being enfolded possessively from behind, a pair of hands resting on her belly. Kisses to her nape. Hips and thighs pressing into her. Hot words in her ear, promises of more to come.

But first, she had to sleep.

❖

Holy shit. Penn sagged against the wall, damp with arousal and sweating from nerves. At first she'd been certain Unity must have seen her crouched in the closet. Those murmured words,

I've been waiting for you, almost gave her a heart attack. She had flashes of Unity tearing cameras and recording devices from their hiding places and calling the cops. She saw herself making up some bullshit as she was handcuffed.

Instead the quiet hum of a vibrator had provided merciful cover as she elbowed her way across the carpet to the haven of the hall and crouched behind a bookcase. Breathing hard, she wiggled her fingers and toes to restore circulation and straightened to her feet by slow degrees. She peeped through the crack in the door. The vibe dangled inertly from its cord, trapped between the bed and night table. Unity lay on her side in the position she'd adopted ten minutes earlier after her noisy orgasm. From the steady rise and fall of her shoulder and the flaccid droop of her hand, Penn was pretty sure she'd fallen asleep.

She trained her stylus flashlight on the floor, methodically arcing the thin beam so she could scan the area. She wasn't supposed to suffer lapses of judgment. She was being paid to act like a professional, and, from what she'd just witnessed, the seduction phase of her operation would be a cakewalk, providing she didn't blow the whole deal by getting caught.

There was just one problem. If Unity had turned on her lamp she would have seen it, a black leather glove lying in the middle of a patterned rug near the master bathroom. Penn eyed the evidence with trepidation. Common sense dictated a speedy recovery and rapid flight from the scene. No guts, no glory. Even if Unity heard her galloping down the stairs, by the time she woke up and got herself together enough to give chase or dial 911, Penn would be hiding in her surveillance van, waiting till the heat died down. She killed the beam and tucked the flashlight in her back pocket. Letting her fingertips rest against the grainy wood of the door, she applied faint pressure, tensing in advance for the inevitable squeak. But Unity Vaughan kept her hinges oiled. The door swung inward and Penn stepped into the room, praying for a sturdy, silent floor. She checked the lump beneath the bed covers. Unity hadn't moved.

Forcing herself to relax, Penn crept across the carpet and recovered the memento of her illicit activities. All three cameras were now working. She was home free. She ducked into the deep shadows next to a chest of drawers and paused, timing her final steps. As she gathered herself, her gaze was irresistibly drawn to the sleeping woman. Unity stirred and her arm flopped away from the pillow. Like a lust-struck idiot, Penn took a few reckless paces closer to the bed, ignoring the drill-sergeant dictates of her mind: *Get out now! Run!*

Moonlight traced the distinctive contours of Unity's face, softly etching her straight nose and high cheekbones. Her mouth was slightly parted, the bottom lip swollen. Penn drank in the sight of her, so vulnerable and kissable. The body she'd seen earlier, as Unity stripped off her clothes, was supple and lovely, built the way a woman's should be. She was a few inches shorter than Penn, with high, full breasts, a narrow waist, long legs, and a great ass.

Penn stood there stupidly, staring down as if she'd never seen a beautiful woman asleep. The emotions that swept over her were strange. She had the odd sense that she was glimpsing something in herself she never knew existed and that her world had shifted in some fundamental way. She wanted to strip naked and slide into bed with this woman, as though she belonged. She wanted to tenderly awaken her and give her exactly what she needed.

Penn curled her fingers into fists, not quite trusting herself to resist the urge. There would be screams of fright if Unity awoke, yet Penn stayed where she was, tempting the Fates. Her body was terrifyingly close to Unity's narrow, limp hand. She reached out, letting her fist uncurl. When her fingertips hovered just inches away, she froze and took a step back thinking: *This is nuts.* She'd already seen far more than she should and she was still invading this woman's privacy.

The prick of her conscience struck her as ironic. How self-indulgent did she want to get? *Yeah, I'm going to fuck you over completely and maybe even destroy your life, but hey, sorry I watched you get yourself off.*

She backed up in small, even steps, slid out into the hallway, and retrieved her duffle bag from the next room. The house stayed silent as she crept down the stairs. No creaking. No sudden pools of light or alarms sounding. The kitchen clock said twelve-thirty a.m. They would be looking for her at Inner Sanctum.

She slipped on the truant glove and let herself out the back door, setting the handle to lock after her. As she jogged back to her van, she made herself a promise. This would be her last dishonorable assignment. Whatever moral tightrope she'd walked as a CIA officer, however arguable the merits of each case, at least she was serving her country back then.

It was time to go home to Langley.

CHAPTER EIGHT

"Where've you been?" Nariko demanded. She hadn't bothered to knock before entering Penn's room.

"I told you, I can't be here twenty-four seven." Penn buckled the belt on a clean pair of jeans and finger-combed her damp hair. "How's Lila?"

"Asleep." Nariko cast a disparaging look around.

She had a compact studio of her own next to Lila's. It was a far cry from Penn's hole-in-the-wall. For a start, she'd replaced the existing bordello-chic with minimalist Japanese décor. The aesthetic was supposed to have a calming effect. Penn hadn't noticed any dividend.

"Is everything okay on set?" she asked.

Nariko seemed restive. "As if you care."

"If there's something I should know, now's the time to tell me."

"They keep changing the script. Mistress Chloe says they're accustomed to working with more nuance."

"Nuance?" Penn snorted. "It's a porn movie."

"Don't assume all erotica is bereft of nuance," Nariko huffily replied.

"You forget, I've read the script." Penn adopted a cool, rational tone. "I don't see a problem if Chloe and Colette want to improvise a little. The story seems kind of...lame."

"All our scripts are lame. Erotica is constructed through visual story."

"And the lovely dommes are doing just fine in that department." Penn started re-threading her boots.

"It would help if you spoke to them."

"About what?"

Nariko sat on the edge of the bed just out of arm's reach. "They want me to play a role."

Penn glanced toward the satiny face in the mirror. "Congratulations."

Nariko glared at her. "It's out of the question. I will not appear on film."

"Then, what's the problem? Just say no."

After a long, agitated silence, Nariko said, "They pity me. They imagine a self-esteem issue concerning my scars and wish to be kind."

"I seriously doubt that."

"Says the student of human nature who can't get past a second date."

"There's no need to get personal." Penn pulled on her boots. "What do they want you to do?"

"A bondage scene. Inverted suspension." Nariko's flippant dismissal implied this was on a par with karaoke.

"I thought you were a connoisseur." Felix had confided this much, along with his view that Nariko needed professional help and was probably frigid.

"My enjoyment of power play does not include being a rope bottom."

Also, not what Penn had heard. "Did you explain that to them?"

"They're very persuasive." Nariko sighed. "In their presence, I find my will neutralized."

"You can't say no?" Penn grinned. She would pay top dollar to see Nariko crumble into speechless compliance. "I'm not seeing how that's my problem."

"You're the associate producer. Inform them that additional actors are not within the budget, and no further changes can be made to the script."

Penn threw back her head and laughed.

"What's so amusing?" Nariko hissed. "Lila is in agreement."

"About what?"

"That you need to speak with them."

"What am I missing here?" Penn was puzzled. Chloe and Colette were far too old-school to pressure anyone into submission. Why bother when they could take their pick? Something didn't make sense.

"The thing is," Nariko said with pained bewilderment, "they wanted *you*."

"Me?" Penn couldn't keep her face completely serious. It was unthinkable, she supposed—gorgeous, accomplished Nariko overlooked in favor of a crass specimen like her.

"I explained your unadventurous nature and dedication to orgasm-focused butch-femme sex."

"Yeah, thanks for that."

"However, there's a problem."

Penn eyed her suspiciously. "Uh-huh."

"I made a bet with Felix." Nariko wrung her hands. "I win five hundred dollars if you do it, but if you don't…he gets a hundred and *I* have to take your place." She flounced off the bed and marched irately back and forth. "That ingratiating worm. He couldn't keep his mouth shut, of course. Now everyone knows and they're all placing bets."

"I spend one evening away and the whole place falls apart," Penn muttered. "You'll just have to tell them it was a joke, won't you?"

Nariko rubbed one of her shoulders, her face averted.

Penn knew that look. "Jesus, there's more? I should have guessed."

"I don't know how this came about, but it was mentioned that you eagerly seek an opportunity to explore your boundaries."

"Wait." Penn smiled coldly. "You're telling me Chloe and Colette think I *want* to hand myself over for some kind of House of Gord bondage scene."

With martyred resignation, Nariko said, "Naturally, I told them I would adhere to the terms of my agreement with Felix and take your place if you couldn't go through with it."

"Thanks for setting me up to look like a wimp," Penn griped. "What were you thinking? You know I'd never agree to anything like that."

Nariko's shrug was a smug little shoulder shimmy that set Penn's mind spinning. Under normal circumstances, she would simply have declined without fuss and no one would care, least of all the European dommes. But Nariko had raised the stakes. The bet placed Penn in a no-win situation. She would feel bad if she didn't "save" Nariko, and worse if she did. Everyone would know about her gallantry deficit because they had bets in place. How humiliating.

Chloe and Colette would graciously agree to forget the whole idea, of course, especially once they knew Penn had never agreed in the first place. But that wouldn't help her reputation. Nariko had, in a single move, checkmated her. Why?

❖

"Jealousy." Chloe took a sip of wine and handed the glass to a fair-haired nymphet whose cheek she patted.

The girl wore a dull metal collar in a Ring of O design some submissives liked. Lately Penn had seen more of these collars on clubbers of the pervy persuasion, especially visiting Germans. The nymphet's small breasts bounced impudently above a blue velvet waist cincher, and a filmy white petticoat displayed her dainty ass and narrow thighs. She spoke only in French, and only when asked. Chloe watched her indulgently, already dressed for the twins' performance in the dungeon at 2:00 a.m. Tonight's look was latex. Its distinctive bitter pungency invaded the room along with the smell of talc and Black Beauty, the conditioner spray that gave the taut garments their wet gloss.

Her sister, Colette, reclined languidly on a cream leather loveseat, a stack of magazines on the coffee table next to her. Beneath her flowing primrose kimono, she looked naked, her breasts and hips smoothly contoured beneath the slippery fabric. She was more laid-back than Chloe, yet Penn had noticed that she was the dominant twin in their dynamic.

"Nariko's not my biggest fan," Penn said. "So when you two expressed an interest in me, I guess she was pissed."

"How could she not adore a strapping creature like you?" Colette remarked in an elegant drawl.

Both twins seemed very French but spoke English without the usual accent.

Chloe's dark, brandy-tinted eyes drew Penn's and her glossy mouth parted slightly, as if a wistful notion had stolen her breath. "Were you lovers?"

"No. Never."

Chloe extended a gleaming ankle boot. The blond nymphet lovingly polished it with a rag. She hadn't looked at Penn once.

"Nariko is trying to gain your attention," Chloe concluded.

"I don't think so," Penn said. "She's really not into me. But whatever the reason for the confusion, I appreciate your understanding. Lila thinks we can use the suspension idea in another film."

Both twins gave polite nods. Close-up, they were not exactly beautiful, but their natural hauteur and exquisite presentation made them incredibly compelling. Like thoroughbreds, they had a wild, high-strung edge that lent a trace of danger to their exquisite poise. Their movements were contained, their voices quiet and polished. Their pale oval faces were mirror images, the features not quite even, yet striking all the same. Dark, melancholic eyes stared out from beneath strong, straight brows. Their lips were lusciously red. Tonight, each wore her blue-black hair in a high ponytail, secured with a plain crimson band. Ruby studs shimmered like drops of blood from their earlobes. Their nails were perfectly manicured and painted the same shade of deep red as their mouths.

Chloe showed hers off in the flick of a hand. "You Americans. Everything must be spelled out. How can romance flourish?"

Penn thought it was rich for a woman in dominatrix gear to judge anyone for being obvious. The dommes laughed, apparently struck by the same irony.

"My sister is in love with love," Colette said. "She pictures you with that timid lotus flower, spreading her petals."

Timid, my ass. Penn smiled. "I picture that, too, fairly often. Then I imagine myself with a black eye."

"Flirtation is a subtle dance," Chloe said. "You may be mistaking her reticence for rejection."

Penn refrained from laughing. "You think she's shy and playing hard to get?"

Chloe gave a wise nod. Despite the constraints of her clothing, she seemed completely at ease in her latex second skin. "Consider the *non-dit*...the unspoken. In your culture so much is spelled out. You rush to analyze. What room is there for mystery?"

Colette translated. "Nariko wishes to be overwhelmed."

Somehow Penn doubted that. The last time she'd tried the direct approach, a year ago after one beer too many, Nariko hadn't spoken to her for a month. In the end Penn had thrown two hundred bucks away on an ikebana flower arrangement. She also wrote a groveling apology in verse, since Nariko liked poetry.

"Only a strong person can compel devotion from such a woman," Chloe said. "So she resists. She's testing you."

Who needed Dr. Phil?

"To be honest, I don't want her devotion," Penn said. "If we got involved, things could get pretty complicated." For starters, Lila would kick her butt.

The twins exchanged a look.

"You prefer to keep it simple?" Chloe seemed disappointed.

Penn had spent enough time in Europe to know that French women played the game by different rules. She'd hooked up with a few of them during stints overseas and never got a handle on what they wanted from her, other than sex. They were more interested in taking their pleasure than being liked, and cared nothing about having her approval. In those brief relationships, Penn never controlled anything, outside of the bedroom. Her lovers exercised power by keeping their secrets to themselves. They didn't seem to need a truly intimate connection, so they didn't invite her in. There was no mutual disclosure of life stories or outpouring of one's deepest yearnings. Penn never felt close to any of them, and that suited her fine. In her line of work heart-to-hearts with pillow friends were not an option anyway.

Sometimes she found her solitary lifestyle difficult. A part of her envied the bond she saw in happy long-term couples, but Penn couldn't imagine herself in a white-picket-fence situation, trying to stay interested in a Suzie Homemaker. She got antsy just thinking about taking out the trash every week and having potlucks with people who couldn't decide between vegan or macrobiotic. But she wondered if she had a deeply buried romantic self whose yearnings were unappeased. She realized that for most women being madly in love and committed to a partner was one of life's great adventures. So far, she'd missed out on anything that even came close.

When she left the CIA she'd half-expected she might meet Ms. Right and settle down, but it hadn't happened and she hadn't really tried to make it happen. She'd vaguely considered the idea of personal ads online, or dating the women she met instead of having sex and moving on. The trouble was, she didn't feel an emotional spark with any of them. She wondered if her libido got in the way. Most of the time she had sex on the brain when she picked up a woman. If she kept their phone numbers and made a date for coffee, she could find out if their attraction went beyond the physical.

She thought about Nariko again. They'd known each other

for five years, although for most of that time Penn wasn't at the club regularly. Over the past year, as Lila's health became an issue, that had changed and they'd seen more of each other. Their relationship had evolved, yet they were no closer to becoming lovers. If anything, the prospect seemed less likely than ever.

With a flash of comprehension, Penn said, "Nariko feels like family to me. That's why I can't go there. And we work together. I don't want to muddy the waters."

The twins studied her with interest.

"You flirt with her," Chloe said.

"It's a habit, a game we play. It doesn't mean anything."

"Does she know that?" Colette asked.

Good question. Penn wondered why the alluring twins were trying to set her up with Nariko. Surely not out of pity. Just in case, she said, "This has nothing to do with her scar."

Chloe dismissed the whole idea with a shrug that was very French. "What is beauty? Certainly not a set of characteristics women can choose from the cosmetic surgeon's menu. This nose, that mouth, these eyes."

Colette nodded. "Beauty isn't about mimicking perfection. It is the reconciliation of imperfections. Without imperfections a face has no character."

"And who can remember such a face?" Chloe pronounced with a disdainful sniff. She and her sister had obviously discussed this topic before. "Production-line prettiness—so boring. Without character, there is nothing unique that lingers in the mind."

"A beautiful woman is unforgettable," Colette agreed. "Nariko's scar takes nothing away from her."

Penn smiled. She saw Nariko the same way. Without the scar, her face would be lovely but unexceptional.

Chloe appraised Penn with sloe-eyed warmth. "You also have an interesting face. Quite singular."

"Well, I definitely don't have that beauty-from-a-jar thing going on."

Colette joined her twin in looking Penn up and down. "You hide your sorrows like a soldier."

Disconcerted, Penn said, "I'm a glass-half-full kind of person."

That sounded like the dismal platitude it was. These women were too perceptive, by far. Their frank stares tugged threads of awareness through Penn's groin. She felt like a meal laid out in front of two dangerous sirens taking time out from gorging on the blood of virgins. If they felt inclined, they would admire the offering, tease their taste buds with tiny samples, then slowly devour every morsel. What a way to go.

Something tangible passed between Chloe and Colette, an unspoken thought that drew identical smiles to their faces. Without warning, the air rushed from Penn's lungs and her next breath seemed inadequate, as though the oxygen had been sucked from the room. Her mouth went dry and she licked her lips. She could hear a trickle of water, the silvery splash of the austere ornamental fountain Nariko had set up in a corner of the room to welcome their guests.

Chloe stroked the head of the dainty submissive at her feet and said, "You may leave us, my pet."

Penn thought it was probably time for her to escape as well, but before she could stand, Colette slid her legs off the sofa and sat up, tightening her kimono belt. The glide of the robe caused a prickle of static that made the fabric float then cling in peaks over each breast. Her nipples pushed into view, dark little shadows beneath the pale yellow satin.

Penn tried to drive hard nails of common sense into her roving thoughts. In a few weeks' time the divine twins would go back to their drafty château and grateful submissives. They were already chic among the European fashion designers and socialites who considered themselves cutting edge. Lila's new film would further cement their ascension to the kink crowd's sexiness hall of fame. Enslaved devotees would shower them with praise and gifts. They would look back with wry amusement on their month across the Atlantic, no doubt decrying the innate prudery of the unsubtle Americans.

If Penn signed up for the dirty job of butch plaything, she would be left with nothing but the wrath of Nariko and an earful from Lila about mixing business with pleasure. And some hot memories.

Trying to lower her pulse rate, she gave voice to the question she often pondered when she surveyed the crowds at Inner Sanctum. "Tell me something. Is it all just theater?"

"You want to know if we merely put on a show for BDSM fashion victims?" Chloe had moved to the dining table and was lifting quirts from an open case, slapping each lightly against her thigh.

"I meant no offense," Penn said.

"You may be direct with us." Colette's smile was warm and genuine. "We're lifestylers, not pro-dommes. We indulge ourselves in Lila's dungeon because we enjoy having an audience."

"We're exhibitionists," Chloe said in. "It's been that way since we were children. Our mother first sent us out on the catwalks when we were three, posing with her models. We got a lot of attention."

"We were a novelty, then," Colette noted with a trace of cynicism. "These days everyone accessorizes with children and small dogs."

The twins exchanged another of their baffling stares, communicating something Penn couldn't interpret. Chloe exchanged a quirt for the long singletail they took turns with. Passing the well-oiled leather slowly through one hand, she said, "You are the opposite, *n'est-ce pas*? You prefer to vanish in a crowd."

"That's me." Penn conceded this perception with a nod. "But I don't have an art like yours. You're very accomplished."

During her time around Inner Sanctum, she'd seen plenty

of whip-wielding incompetents leave unintended bruises on wannabe submissives. To watch Chloe and Colette wrapping their "victims" intentionally, bestowing delicate fan patterns without drawing a drop of blood, was an education.

"We learned from the best," Colette said. "Mistress Ulrika of Munich."

With a sigh, her sister murmured, "She Who Must Be Obeyed," and they spent a few silent seconds in wistful contemplation.

"It was my sister's idea to involve you in the shibari scene," Colette said. "I would use you differently."

Penn's spine reacted with a small jolt. "Really?" She watched the slow-dance of Colette's mouth as she spoke again.

"A careful flogging." Her dark eyes bored holes. "To warm you up."

"I'm honored," Penn said evenly. "But somehow I don't see myself getting up close and personal with an X-frame."

"You're not comfortable surrendering control?" Colette studied her face intently.

"There is that. And pain doesn't do it for me."

"This is something you've explored?"

"Not in a ritualized manner." Her year at Camp Peary wasn't exactly pain free. The intense paramilitary training received there had taught her never to place herself in a vulnerable position. Penn knew her highly developed self-preservation instincts put a crimp on her personal life, but she couldn't alter what had become second nature. A lot of case officers left the CIA for that reason.

"We found out a lot about ourselves when we were with Mistress Ulrika," Colette said.

Penn kept her thoughts to herself. She could see the appeal of power play for people in nice, soft lives whose boundaries and limits were never tested. Endurance and chemical highs weren't a part of everyday life for Jane Citizen, yet human beings were hot-wired for fight/flight. It made sense that a few adventurous types craved the heightened intensity and role-play they could experience in power exchange. She felt a pang of regret that the opposite was true for her. She didn't want her work to impact on her erotic self, and yet it had. Occasionally she wondered what it would be like to surrender her will completely. It was never going to happen, of course. She couldn't imagine having that kind of trust in another person.

Penn chuckled inwardly, picturing herself bleating out a safe word after about thirty seconds. Oh, yeah—really hanging tough.

"Are you curious?" Chloe approached, the singletail furled in her hand. She rubbed the distinctive red Lucite tip of the handle up and down her thigh.

Penn's first impulse was to take the whip from her and back her against the wall, but it would probably be smarter to juggle knives. Chloe's commanding femme-fatale stance was like an invitation to single combat, not an ounce of wasted energy. Her latex dress was a simple mid-thigh-length design with a high collar and long sleeves. It molded her so snugly, every move emphasized the sensual symmetry of her form, from the upward thrust of her breasts to the modest flare of her hips and her long, lithe legs. They were naked, the feet narrow and elegant in the freshly polished ankle boots.

Normally, Penn enjoyed the feel and smell of leather more than latex, but Chloe's look was so sexy it took her breath away. She shifted in her chair, trying to ease the pressure where her crotch seam rubbed insistently. Her arousal had dulled as she drove back from Unity Vaughan's house, but she was swollen again, her body making its needs known. The idea of being "used" was sounding better and better.

She realized the twins were waiting for her answer. "Curious? Yes, sometimes. But I know who I am. Putting on cuffs and getting a pain fix isn't going to tell me anything new."

She'd been there, done that, had the T-shirt. On the Farm, trainees were subjected to harsh interrogation techniques. By comparison, being flogged in a consensual situation, when she could stop the play at any time, would be a cakewalk. Penn reached for the wine she'd forgotten about. Her hand shook slightly.

Colette noticed. "You seem nervous."

"I'm drinking wine with two very sexy women. If my pulse rate didn't increase, I should be on a gurney."

Chloe sat on the arm of the love seat and crossed her long, slim legs. She looked like a pinup. The bold flirtatiousness had left her face. Her eyes were unexpectedly velvet-soft and sweet as a child's. In a conspiratorial hush, as though referring to some shared wickedness they hardly dared express, she invited, "Tell us the truth. What kind of offer would be irresistible to you?"

For a few tingling seconds Penn was captivated. "An offer?"

The twins smiled, in on a secret hidden to outsiders.

"We'd like to share you," Colette said.

Penn guarded her reaction. If her delicious companions weren't sisters, the decision would be a no-brainer. And if she were only attracted to one of them, she wouldn't be sitting here tongue-tied, wondering if she was as adventurous as she thought. Trying to clarify what exactly was on offer, she asked, "Are you talking about a threesome?"

They laughed.

"What do you think we *are*?" Colette's midnight-satin voice got low and husky. "Perverts?"

Penn felt a shivery relief. "Now that you mention it—"

"You sound so disconcerted." Chloe's smile was that of a fairy-tale enchantress with wicked intentions. "Don't worry, we have our own boundaries. While one plays, the other may only watch."

Penn couldn't be certain if this information was reassuring, disturbing, or a turn-on. Perhaps all of the above. A manicured hand stroked her knee.

"We haven't had a butch for quite some time," Colette said. "And dear, sweet Violette tells us you're delightfully traditional in that role."

Penn flushed. Obviously Thalia had spilled the beans and Violette now knew they'd hooked up for a night. She wondered how much detail was circulating. Had everyone at Inner Sanctum heard a blow-by-blow account? What was her scorecard? She didn't have to hold her breath waiting to find out.

Chloe slid off the sofa and bent over her, letting her taut latex-covered breasts brush Penn's face. In her ear, she murmured, "You left her very sore."

Penn turned her head until their lips came heart-stoppingly close. "She was begging for it."

"Don't they all?" Chloe's breath rolled across Penn's face like a warm, minty fog. She glanced back at her sister. "May I have her first, *chérie*?"

"Only if you explain what you want from her," Colette teased in reply.

Desire writhed deep down in Penn's gut. "Hold that thought," she said roughly "I have to go to work."

Weakening with every second, she fled the room with unbecoming haste. It occurred to her, as she clomped downstairs, that she should change her briefs, maybe even her jeans. The thought made her grin.

CHAPTER NINE

"A re you sure it was following you?" Neil Stambach looked as dazed as a man who'd just woken up from a coma. "What if it's the Koreans?"

"I don't know what's worse. Their creepy people or ours," Unity said as they continued along the breakfast buffet.

She had no appetite. All she could think about was that big, black Cadillac Escalade with the tinted windows that had stayed two cars behind hers all the way across town this morning. She had no idea who was inside. And maybe it was just a coincidence that the SUV had followed her from her street in Bethesda to the Marriott parking lot. A remarkable coincidence.

The SUV wasn't the only thing that had unsettled her this morning. She'd been in her walk-in closet, choosing an outfit for the day, when she saw something very odd. A fine film of pale dust covered all the shoes on one of her racks. Was it possible, in the two days since her maid service on Monday, that this amount of dust could accumulate? Or had Mrs. Jackson suddenly forgotten to clean inside the closet?

Unity had a hard time believing either scenario. She searched her closet, then her bedroom, then worked her way around the house. Nothing seemed to have moved or changed, yet she had a strange feeling that someone had been in her house again.

"It could be the Russians," Neil said, blinking like crazy.

Unity made a show of disingenuous surprise. "How could that be possible? Our president looked Putin in the eye and got a sense of his soul."

Neil snickered.

"The Russians are too busy killing dissident journalists to send spies to Bethesda to steal our secrets," Unity said. "But jokes aside, I'm pretty sure someone was snooping around in my house last night while I was here."

"What do you think they were looking for?" Neil inspected a cheese Danish before adding it to his piled-up plate.

"I don't know. It doesn't make any sense. If it was a regular burglary they'd have stolen my DVD or laptop, wouldn't they? But if it's about Vaughan Biotech, then why look in my house when we have a secure building? Obviously anything important would be there."

"Good point." Neil's cheeks took on a slight flush. His next comment was cautious. "You, know, a lot of people feel vulnerable after a break-in. When are they coming to install the new security system?"

"Friday, this week."

"You'll feel better as soon as that's done, I guarantee it."

Unity knew he was talking common sense, and if it weren't for the dust, she would assume she was just being paranoid.

"Have you actually *seen* anyone?" he asked.

"Guys with trench coats, thick glasses, and foreign accents?" Unity laughed. "Hell, yes. Look around."

They carried their meals to a vacant table.

"I'll get the coffee," Neil said and strolled off across the yellow-striped carpet.

As he stopped to greet a couple of colleagues, Unity scanned the room for Professor Maass. Her heart jumped when she spotted him being helped from his wheelchair into a seat at one of the larger round tables. The gaunt, powerful man assisting him looked like a bodyguard, but there was no sign of the woman who constantly snuck into Unity's thoughts. Maybe the professor's team worked shifts and the evening guard would arrive later in the day. Refusing to speculate any further, she sliced an apple and nibbled on a piece. Neil returned and was handing her a mug when someone bumped him and a splash of hot coffee careened across her pristine white cuff.

"Damn, I'm sorry." Neil set the mug down and started fumbling with a napkin.

Unity took the scrunched paper from him and mopped at the stain. "Don't worry, it'll come out. But I think I'll switch this for a fresh blouse before the stem-cell panel." She'd picked up her cleaning en route this morning so there were several changes of clothing in her car. Rising, she excused herself, insisting, "Go ahead without me."

She left the breakfast area in a brisk walk and was joined by a chunky man in dark glasses as she rode the elevator down to the parking level. He was on his cell phone the whole time arguing with someone in a low tone. The smell of car fumes, rubber, and oil hit her as soon as she stepped out of the warm, carpeted interior. Hunching her shoulders against the cold, she listened to the rapid clip-clop of her heels as she took the long diagonal route to her Lexus.

It would be easier to change in the car than have to carry her soiled garment around with her for the rest of the morning. Unity located the clean blouse she was looking for and pulled it free of the wire hanger. She locked the trunk and slid into the passenger side, automatically flipping open the vanity mirror so she could check her hair and makeup. She started in fright when a dark shape passed across the back of her vehicle. Before she had time to react, the driver door opened and the chunky man from the elevator dropped into the seat next to hers.

Panicking, Unity tried to get out of the car, but her door wouldn't budge. A second man stood outside, leaning against it. All she saw of him was the back of a hand that brushed the window. The wrist was tattooed and the skin probably belonged to an African-American.

"I'm just here to have a talk, Miss Vaughan," said the bulky stranger next to her.

Unity thought her pounding heart must be visible. Her cheeks were hot and her hands started to shake. She hardly dared to look at the man's face. From her darting glances, she imprinted a tanned, acne-scarred complexion and a fleshy nose and mouth. His hair was salt-and-pepper, very short and smooth as though he'd taken the time to comb it before carjacking her—first impressions being important. She couldn't see his eyes behind the dark glasses.

"Who are you and what do you want?" She hoped she sounded strong and assertive, not terrified.

"My identity doesn't matter." There was a rehearsed quality to the words, like he routinely delivered the same reply to the same nervous question. "My employer is willing to pay a significant sum for all rights and patents for the Unity Protein."

Speechless, Unity lowered the blouse she had clutched to her chest. Hardly a soul knew she'd settled on the name. Just Neil Stambach, Prof. Gustafson, her attorney, and a couple of senior people at *Nature* magazine. She hadn't even added the name to her patent application yet. How could the information have leaked out so fast?

"Who's your employer?" she demanded.

"I'm not free to disclose that information."

"Then we have nothing to discuss," Unity blazed. "I will not sit here and be intimidated by a couple of hired…musclemen, or whatever you are. Get out of my car now before I call the police."

To her dismay, the brute next to her didn't budge. With the slick confidence of a man who knew things could get worse before they got better, he said, "You're a smart lady." The formality of his opening statements had gone. He was ad-libbing now, his accent pure Baltimore. "My advice is to get ahead of the game right now. You got something people want. My employer, he's not the only party interested."

"What do you mean by that?"

"You could say he's a middleman. He's been approached by certain people who want the property. Serious people."

"Then why don't these *serious* people come and see me? I'm in the phone book."

"All I can tell you is you'd be better off taking the money and letting my employer take care of business." He softened his voice, as if talking to a small child. "You don't want problems in your life, sweetheart. You got a nice house. A good job. A pretty face. If you was my sister, I'd give you the same advice. It was real easy for us to get to you. Think about that."

Unity felt bile rise in the back of her throat. His meaning was clear. If this thug planned to hurt her, not just scare her, he and his sidekick had ample opportunity. She clasped her damp hands together, refusing to allow him to see them shaking uncontrollably. If she'd learned one important lesson while growing up in the daily crime and grime of West Baltimore, that was never to show weakness.

Reaching for something buried down deep, she turned in her seat and faced the man squarely. "How much?"

He gave an off-center grin that displayed poorly capped front teeth. "See now, that's your common sense talking. Twenty million wired to the offshore bank account of your choice. We can even set that up for you, since a lady like yourself probably doesn't have the usual financial apparatus in place."

Unity nodded, trying to look calm but interested. "That's quite an offer." She let out a small sigh, a brief show of feminine nerves. "And I see your point. I have a lot to lose."

He nodded with the benevolence of a hireling soon to deliver good news to his boss. "Twenty million bucks for a science project." Chuckling, he said, "Nice work if you can get it, huh?"

Kiss my ass, fuckwad. Unity concealed her anger behind the ditziest smile she could feign. "Here's what I'm willing to do.

You can tell your boss I'll think seriously about his offer, and in the meantime, I won't sell my company to the people who just made a legal bid."

"You got another offer?"

"Yes. Fifty million." She shrugged. "So, you see my problem, don't you?"

He took a moment to think about that fact and made the interpretation she was hoping for. "You'll be looking for more money, then?"

"You said it, yourself. I have something a lot of people want."

"Lucky you, huh?" He reached for the door handle. "We'll get back to you after the weekend. And remember what I said. You got some protection if you deal with us. Word is, you're gonna need it."

❖

"Seth, how are you?" Unity switched her cell phone to her left hand while she slid her right thumb into the reader. The door to her office unlocked automatically.

"Hey, baby. I'm doing good. What's up?"

"I need some help."

"You got the right man for that." Her mother's ex had the warm, deep bass of a blues singer. Seth Williams was one of the only decent boyfriends Ellen had ever had, and had done his best to stay in Unity's life after he was dumped. He was the only person there for her at her high-school graduation; Ellen had been drunk that day and forgotten. He'd lent her money when she was in college and visited her whenever he could. In recent years they hadn't seen so much of each other. She felt bad about that.

Seth's mom lived with him now. The old lady was in a wheelchair and needed someone there with her all the time. Seth's sister took care of her when he was at work. The rest of the time, he was the good son so it was impossible for him to get out of Baltimore. Unity should be driving up to visit, and she kept meaning to, but time slipped by and good intentions had taken a backseat to life. She knew she had some making up to do, but Seth never made her feel guilty. He loved her.

"What you got going on?" he asked.

"It's a long story. Remember I told you about that special research I was doing to help make wounds heal faster?"

"Sure I do." Excitement entered his voice. "You got that happening in your laboratory?"

"Not exactly, but I've made an important discovery in a related field. I can't go into details and to be perfectly honest, it's not easy to explain." She took a stab at something he might be familiar with. "You've heard about the human genome, haven't you?"

"Oh, yeah. All you blue-eyed people with the same ancestor. I always knew there was inbreeding responsible for some folks."

Unity laughed. "Well, I've invented a special kind of cell that could have an impact on genes, just like the blue-eyed mutation did." Not exactly, but more or less in the ballpark. "And the thing is, I've patented this cell and now a lot of people want to buy the ownership from me. Some of them aren't good people."

"Who you talking about, baby?"

"That's the problem. I don't really know. I got an offer from a big company to take over my business last week." She didn't mention Merrill's name. Seth had loathed her and the feeling was mutual, another reason he and Unity had seen less of each other over the past few years. "But I don't want to sell Vaughan Biotech because I wouldn't be my own boss anymore. Then, this morning I got another offer. And that's what I'm worried about. The man who made the offer, he's like Lenny Olsen."

Lenny was a local scumbag now serving twenty-to-life. He'd been Ellen's boyfriend before Seth and liked to throw punches when he was drinking. During the two years he lived in the Vaughan household, Unity had spent most of her time hiding from him.

"Did he hurt you?" Seth's voice got harsh. "If he laid a finger on you, he's a dead man."

She could practically feel him blazing through the ether into the small metal phone in her palm. The device seemed to heat up instantly, and she swapped it back to her right hand as she sat down at her desk.

"No, he didn't hurt me. But I felt threatened. That's why I called you."

"What do you need, baby? You know I'm always here for you. Just tell me what you want."

"I thought you might know someone from back when you were a marine. Kind of a tough guy. I need someone who can watch my back and maybe find out some information about the men who scared me." She paused. "I think I'm being followed, and my house got broken into the week before last."

"You talk to the cops?"

"Yes, and they told me to get a new alarm system. But nothing was stolen, so what are they going to do?"

Unity thought about the Escalade. She wasn't imagining things when she'd noticed it tailing her back then; the two thugs had driven away in it. The chunky guy was right. Getting to her was easy. If they could do it, so could anyone.

Seth was muttering, upset that she hadn't called him sooner. "Shit. You got a home invasion and I don't hear about it till *now*?"

"I should have called. I know."

"You damn right you should have called." With a trace of suspicion, he asked, "You seeing her again? Is she back there living with you?"

"No, absolutely not."

"Well, that's one piece of good news, that you haven't gone and *lost your mind*."

"She's history, Seth. You know that." Unity moved back on-topic. "So, do you think you can help?"

"Maybe. A couple of boys in my unit ended up in special ops. I'll talk to them."

"Thanks, it means a lot."

"Where you at now, baby?"

"In my office. Don't worry, it's pretty safe here. We've got all kinds of security in this place."

"Don't go anywhere, you hear me. Just wait there and I'll phone you back soon."

"You got it." Unity felt her shoulders loosen with relief. "I love you, Seth."

"Well, don't you forget it. And next time someone breaks into your house, I want to hear about it right away."

"Yes, sir."

"Now, I love you, too, baby. Don't you worry about a thing. I'm gonna take care of this."

❖

Unity entered the address Seth read out into her GPS and headed for the George Washington Parkway via the Beltway. Neil had been shocked when she called to tell him she wasn't coming back for the afternoon sessions. But she'd detected a note of excitement. She'd asked him to present the short paper she'd prepared as a profile-raising exercise. Vaughan Biotech was one of a new generation of small research corporations trying to carve out a name in an industry dominated by global heavyweights. If she was completely honest, one of the reasons she didn't want to sell to Fortis was about ego. She didn't want to be gobbled up before the Vaughan name became a household word, at least in the households of her counterparts around the world.

The traffic was light, by DC standards, and she reached Eighth Street in less than forty minutes. The building she was looking for was not residential, but appeared to be some kind of nightclub. She turned into the adjoining parking lot and took in her surroundings. With the exception of a few cars parked in a roped-off VIP area, the place was deserted. Unity looked twice at the vehicles. Tucked between a couple of absurdly huge SUVs was a red BMW M6 like the one she'd seen in her street a few times, parked in front of the Kershaws. She managed not to read anything sinister into the coincidence. There had to be hundreds of that model driving around DC.

A security camera mounted on the brick building was angled toward the cars, so Unity pulled in close to them. At least if a guard was watching, her Lexus would be safe. She took the note she'd written earlier from her purse and scanned the information again, still not quite believing that she was trying to hire someone Seth had described as "one scary motherfucker." According to his contacts, Penn Harte was some kind of freelance hired gun with a shady past that could involve CIA black ops or the criminal underworld. No one really knew for sure. They'd just given Seth the name, which came from a friend of a friend who knew some colonel who ran a team of people with unusual skills. This Harte individual supposedly worked contracts for the colonel. The story sounded like something from an espionage novel.

Unity stared up at the building. Seth said no one knew Harte's address, but this place was a known hangout and maybe someone here knew where to find him, or could deliver a message to him. According to the unlit neon sign over the club entrance, Inner Sanctum was normally open till five a.m., so the staff probably didn't start arriving until the late afternoon. Unity wondered if she should come back then. She could go have lunch over at Eastern Market a few blocks away, do some shopping, and then try her luck.

She peered behind her toward the road. So far she hadn't seen the Escalade. No doubt Crater-face and his tattooed friend were reporting in to the guy who wrote the checks. With any luck they would be off her tail for a few days while their boss came up with more money. Yet again she agonized over her options. She had serious reservations about putting someone with a dubious background on Vaughan Biotech's payroll. What if this Harte individual had a rap sheet and the kind of history that could attract the attention of Defense Security Service pen pushers? Unity couldn't afford a blemish on her company's employment record that could affect clearances. She was supposed to submit the name of everyone she employed. If a background check on Harte raised awkward questions, she could be in real trouble.

She pondered the alternatives. She could "forget" to submit the name and hope Harte would be long gone before anyone noticed his brief presence on the payroll. Or she could hire a security firm with the right clearances and keep everything aboveboard. Or, if she got desperate, she could accept the offer from Fortis and let them deal with the problem. What she was doing seemed crazy in the face of safer, more practical alternatives. Unity leaned her head on the steering wheel and tried to think.

If she hired the right kind of firm, it would cost a fortune and she would just get a glorified bodyguard. She wanted more than that. She wanted someone who would get her back, but also find out who was offering twenty million dollars for the Unity Protein. A foreign government? Criminals? Terrorists? She couldn't ask a security firm to handle that kind of investigation.

She stared at the club again. Maybe the assignment would be out of Penn Harte's scope, or maybe he wouldn't be interested. Could a washed-up former spy handle this kind of work? Unity put the slip of paper back in her purse and decided to think about that some more while she ate a falafel.

CHAPTER TEN

The script said: *Bacchanalian orgy at Lady Shulamith's mansion in the Garden District of New Orleans. Sexy cops Kylie and Pat arrive, expecting a crime scene. They fuck Lady Shulamith while her hot man-meat slave watches and whacks off without permission. He gets punished.* A page of dialogue was followed by the instructions: *Oral, oral, dildo/mouth, dildo/pussy, humiliation, flogging, lez threesome, pop shot.*

To save time, Lila had decided to shoot part of her next project, a more traditional semi-kink moneymaker called *Sweet Evil Cops*, at the same time as her twin dommes project. A new set that would work for both productions had been built on the soundstage, and a swarm of club regulars had shown up in response to an open call for extras. Those who wanted their naked butts immortalized would be fed a catered lunch in exchange for several hours of groping in a dark, freezing room. They would also get free tickets for the next Hedonism party. They seemed grateful.

Penn surveyed the bodies writhing like snakes in a pit. She wondered if that was the artistic impression Lila wanted.

"Okay?" she asked the director while the cutaway footage was being shot.

Quebec, or "Q" to those fortunate enough to be counted among this artiste's circle of acquaintances, was a Canadian who rejected gender. S/he wore a stylized "Q" on a heavy chain around a throat that seemed too slender for a man's. His/her features belonged to a baby-faced butch, but the voice was a soft, masculine bass.

"We're good," s/he told Penn and signaled the talent who were sitting in deck chairs on an Astroturf mock-patio drinking coffee and writing new lines for themselves.

Penn had been amazed to find out from the guy playing Lady Shulamith's humiliated slave that this was normal. Porn movies of yesteryear had minor plots and actors worked with a script. These days, they only got a few lines scrawled on a piece of paper. Most tried to improve upon these as they went along.

Q took a moment to inspect the pulsating sexual frenzy, then said, "See that ass with the major pimples. Keep it out of the close-ups."

There ensued some discussion between Q, the two cameramen, the boom operators, and the lighting technician; then they kicked off the dialogue rehearsal. The team seemed to figure out the blocking and camera shots as they went. A guy from an adult magazine snapped still photos between times, politely urging, "Look at me" and "Spread those cheeks." Someone hit the volume on a portable CD player and "Like a Virgin" pounded out. Most of the orgy participants immediately lost it and started laughing hysterically.

Penn moved back behind the lights as everyone got ahold of themselves. Chloe and Colette usually didn't arrive on set until two, so there was time to wrap up today's *Sweet Evil Cops* shoot first. Then all the extras would have coffee and cigarettes, while the dommes rehearsed with the director. Most of their scenes were completed in a single continuous take, a fact that impressed the production crew, who were used to the usual stop/start delays to change position, add lube, blow noses, and wait for males to get hard.

Q called for silence, then instructed, "Okay, everyone start fucking," and the taping began.

The sexy cops threw open a cardboard door and rushed in, guns drawn.

"Who called 911?" the smaller of the pair demanded, turning her head wildly so her hair swung.

A busty goddess in a blue sequined gown stood up from a velvet couch and sidled over. "I did. I'm Lady Shulamith. Welcome to my party."

The other cop, a nicely built brunette, holstered her gun. She spoke with a lisp. "I hope you aren't wasting our time when we have real crimes to solve."

Her sidekick waved a pair of handcuffs and flicked her honey-auburn hair some more, using the hand with the gun. "If you've made a false complaint, we'll have to place you under arrest. Turn around and spread your legs."

Lady Shulamith said, "I can't. My dress is too tight."

"Take it off," said the brunette.

She and her partner started kissing and fondling each other as Lady Shulamith sensuously stripped. She was once an exotic dancer, and it showed. Q made a signal to keep on rolling and cued the man-meat slave. He looked on as Lady Shulamith was patted down extensively by both cops.

The strawberry blonde untangled her gun from her hair and poked it into its holster. "You're in trouble with the law. But maybe there's a way out for you."

"Let me guess," came the languid reply.

Just in case there was room for doubt, the brunette announced, "You have to do everything we want." She unbuckled her belt, slid it from the loops, and trailed it over Lady Shulamith's full, round breasts. "We're going to lick that hot pussy of yours and fuck you with a big dildo."

I'm shocked, Penn thought. One of the crew passed her a camera and asked her to take continuity shots, a production value Lila was particular about. Nariko normally did them, but she was with Lila today, at her chemo appointment. Penn avoided those. She got stressed and emotional, and no matter how well she hid her feelings, Lila wasn't stupid. An anxious companion only made things worse for her. Nariko had the gift of serenity, so she was the one who went along on all the hospital visits.

Penn's neck prickled as she felt a new presence in her personal space. She didn't have to turn around; she knew from the sudden tension and darting glances that the twins had arrived. They couldn't walk into a room without creating a stir of envy and desire.

"It would please us to hear you talk dirty like that," a voice in her ear murmured, and Chloe's body brushed against her. "Perhaps more eloquently."

Penn pushed the small digital camera into the front pocket of her jeans. "That could be arranged."

She felt a hand on her butt. A slow squeeze. Colette stood directly behind her, so close her breasts were pressed to Penn's back.

Trying not to disrupt the shoot, Penn said in a whisper, "You two are here early."

"We wanted to watch." Colette moved in even closer.

The sisters were dressed for their next scene, in military-style khaki leather, a short snug-fitting jacket fully buttoned over a slim knee-length skirt. Penn knew what lay beneath the conservative sexiness. They stripped down to a matching Victorian corset and tiny shorts as their scene progressed. Just thinking about it made her weak, and she had a tough time concentrating on the tableau before her.

The porn scene was clichéd but still hot. Lady Shulamith's pale, lush body and platinum hair glowed against the narrow red-velvet couch, her arms flung sideways, her legs wide apart. Between her outspread thighs knelt the strawberry blonde, still in her uniform, minus the cap. Her small hands pushed against the mistress's knees. The wet sound of her licking and Lady Shulamith's moans were audible, even from where Penn stood. The women seemed to be genuinely enjoying themselves.

Standing over them, the brunette cop undid her shirt and

threw it aside. She wore a black sports halter bra and looked like she worked out. Her dark eyes rested on the other women with unusual intensity. Either she was a good actress or she was really turned on. She stepped back, changing her stance as a cameraman slid to the floor at her feet, zooming in for a close-up of tongue on clit. In profile, the brunette's close-fitting uniform pants revealed the solid arch of a dildo.

Chloe scraped her fingernails down Penn's denim-clad thigh, sending a shiver through her. "She's Shulamith's lover in real time."

Penn damped her dry lips with her tongue. "That's hot."

"She had a fit when Q wanted the blonde to wear the dildo for this scene." Chloe's knuckles ground lightly against Penn's fly as she withdrew her hand. Her cinnamon-tinged breath warmed Penn's cheek. "Jealousy is an interesting emotion, isn't it?"

Penn wasn't sure if she could do philosophy right now. She placed a finger to Chloe's lips and pointed at one of the cameras. Chloe responded by sliding her tongue over Penn's fingertip and slowly sucking. Watching them, Colette wore a smile that fell short of soft and sweet. Her expression was hungry and speculative. She toyed with the deerskin flogger she was carrying, letting the soft tails run over her palm and between her graceful fingers. The gesture was full of sinister promise, and for the first time since they'd met, Penn understood that she was looking at the true sadist of the pair, the woman whose will defined both of them. Chloe only took control when Colette found it pleasurable to observe.

The thought made Penn uneasy but aroused her, too. She touched the flogger, sliding a finger through the limp, heavy strands. Colette's eyes met hers. The aggressive dominant stared out from those mysterious depths, holding Penn mentally pinioned. Colette lifted the flogger to Penn's face, letting a soft swath of deer leather slide past her neck and cheek. Refusing to be the first to look away, Penn clamped her hand over Colette's, completing the electrical circuit surging between them. Warmth coursed into her cheeks. She drew a sharp, shallow breath, getting hotter by the second.

With a cynical smile, Colette slid from her grasp but left Penn in possession of the flogger. "You look good holding that." Her voice was so quiet Penn had to watch her lips to be sure she was hearing correctly. "A natural."

Penn's heart pounded. Her legs were almost cramping from the control she'd imposed to prevent tell-tale quivers. Seeking a way to break the tension without conceding Colette's power, she remembered she was supposed to be taking snaps. She drew the camera from her pocket and forced a casual grin, as if she wasn't churning inside.

"I'm on continuity," she explained. "I better concentrate."

Colette said, "Be careful what you wish for."

Penn brought the camera to her eye. What she saw made her gulp.

❖

With a shock of recognition, Unity took in the sight of 5' 9" of lethally attractive woman with a flogger in one hand, a camera in the other, and a pair of corseted twins fondling her body.

"That's Penn, with the camera," said the man who'd led her into the dim industrial space.

Unity stared harder in case she'd made a mistake. The woman in the boot-cut jeans and black turtleneck wasn't the washed-up spy she was expecting. She was, without doubt, Pat Hunter, the distracting butch bodyguard Unity couldn't get out of her mind.

"Penn?" she repeated vaguely.

"The one and only." The man with the chandelier earrings looked her up and down quizzically. "You're a *friend* of hers?"

The word "friend" was delivered with wry emphasis, implying many shades of meaning. Unity took a card from her purse. In a tone that was strictly businesses, she said, "Would you give this to her, please, and tell I need five minutes of her time. It's urgent."

As he sauntered away, she made a point of looking anywhere but at *her*. Three hotties were having energetic sex on a couch beneath intense white lights. Unity feigned interest. A brunette wearing a strap-on was fucking a glamorous platinum blonde who was going down on a small, tanned woman whose unwieldy breasts bobbed on her chest like flotation devices. Near the threesome stood a hunky surfer dude jerking off while he watched them. Ick. All over the floor, naked limbs tangled in a sweaty, heaving orgy that both repelled and fascinated Unity.

She tried to behave nonchalantly, like she saw this much flesh on a daily basis, but she couldn't control her heart rate or the film of perspiration that glued her bangs to her forehead. She looked up past the sexual Disneyland, directly into Penn Harte's eyes.

Even from across the room her intensity was disquieting. There was no sign that she was embarrassed by her surroundings. If it worried her that she'd used a false name when they met, her demeanor held no trace of apology. She said something to the dark-haired twins standing next to her, handed them the flogger and camera, and strolled around the outside of the set. Her boots were Western ropers that made her legs look longer and lent a trace of swagger to her walk. The effect was maddeningly sexy.

When she reached Unity, she said, "What an unexpected pleasure, Dr. Vaughan."

"Is it Pat or Penn?" Unity asked, determined not to lose herself instantly in those smoky topaz-chipped eyes.

She focused on Penn's mouth instead. Bad idea. The tiny hollows at each corner deepened, as though something had made her smile inwardly. Her lips weren't girlish. They had a firmness that went with the rest of her face. Unity wondered how they would feel pressed to her own. In the worst way, she wanted to find out.

"It's Penn when I'm not on an assignment."

Unity glanced past her as someone had a noisy orgasm.

"Let's walk and talk." Penn's voice was husky, and her scent was different from last time.

Unity blushed when she realized what she'd detected. Penn smelled of sex, the way people smelled of smoke when they'd been around cigarettes. The aroma buzzed across Unity's senses, unsettling her completely. She'd been able to rationalize the urges she'd felt last night by reminding herself that she was tense, lonely, and sexually frustrated. It was infuriating to find herself having the same responses now, at a time when she needed to have her brain switched on and her libido in hibernation.

This woman came highly recommended. The fact that she looked like sex on tap was irrelevant. Unity was possibly in danger, or at the very least her livelihood and reputation were on the line. Telling herself to get a grip, she followed Penn up several flights of stairs, staring down at the risers so she wouldn't notice the way Penn's firm butt moved in her jeans. Thankfully they reached a narrow carpeted hallway before she could shame herself by whimpering or falling over.

Penn opened a hammered steel door, and they stepped into an empty lounge bar. Several recessed lamps had been left on, so the room wasn't in complete darkness.

"Drink?" she asked.

Unity decided she needed one. So far it had been quite a day. "Grand Marnier on the rocks, please."

Unable to help herself, she followed the slight roll of Penn's hips as she walked to the bar. Her every move had an economic grace and self-assurance Unity couldn't imagine possessing. Feeling sorry for herself, she flopped down into an armchair. Only last night, she'd seriously thought about taking this woman home, and if she was honest, she wished she had. She'd decided already that if "Pat" was at the convention tonight, she would set aside her ambivalence and have some fun for a change. But everything was different now. Sex with an employee wasn't an option, assuming Penn was willing to work for her.

Unity stared down at her hands. They were shaking, and not only because she was in the grip of lust unlike any she'd ever known. The adrenaline rush of the morning had drained away, but her muscles still seemed out of control. She couldn't stop shivering. Her nerves were poised on a fine edge, her usual methodical thinking disrupted.

Bitterness rose in her throat. This should be the best time in her life. She'd done what most scientists only dreamed of, and she was still young. There was time to do so much more. She had a successful business and a beautiful home and was finally building a relationship with her mother after years of disillusion and acrimony. And Merrill was history. Unity stroked the ring finger of her left hand. The pale shadow of the band she'd worn had finally gone, but she could still feel its ghost presence, just as she felt the lingering effects of those lost years.

Merrill was like a bad case of measles—not toxic enough to kill her, only to prompt immunity. The disease had left her altered somehow. She felt incomplete, as though a stranger had displaced her former self and now occupied her mind and body. Her mother always said she cared too deeply about things. That was no longer a problem. The new Unity didn't experience the world, or others, with the same intensity. The place in her heart once given over to deep emotion was like a padded cell. Nothing got in, or out.

Which was why her present state made no sense. It was as if, after a year on "mute," the volume had suddenly been turned up loud and her ears were ringing. Unity looked up sharply as a pair of booted feet came to a halt in front of her. It wasn't her day. Penn's crotch was at eye level. With her lean hips and strong thighs, she was built for jeans. She had no waist, and Unity knew from the brief collision of their bodies that she was hard and muscular where there were usually soft curves.

"Enough ice for you?" Penn offered the drink she'd poured.

Unity closed her hand around a cold glass, slippery with condensation. The ice cubes bobbed and clinked in the dark amber liquor. She wanted to smear one across her brow. "Perfect, thank you."

Penn sat down in the armchair at forty-five degrees. Her knee brushed Unity's, but she didn't adjust her spread posture to avoid further contact. "How did you find me?"

"A friend of a friend sent me. I was told to give you this." Unity handed over the note Seth had dictated. All it said was *Vae Victis,* a Latin phrase that meant "woe to the vanquished." Unity wondered at the significance. Was this a special password used by spies, something like those weird handshakes Freemasons exchanged?

Penn took a lighter from her pocket, put a flame to the paper, and set it in a decorative ashtray. Unity wanted to laugh. She half expected to hear the theme music from *Mission Impossible.*

"What do you need from me?" Penn asked.

Unity could have answered: *Twelve hours of your undivided attention between the sheets.* But her sensible self replied, "If you were listening to convention gossip yesterday you've probably heard my company has been working on a de novo protein design."

"This is the one you've patented?"

Unity sighed. So much for nondisclosure. She wished she had some idea where the leak was coming from. She trusted Neil implicitly, and she doubted Professor Gustafson would ever blab about work that would also make him a star. No one else, other than her attorney, knew enough to fuel such accurate rumors. Her mind strayed to Merrill. Could she have learned more than she was letting on. If so, how?

"Yes, I've filed for a patent."

"And this special cell is a hot property?"

Unity let the scientifically inaccurate description stand. By the time her discovery went public, the Unity Protein would probably be described as "a superbug" and Unity would be asked if she had the vaccine for it.

"Because of the discovery my company is a target for takeover. A large corporation made a bid last week, and as of this morning, someone else is in the market. I was offered twenty million in cash to do the deal."

Penn gave a low whistle. "Quite a payday. Do you want to sell?"

"No, but I want to know who's trying to buy. That's where you come in."

Frowning, Penn traced a finger over the neck of her beer bottle. "I'm not sure if I can help."

"It's not just about digging around. I need some personal security, and you're a bodyguard—"

"Not exactly. Professor Maass is just a cover for another assignment at the convention. He has a security team, but I'm not a part of it."

Unity's lungs burned. She supposed she should be grateful that she wasn't the only scientist dealing with a crazy situation. Apparently Penn had other clients in her field. All the more reason why she would be exactly the right person for the job.

Trying not to sound as desperate as she felt, Unity said, "Look, my house has been broken into. I'm being followed. I think someone on the inside is leaking information about my research, but I don't know who. And a couple of creeps who see Tony Soprano as a role model are threatening me. It's unbelievable."

Penn's expression was hard to read. "How do you know you're being followed?"

"Because I've seen the same black Escalade with tinted windows for the past two weeks, and the thugs from this morning drove off in it. That was after they told me I should do business with their boss or I'd end up with a broken face."

"Did they say who their boss is?"

"No, or I wouldn't be asking you to find out," Unity said patiently. "I got the impression he was a go-between for the real buyer."

"Entirely possible." Penn took a quick slug of her beer. "Do you think the same men broke into your house?"

"Probably. Who knows?"

"Was anything stolen?"

"I don't think so, at least not the first time, although I haven't had a chance to look properly."

"You've had more than one break-in?"

"I think so. It's hard to say for sure, but I'm sure someone was in the house again last night."

"Last night?" The tone was very flat.

"Yes, while I was at the Marriott *flirting with you*." The words were out before she could stop them.

Penn's eyes glinted. She set her beer bottle on the side table between the chair arms. Her expression was pensive. "Just on that, what made you back off?"

"As I recall, you were the one who had other plans. But it doesn't matter, now. I'm here because I'm interested in your services."

Penn stretched her legs out in front of her, dropping one foot casually over the other. "Which services do you have in mind?"

The question was sardonic, and something in her face sent Unity's pulse racing out of control. She should have known better than to meet those dangerous eyes. In fact, she should have left the building the moment she saw who she was dealing with. They could make the necessary arrangements on the phone. She didn't have to sit here with a woman who had the power to short-circuit her common sense. To make her want what she would never have.

Penn smiled at her and something visceral passed between them. Virtually paralyzed, Unity pushed a breath past her stuttering heart and out through the narrow fissure between her lips. The words she groped for failed to emerge. In their stead came a low, hoarse sound like the grunt of someone winded after a belly-punch. She felt like folding in two.

Penn propped her elbow against the chair arm and rested her cheek against her loosely curled fist. Her expression altered and Unity felt safer, suddenly, able to let her spine relax without fearing her whole body would collapse. She saw tenderness and a trace of regret, and she had the odd impression that Penn knew exactly the effect she was having. And had decided to be merciful and turn down the heat.

"Do you know what you want?" Penn asked, so gently Unity let the brazen truth spill out.

"To kiss you."

Shocked, she set her glass down with a thud. Grand Marnier sloshed over the side. Licking the fluid from her fingers, she lurched to her feet and headed for the door. She could hardly believe what had just happened. She felt like she'd stepped out of her skin and into another reality where her frail, naked self was horribly exposed.

"Unity. Wait." Penn didn't grab her arm or get in her way. She followed, but stopped a few feet away. "Please. Don't go."

Unity couldn't stop herself. She turned around. Apparently still under the spell of the truth elixir, she blurted, "This makes no sense to me. We're strangers."

"I don't know what to think, either." The candor in Penn's voice was reassuring. She seemed almost as befuddled as Unity.

"Lust," Unity said. "Obviously."

Human attraction was mysterious by definition, but one thing was certain. Nature had rigged the odds so some pairs would feel the urge to mate and others would not be attracted at all. She and this woman had evidently hit the chemical jackpot. The pheromones would settle down eventually. In the meantime, they were adults, not teenagers. They could choose not to act on sexual attraction.

Penn studied her with implausible calm. "Lust."

She seemed affected by the word. Emotion clouded her

face and she stared at Unity as though she were lifting layers and peering beneath. She took several steps closer until Unity could feel the heat emanating from her body. Unity didn't move. Her breathing was uneven. Her fingertips slid against her damp palms. She knew she should say something to draw down the veil of normality between them, but by some unspoken accord they stepped into each other.

Penn rested her hands on Unity's hips. The fingers were trembling. Unity brought a hand to Penn's face. At first she barely grazed the firm plane of her cheek, her fingers quivered so much. She watched the muscles in Penn's throat tense as she swallowed. Her eyes were bright and dark, the pupils voiding all color but for a thin ring of silver-green. Her mouth opened a fraction as Unity brushed her thumb across the bottom lip.

Around them, the room seemed to shrink, the shadows shifting as colors receded into a dull haze. There was no sound but the hushed shuffle of converging breaths as their faces drew closer. Penn's lips smothered the sigh that rose from Unity. At the first brush of their moist flesh, they drew back, staring at each other. Then they kissed again, and Penn enfolded her and walked her backward. Her tongue parted Unity's lips, tasting of beer. She pushed her hard against the door. Crushed, Unity tilted her head back and opened wider, taking Penn's tongue deep inside. Their hot, hungry, slippery kiss became desperate. Unity bit Penn's lower lip hard.

There was nothing measured in the way they clung to each other. Blood pounded in Unity's ears. She closed her eyes and fell into a darkness so complete it consumed all that wasn't flesh and heat and the startling joy that broke her open at every seal. She tasted metal and realized they were almost gnawing as they kissed. Her mouth was bleeding, or was it Penn's?

They slid down the door, their legs giving way in the same moment. Penn kissed Unity's throat, forcing her head back. They pulled at their clothes. Unity cried out as a talon of pleasure pierced her nipple. She looked down as Penn's mouth consumed then released her bunched flesh. Her bra was in a roll beneath her breasts and her shirt was half-off. She couldn't speak, afraid to breach the wild enchantment that held them captive.

Panting, she slid her fingers through Penn's hair and pushed her head down. Something banged against the door. Her shoulder, Unity thought. She felt the soft rasp of denim sliding between her thighs and the prickle of moisture exposed to air.

Penn cupped her hard, fingers probing against the soaking fabric of her panties. She said, "I have to have you."

Unity almost sobbed. She hitched up her skirt and pushed clumsily at her panties.

Penn dragged them down, moving aside so she could tug them away from Unity's ankles. "I'm sorry about this place." She glanced distractedly around. "It's not what I had in mind."

"I don't care," Unity choked out. She let her legs splay wide.

Penn stared down, taking her in. "You're so wet."

Her face was very still, her awe tangible. Naked intent rolled in like a storm, obliterating the surface tranquility. Her eyes gleamed and her teeth showed between lips drawn taut. She placed a fingertip at the rigid, aching apex where Unity's flesh parted. A strange sound was drawn from her, a low animal growl that found an instinctive reply in Unity. The groan she heard from her own throat was dark and foreign. She stared up at Penn, spellbound, and recognized something ancient and unnamable. A heady languor stole over her, then, slowing the passage of blood through her veins.

She whispered, "I've been waiting for you."

As she spoke, she realized she was moving. Not in a good way.

Penn jerked upright and slapped her hand against the steel divide behind them. Cursing, she said, "Someone's out there."

"Oh, God." Unity froze, then elbowed herself up.

Leaning hard against the door, Penn yelled, "Wait a second," and helped Unity to her feet. Her cheeks were pale and her mouth had a look of pinched desperation.

Unity pulled on her cold, damp panties and rearranged her clothing. She felt numb.

Penn tucked in her turtleneck. As she refastened her belt, a couple of thumps landed on the door. She touched Unity's shoulder. "Ready?"

All Unity could do was nod and frantically smooth her hair. She scuttled toward the unlit bar, then realized how stupid it would look to perch on a stool miles away from her drink. She didn't have time to get back to the armchair before Penn moved toward the center of the room and their coitus-interrupter marched in. She was stiff-backed and Japanese, narrow all over. Halting just inside the door, she stuck her dainty hands on her nonexistent hips and swept Unity with a look that would shrink the most stubborn clit.

In a voice that dripped with haughty indignation, she said, "Your shirt is wrongly buttoned."

Unity knew she was already bright red. This rudeness from a total stranger added anger to her embarrassment. "Nice to meet you, too…er—"

"Nariko." Penn's expression would have been comical if Unity were in any mood to laugh. "Unity is a client of mine."

This disclosure was met with a scathing snort. "I suppose it was only a matter of time before you marketed your *services*."

Unity was not sure if she was reading too much into the snide remark, but she wanted to set the record straight. With as much dignity as she could muster, she said, "I'll leave my card, Penn. Thank you for your time. Please let me know if you can help."

Nariko laughed.

Who was this woman, anyway? The answer dawned on Unity instantly. If this was Penn's girlfriend, she wasn't happy. Unity rebuttoned her shirt, crossed the room, and picked up her satchel. She decided she should be thankful. At least they hadn't had sex, not entirely—assuming an orgasm was the litmus. She had trouble defining their encounter. Were they just making out? Something in her chest cramped in protest at the idea, and she expelled a short, sharp breath. She could feel Penn's eyes burning into her shoulders, but she couldn't turn around. She pretended to rifle through her satchel for the car keys she'd already located. When she finally felt composed, she produced the placid smile she relied on during arguments with Merrill and breezily pivoted toward the door.

"If there's anything you need to know before you begin, you can reach me on my cell phone," she said.

"Will you be at the ball tomorrow?" Penn asked, walking her into the hallway.

Unity shrugged. "It's not a priority. I have work to do."

"Then I'll call you. I'm going to need more information." Penn's voice was not entirely even, attracting a sideways look from Nariko, who had followed them.

Whatever the cranky possible-girlfriend saw, it disconcerted her, and she studied Unity through narrowed eyes.

"I'll walk you to your car," Penn said.

Before Unity could respond, Nariko said, "You're needed on the set, Penn. That's why I was looking for you."

"They can wait."

"No, it's fine," Unity said. "I can find my way out."

"I'll escort you," Nariko offered pleasantly. "I have to get something from Lila's car."

Sensing that Penn was about to lose her temper, Unity touched her arm and insisted, "Go. I'm fine."

Penn's hand closed briefly over hers. In a murmur meant only for her, she said, "It's not what you think."

Oddly, Unity knew exactly what she meant and believed her.

They said a strained good-bye, and she and Nariko descended the stairs in silence.

When they reached the parking lot, Nariko had the grace to say, "I apologize for my tactlessness."

"Thank you." Unity hit the remote and the Lexus blipped its unlocked signal.

"I didn't understand, at first," Nariko continued.

"Understand what?"

The beautiful mask of Nariko's face seemed to slip. "That you and Penn are in love."

Unity stifled her laughter. "I'm not sure what you think you saw back there, but I assure you, it wasn't love. We only met last night."

Nariko smoothed her hair back with both hands. Her fingers fluttered like drunken butterflies around her face. "Oh, that is even worse."

"Now you've really lost me."

Nariko stared at her as if *she* were the delusional one. "Love at first sight." She shook her head. "I cannot believe it."

"Relax." Unity dropped into the driver's seat and buckled up. "There's no such thing."

Nariko's little fingers had surprising strength as they dug into her shoulder. Leaning in the open door, she said with scary composure, "If you are cruel to her, I will kill you."

"Well, that sucks," Unity said dryly. She started the car.

Nariko backed off, but called after her, "I'm not kidding."

It was wise to speak gently to big dogs and crazy people, so Unity said, "Okay, I'll be nice." She almost expected a rock to smash her rear window as she drove away.

"Love at first sight," she muttered.

Could her day get any more surreal?

CHAPTER ELEVEN

The twins wanted her body. How lucky could a woman get? Penn poured herself another whiskey and scanned the mating rituals taking place around her. Tonight the crowd's usual restless, sex-soaked fever failed to stir her. The silvered sway of breasts, the pale smooth planes of flesh, the gliding bodies and searching hands left her strangely detached.

"I think I'm getting old," she told Nariko, expecting no reply. Her nemesis had been moody ever since the episode with Unity that afternoon.

Nariko said, "Don't you have better things to do than hang around here? Felix can take care of the mundanes."

"I asked Lila if she wanted to play cards."

"She's exhausted."

"It's incredible news." Penn was still grinning from her conversation with Lila a few hours ago. The tumor on her liver had shrunk enough to be operable. It looked like her chemo was finally having results.

Penn was so thankful she'd rushed down to Lila's church, the Parish of St. Monica and St. James, to make a donation in her name. She was lucky to escape without being roped in to the choir. Lila was a member and Penn had often sat in on their Wednesday-night practices. A few of the singers came by the club every week, bringing gifts and flowers. Lila was hoping to be well enough to sing at Midnight Mass on Christmas Eve. For the first time in months Penn allowed herself to think that far ahead.

Her cell phone vibrated and she snatched it from her pocket. She'd called Unity hours ago and left her number, suggesting they get together ASAP to discuss the security issues so she could start making inquiries. So far, Unity hadn't called back. Penn figured she was probably stuck in her laboratory examining bugs under a microscope.

She checked the incoming text message and excused herself. She'd already spoken with Gretsky to break the bad news that Kyle Roth's client wasn't the only suitor for Vaughan Biotech, and the new players sounded dirty. He said he would shake some trees. Penn dialed the number he provided as she took the stairs to her room.

"What have you got?"

"Eddie DiMaria," Gretsky said. "Baltimore LCN. Gambino family."

"Isn't biotech kind of a reach for the mob?" Penn said dubiously.

"Eddie's the new breed. A middleman. The feds have him shifting big-ticket commodities to the Chinese. Stolen art. Looted museum pieces from Baghdad. You want it, he gets it."

Penn settled back on her bed. "So the Chinese are shopping for this protein cell Unity Vaughan invented?"

"Used to be that they only stole intellectual property. I guess they're buying what they can't steal these days."

"Have you told KR?"

"Oh, yeah. And let's just say he's unhappy. How close are you to fixing this?"

"I'll have the raw footage tomorrow night."

"Excellent. We need to deliver."

"Any idea where the leak came from?" Penn asked.

"Not so far."

One possibility had occurred to Penn, but she didn't mention it. KR's client was playing hardball. Would that include leaking proprietary information gleaned during negotiations with Vaughan Biotech? Assuming the client was the DoD, maybe they wanted an unsuitable buyer to jump into the mix to make the Fortis offer seem more tempting. If they thought the Chinese were involved, the stakes would be even higher. The Pentagon was getting antsy about the military technology grab.

Penn thought it was a bit late to put that genie back in the bottle. American cash had built the Chinese economy, and the money shipped over to pay for lead-corrupted kids' toys and poison pet food had now been borrowed back to pay for Iraq. The US owed China about 1.4 trillion dollars, and the Chinese were also buying about 36% of the US personal debt every month. Pressuring Beijing over anything was virtually impossible. Mindful of this unfortunate practicality, the DoD had even created the requisite access control lists to deep-six the entire Chinese IP address space—leverage if they needed some. They were fighting hard to keep advanced weapons technology out of Chinese hands.

Obviously the DoD and Fortis had mutual interests. They were probably sharing information. She thought about tomorrow and felt sick again.

"About the DVD," she said. "I assume I won't be compromised? Unity won't know I'm the source?"

"There's no way for her to connect the dots," Gretsky said. "She already knows there are criminal elements involved. Her house was broken into. She's going to think the bad guys are responsible."

"Are you sure we still need it? I haven't spent any of the cash. I could take a pass on this one, you know what I'm saying?"

"Yeah, hey, it chaps my ass, too, that KR will have you butt naked on his computer."

"Don't go getting all choked up on my behalf," Penn said sarcastically.

Gretsky laughed. "Speaking of heartburn, I heard you've been talking to Simmons."

The senior NCS officer was an old friend of his. Penn had more or less assumed they would compare notes. "I think it's time I surfaced."

"They'll send you back to Russia. That's a different operational climate these days."

"I'll cope."

Penn flicked aside a small barb of panic. If she returned to the Clandestine Service as a case officer, she could end up running cutouts in Iraq. Switching from the NCS to the Directorate of Intelligence was an option. They needed intelligence analysts with her skills. It wasn't the most exciting work, but she could stay in DC.

Gretsky signed off, wishing her good luck for tomorrow. Penn tried to sound enthusiastic. She felt like shit. There was no voice mail or text message from Unity. She considered placing another phone call, but what would be the point? Unity would get in touch when she was ready. Their afternoon encounter probably had something to do with the lack of communication. Penn had thought about little else since, even with the good news about Lila.

Normally she didn't look for deeper meaning in acts driven by the most basic human urges. She didn't replay a kiss over and over, letting herself indulge in romantic speculation. But normally she didn't feel the way she did now, strangely thrilled and churning with anticipation at the thought of seeing Unity again and finishing what was started. Normally she didn't agonize over her own ability to please and give pleasure. But the thought of making love with Unity, taking all the time she wanted, was damn near terrifying.

She would only have one chance, and she had no idea what "perfect" would mean for Unity. After their chaotic fumblings downstairs in the club bar, she probably thought Penn had no finesse at all. A second encounter was, doubtless, the last thing on her mind. Maybe she was right now thinking she'd had a fortunate escape from a clumsy desperate, like all the others who wanted to grope her.

Penn couldn't believe her ineptitude. She'd felt like a teenager in the backseat of a car, allowed for the first time to see a pair of breasts and touch a woman's body. Sure, they were both aroused and Unity wasn't making any objections, but with the benefit of hindsight she must be looking back wondering if that's how sex would be. She hadn't called. Was she just too embarrassed?

Penn slowly rubbed the thumb and fingers of her right hand, recapturing the feel of Unity's wetness. God, she'd been so desperate to get inside her, she couldn't think straight. Next time she would get her act together and behave like she knew what she was doing. She would make sure Unity had no regrets about spending a night with her. Penn wanted to give her everything she needed, and more. The thought made her ache with a yearning so profound her eyes stung.

Burying her head in her hands, she mumbled, "Shit."

She could sit here ducking reality forever, escaping into self-indulgent fantasy about making sure the woman she planned to betray would actually enjoy herself in the process. Penn felt disgusted with herself. Instead of imagining how Unity would taste and feel, she actually needed to plan how to position her for the cameras. The concept revolted her so much, saliva flowed across her tongue and she almost gagged. What the fuck was she thinking?

She checked the time. It wasn't too late to put Gretsky's money back in the lockbox and tell him KR could take his "biographical leverage" and shove it. What was the worst thing that could happen? She let that thought tick over. The worst thing wasn't her reputation in shreds or her return to Langley under a cloud because Gretsky would think she'd gone soft. The worst thing, by far, was the fact that some other hot woman would be sent in to do the job, and Unity was just lonely enough to give in.

Penn's stomach clenched and her hands shook. The thought of one of those stone-cold bitches touching Unity made her crazy. In fact, the thought of *anyone* touching her was a problem. Dazed, Penn flopped back against her pillows. Something was wrong with this picture. She didn't *do* jealousy. She didn't do guilt, either. In the past sixteen years, she'd never lost a minute's sleep over her work. There was no conflict of interest, no messy emotional investment that could compromise an outcome. North, on her moral compass, pointed to the flag. There was no opposing pole, no force she had to resist.

Occasionally, she heard about officers who lost their way. Some sad schmuck living in a hellhole would form an attachment he couldn't let go of. Once or twice Penn had extracted those poor fools and dragged them in to the station chief to have their heads read. Most were cut loose. An officer who had his priorities ass-about-face couldn't be trusted anymore. There were no shades of gray at the agency. Loyalty was everything. That was why Penn had walked away. She couldn't be loyal to Porter Goss and his moronic puppet masters, as well as to her country; the two were mutually exclusive.

She heaved a sigh, thankful that her current dilemma only involved a freelance assignment. She should have turned it down in the first place. Even if she felt nothing for Unity, the job was distasteful. It ate at Penn that she was working the sleaze shift for Kyle Roth, sharing the gutter he occupied. For money. She felt dirty, but if she backed out now, it would make no difference. They were going to bring Unity to heel any way they could, and things could get a whole lot uglier than a sex tape.

The only way she could handle this with any belated decency was to make the final cut herself, editing the content to expose Unity as little as possible. They only needed enough content to compromise her. Unity would do the deal because she had no choice. Just knowing they had the DVD and could use it would be enough to persuade her.

Penn would destroy the master copy herself, or make sure Unity received the original and knew it was the only one in existence. Penn could do that much, at least. A pinprick of uncertainty muddied her thoughts. If she was going to be stuck undercover for the next few years, maybe it would be nice to have her own private copy as a memento. She set her cell phone aside, troubled by that idea. What exactly did she think she would want to relive? She had no desire to watch reruns of her sexual encounters with women. Why would this be any different?

Even as she asked herself the question, she knew the comparison was flawed. She felt a connection to Unity that was more than physical. There was no denying the chemistry between them, but lust alone could not account for her belief that they meant something to each other. She couldn't escape the feeling and kept coming back to it, trying to make sense of the irrational. They'd had a couple of brief conversations and a botched sexual encounter. It was crazy that words like "destiny" kept popping into her head.

People saw what they wanted to see, she supposed, and she'd reached a point in her life where, for once, she was thinking about finding a long-term partner. Was she seeing Unity through the prism of this new nesting urge? Had the hunt for a mate finally overtaken the quest for a fuck? If so, why on earth would she want to rush back into counterintelligence work? Did she really want to hide her true self from someone she loved?

Penn drew a sharp breath, tripped up by the word "love." She was losing it. Working freelance, without any sense of purpose, had messed with her mind and disarranged her priorities. Former officers went through stuff like this when they returned to civilian life. They looked for ways to fill the vacuum. Some drank. Others gambled. And there were plenty who adopted a glossy new cover, that of the perfect partner in the perfect relationship. Lost in love, because it was better than being simply…lost.

Penn dragged her locked steel box out from beneath her

bed and extracted Unity's folder. The photo didn't do her justice. It failed to capture the winsome tenderness of her smile or the emotions that flowed like a rip current beneath her deceptive cool. Penn was aware, with every moment they were together, that she was in danger of being swept away. The feeling was completely new to her. She moved her fingertips over the face in the picture, rebelling against the glossy texture of the paper and the flat, frozen half-truth of the image. Unity was much more than a pretty face. The camera had failed to capture all that was elusive and complex and incredibly sexy about her. In the split-second distillation of a frame, the real Unity was absent. Entirely out of reach.

Penn wouldn't have expected anything else.

❖

It was too late for a phone call. Unity had put it off long enough that the option no longer existed. Who made business calls after midnight?

She'd avoided picking up the phone at a reasonable time. The truth was, she wanted to snap the mysterious cord that seemed to tie her to Penn Harte. She thought distance and the passage of time would serve her the way a holding cell served drunks who got into fights. She would get a chance to chill, as sobriety overtook her, and reflect on her misguided behavior. She would see the kiss that afternoon in context. She wasn't the first sex-starved woman to fall into the arms of the first attractive woman she stumbled across. Pathetic, but true.

There was nothing to stop her and Penn behaving like adults and getting what they wanted from a business arrangement. Penn had the skills, and Unity could afford to buy them. It seemed so simple, yet a siren song beckoned her toward a more reckless path, whispering that she could have it all. That she wanted to know Penn sexually, and why not allow herself that adventure?

Did she deserve to feel the way Penn made her feel from the first moment they met? Desired. Aroused. Ready.

The sheer improbability of their attraction made her hesitate to crush her feelings. She'd doubted herself capable of such intensity with another person again. She felt maimed, after Merrill, convinced that even if she ever met another woman she could settle down with, the relationship would be tepid and safe. There would be no pins and needles. No extremes. The thought comforted her.

Penn had the opposite effect. Unity could rationalize the how and why of that fact as much as she liked, but nothing would change. She had a straightforward choice to make. She could ignore their attraction and stay on course, or act upon it and risk a diversion.

She approached the problem logically. Right now, her company was all-important. She couldn't afford to get squeamish about taking the necessary steps to safeguard Vaughan Biotech. A team of people depended on her for their livelihoods, and she'd worked her whole life, against long odds, for what she'd achieved. Only a miserable coward would back off over a case of girly flutters. If Unity couldn't play hardball when it mattered, she might as well phone Sullivan Brady right now and take his offer.

She was going to employ Penn, regardless. And maybe she would sleep with her. So what? Other people had a love life at the same time as running a business. What was she afraid of? Unity could answer that question without thinking twice. She had baggage. When she fell for Merrill, she'd virtually put her life on hold. Everything took a backseat. She couldn't allow herself to make the same mistake twice.

She stared down at the number on her cell phone and cut herself some slack. She was older and wiser these days. There was no chance that she would throw herself under that train again. Why not enjoy herself? She wouldn't need Penn's help with security issues indefinitely. Maybe they could date for a few months until the chemistry fizzled, then part as friends. The more she thought about that possibility, the more reasonable it seemed. She hit "send" and prepared herself to talk to voice mail.

"Unity?" Obviously not a recorded message.

Her mouth went dry. It was still sore where the pressure of their kiss had slightly split her bottom lip. "Oh, you're there."

"Yes."

Unity crossed her legs. "I'm sorry I didn't get back to you sooner. I was tied up." Poor choice of words. She added, "We should talk…about the job."

"Agreed," Penn said softly. "Want me to come over?"

"Now?"

"I'm used to working late."

Unity swapped the phone from one damp hand to the other, thinking, *Don't say yes*. Tonight was risky. She felt weak-willed. "Let's cover some bases on the phone and meet tomorrow."

"No problem." Penn sounded indifferent, a response that bothered Unity way too much.

"I'll be busy all day tomorrow. There's a U.N. delegation coming." She'd also heard from Neil that Merrill was going to be on the panel for that session, a last-minute replacement for the Fortis representative on the program. "I can escape from the ball for a while, if you're free later."

"Done," Penn said. "I made some calls, by the way. Does the name Eddie DiMaria mean anything to you?"

"No. Should it?"

"He's a middleman who deals in commodities like yours. The goons you saw sound like his men. They're not all made guys."

"Oh, my God. Are you talking about the Mafia?" Unity clutched the phone so tightly her nails bit into her palm. "I thought they just did drugs and prostitution."

"They've moved with the times. Some of the new breed are into cybercrime and big-time theft."

A cold bead of sweat meandered down Unity's spine. "I feel sick."

Penn's voice came back, soft and reassuring. "You don't have anything to worry about. This is in play and they think you're listening. Did they say when they'll contact you again?"

"In a couple of days."

"When you hear from them, set a meeting time. I'll come with you and do the talking."

"Who will I say you are?"

After a moment, Penn replied with mild humor, "Your *consigliere*."

Unity wasn't sure if she was joking or not, but the warmth of her tone inspired confidence. "Are you sure you want to do this?"

"Absolutely."

"Your fees," Unity began. "Do you want—"

"No. You don't owe me anything. Just call it a favor between friends."

The offer hung in the air. Uneasily, Unity said, "I'd rather we kept this strictly professional."

There was a long silence, then, "Is that your way of telling me I have to keep my mouth away from your beautiful nipples?"

Unity gasped. Memory immediately ambushed her prosaic intentions. She could still see the look on Penn's face and feel that finger poised on her clit. Her throat closed over the words she forced out, blurring their sharp edges. "Yes."

"Are you sure about that?"

"Things happen." Unity was irritated to hear her voice waver. Sternly, she said, "To be perfectly honest, I don't know what got into me."

"I wish I could say *I* did."

"Stop." On a gulp, Unity said, "I'll see you tomorrow night."

There was no answer. She heard a muffled noise. Maybe the sound of a drawer opening.

"Are you there, Penn?"

"Yes." Another sound. A zipper? "Sorry, just changing my clothes. I have to go down to the club soon."

An image flashed through Unity's mind. Penn, with those stunning twins. She flinched. "Well, I won't keep you."

Penn didn't say good-bye. Her breathing was a soft shuffle at the other end of the phone. "Are you still wet?" she asked, like it was an everyday question.

Unity squirmed. The pulsing pressure at her core tugged at the ripening flesh on either side. She felt strung out and restive. "Look, I have to go now."

"I have a better idea." Something jangled near the phone. "Those are my car keys. I'm not really needed here. I could be at your place in forty minutes."

Unity said the first thing that jumped into her head. "How do you know where I live?"

"I looked you up in the phone book." A long pause. "Well?"

Don't answer. Unity pressed her fingers hard against her sore lip.

"Forty minutes," Penn repeated. "And I'll give you anything you want."

Unity expelled a sigh of frustration. "We can't do business if you're going to tease me all the time." Oh, God. She sounded so prim.

"I'm not teasing. I'm very serious."

"You don't give up, do you?"

"We both know I want to fuck you," came the laconic reply. "Why pretend otherwise?"

Unity couldn't think of one good answer that wasn't a lie or a feeble evasion. She changed the subject. "It's black tie tomorrow."

Penn laughed. "I figured."

"People will be dancing. The old-fashioned kind." Great, now she was burbling.

"Works for me."

"My ex will be there."

Something changed. Unity sensed the recalibration before Penn said a word. When she spoke, her tone was cautious.

"How do you feel about that?"

"She's the CEO of Fortis." Unity knew her voice was higher than usual, but she couldn't relax her throat. "That's the company that made the takeover bid. She'll probably want to talk about their offer."

"Are you having second thoughts about refusing to sell?"

Illogically, Unity thought she detected a hopeful note in the question. Maybe the Mafia angle was more scary than Penn had let on, and she thought Unity could save herself some grief by selling to Fortis.

"I'm not sure," she said honestly. "Maybe I'm just being stubborn because...of her. There's a history."

"We don't need to go there," Penn said gently. Her withdrawal was tangible.

A heavy lump of regret settled on Unity's chest. "Penn, I wish we hadn't been interrupted...before. I mean, this afternoon...you know."

"Yes, I know. Don't think about it anymore."

Easier said than done. Unity blinked away a fine dew of tears. "I'll see you tomorrow."

"It's a date."

For several seconds Unity kept the phone pressed hard to her ear. She wanted to say something else, but by the time she found the right words Penn had already gone.

CHAPTER TWELVE

Her dress was the color of black roses, a deep, dark red that spoke of blooms in the pitch-black of night. By contrast, her skin was milky moonlight, dancing against the undulating caress of her low-cut gown as she swept a hand or exposed her throat, laughing over some unfunny joke. From across the ballroom, Penn stared at her and couldn't stop. She was as unavoidable as the weather.

The crowd was pinkly scrubbed and perfumed for this evening of awards and valedictories. There were probably three hundred people. Penn couldn't see a big guy with acne scars or an African-American with a tattoo on his wrist, the goons Unity had described. In her new capacity as Vaughan Biotech's supposed security czar, she scanned the guests with mechanical efficiency, yet all she really noticed was Unity gliding smoothly from one group of suits to the next, rolling like a relentless tide through the room, leaving a trail of flushed faces and bitter wives.

Penn wanted to drag her away down some back alley and press her hard against a wall. She wanted deep, urgent kisses they would have to steal since they couldn't escape to the privacy of a room. She wanted to stare straight into Unity's eyes, hoist her skirt, open her legs, and fuck her hard. And when they were both panting and groaning, slicked in sweat and writhing against each other, she wanted to feel hot contractions suck her fingers deep before spilling them out.

The thought made her nerves twist, and she dragged herself present, teasing her mind with tamer fantasies of suavely peeling off stockings and teasing flesh through lace panties like the ones in Unity's lingerie drawers. Of digging down beneath Unity's careful dignity and seducing her away from the safety of her intellect. Unity liked having her boundaries in place, that was obvious. It was equally clear that she needed someone to push them aside and lead her to the sensual river that flowed deep within. She was one of those women afraid to drown, so she didn't give herself permission to swim. The voice of reason presided.

Penn wanted to make her put her wiser self on hold. She wanted to summon the other Unity, the one she'd rolled on the floor with the day before. Seeking glimpses of her, she hovered at the shadowed margins of the room, knowing she hadn't been seen yet. And Unity was looking. Penn could tell from the oblique back-and-forth shuttle of her head and the expectant air every time she glanced toward the main doors.

She was on the point of moving into view when she realized someone else was also watching Unity. The woman was tall and elegantly dressed, in a black evening suit and a crisp white shirt. Her hair was cut to flatter a well-shaped skull, and her features were smooth. Her expression and body language exuded the firm, friendly authority of a woman in charge. And she could not keep her eyes off Unity. Penn loathed her immediately, but couldn't blame her.

When the woman advanced toward Unity, Penn kept herself in check. But when she had the audacity to place a hand on Unity's waist like it belonged there, Penn made an instant damage assessment. No contest. She could knock her out in five seconds. Kill her in fifteen. Not that she was feeling primitive or anything.

At the brush of that hand, Unity turned in a vivid, joyful blur that melted like candle wax when she saw who stood there.

Everything fell. Her face. Her naked shoulders. Her full, red mouth. She backed out of reach. The woman followed and Unity shrank into herself like a sea creature taking countermeasures. The response was so deeply conditioned, Penn didn't have to guess at what she was seeing. She hoped there would never be a time in her life when a woman shriveled in her presence, becoming the diminished creature that had assumed Unity's form.

Penn left her shrouded corner with an avenger's gait. People got out of her way. But before she entered Unity's sightline, she witnessed something that halted her determined strides. Unity's drooping head jerked up, her spine straightened, and her eyes flashed with rebellion. With her shoulders flung back and her arms at her sides, each hand unconsciously poised, she looked like a gunfighter anticipating the draw.

Watching her reclaim herself, Penn was captivated. Her heart beat crazily. A flash of memory drove her back in time to a holiday in Ottawa when she was thirteen. She could still feel her dad's hand clasping hers as they ice-skated in lazy figures of eight. Later that day, when the rink they were using was closed to the public, she saw something she would never forget. Her father had met a man there, a German. As they talked, a woman skated alone on the ice to Bizet's voluptuous *Carmen*.

She was lithe and dark-haired, so beautiful she could have stood completely still and Penn would have been spellbound. Instead she rolled into motion, claiming for her own the ethereal space between the ice and the music, spinning and jumping in sensual bursts like a rolling flame. Her flowing elegance blended artistry and power. She possessed the supreme confidence to translate what could only be imagined into physicality, through sheer force of will. Penn watched that strength play out right in front of her until the dream of the routine was shattered as the skater glided into a double Axel, then mistimed her jump. Unable to gather flight, she failed to complete her rotations and landed heavily, panting and clutching at the merciless ice.

Penn lurched out of the gate and onto the rink to help the

stricken goddess and instantly fell, splat, on her face, biting through her lip. As she looked up in mortification, the skater also lifted her head and seemed to shake herself, throwing off the cloak of defeat that threatened to crush her. Eyes dark and fierce, she rose on her blades again, flatly refusing to concede an inch to self-doubt, pain, or human weakness. She reached for Penn's hand, plucked her off the ice, touched her bleeding mouth with a small, regretful sigh, and said something to her in German.

Penn stumbled back to her seat just in time to watch her circle, gather speed, and make the jump again, this time with flawless grace. Only later did she learn that the skater she'd encountered that day was Katarina Witt before her 1984 world championship. She had to laugh as she watched Unity face off with the guest who'd unsettled her. Some things never changed. After all these years, Penn still had the same urge to rescue an extraordinary woman who had already rescued herself.

Skirting a large, noisy clique of science-nerds, she donned a relaxed smile and strolled casually toward Unity and her ex. When Unity saw her, a rosy tide claimed the pale expanse of her throat and caught fire in her cheeks. In the same instant, the ex turned around, puzzled and plainly irked.

"Merrill, this is Penn Harte." Unity sounded breathless. "She's in charge of security for Vaughan."

The ex looked underwhelmed. Her handshake was mechanical at best. "Merrill Walker, CEO of Fortis Biosystems. If you'll excuse us," she said coldly, "Dr. Vaughan and I need a moment in private."

"That won't be necessary," Unity contradicted her. "I prefer to have Penn present for discussions that concern company security."

Penn took in the tilt of her streamlined jaw, the arch of her neck, the vulnerability of her throat. Her breasts rose and fell a little too quickly against the low scoop of her neckline. Penn wanted to believe the excitement was for her, rather than a stress-reaction to the ex.

"I understand your people made a bid for Vaughan Biotech last week," Penn said.

"We did, although I'm unclear why you're interested."

Merrill's withering appraisal was calibrated to insult, and like any self-respecting butch, Penn was angered. But she had enough self-discipline and experience to suppress her reactions. In a pleasant tone, she said, "It appears that confidential information shared during the negotiations is now circulating. I need to find out how that could have occurred."

"Are you suggesting Fortis was responsible for breaching a nondisclosure agreement?"

Penn shrugged. "Were you?"

Merrill cast an accusatory look at Unity. "Are you kidding me? Who is this person?"

"Hired muscle?" Unity suggested mildly, then laughed. "We're not in Kansas, anymore, Merrill. I decided it was time to employ someone to watch my back."

"Yet your new employee seems preoccupied with your front," Merrill quipped.

The color receded from Unity's face and a smooth, hard mask slipped into place.

Before she could speak, Penn stepped in closer to Merrill and said, "Back off. You're out of line."

"Oh, please." Merrill didn't budge. Creasing one of her white cuffs with too much force, she said, "You know, you're way out of your depth, Unity. You've leaked enough information to bring in bids from every rogue government this side of Pyongyang, and you really imagine you can hire some amateur to pin that on my company? Think logically, if you can. How is it in our interests to leak sensitive information when we're still planning to take over Vaughan Biotech?"

"Please lower your voice," Unity said. "I prefer not to broadcast our internal dealings to the entire room."

"Then let's continue this discussion elsewhere."

"I don't think so. I have nothing new to say to you."

"No one's making any accusations, Ms. Walker," Penn said.

"Don't be disingenuous with me." Merrill's eyes narrowed as they drifted from Penn to Unity. With mocking insolence, she jibed, "Security? Are you really that desperate for attention?"

Penn's nerves felt like ice crystals slowly cracking after caustic rain. A warning hand twitched at her sleeve and she realized she had her fist balled, ready to plant Merrill. Keeping her voice even, she said, "We're done here."

With mock gallantry, Merrill waved a hand, as though conceding permission for them to leave. "It's been an education." The look she gave Penn was contemptuous.

"Just ignore her," Unity whispered, slipping her arm into Penn's. "She's angry with me because I won't take her deal."

Penn thought there was more to it than that. "This seems personal."

"Merrill has some hard feeling about our breakup."

"She wants you back. It's written all over her."

Penn steered Unity through the ballroom. The music was a lugubrious big-band foxtrot, the kind Penn was familiar with from the embassy circuit that formed part of every undercover officer's basic training. She'd had no luck passing as an eager secretary luring horny attaches into boastful disclosures, so the station chief had eventually sent her in as a man. She scored big with bored wives and closet queers. That went over fine with the agency. "Whatever it takes" was the motto in humint.

"Yes, she does want me back," Unity conceded tonelessly. "But that's not happening and she just has to get used to the idea."

Penn cast a quick glance at Merrill and decided to speed up that process. Taking Unity's hand, she said, "Dance with me?"

On a pent-up breath, Unity slipped into her arms. "I thought you'd never ask."

Penn encircled her waist just enough to lead her into the basic walk even a nondancer could follow, but Unity was far from that. She fell instantly into tempo, adjusting to Penn's step length and swaying just enough to add a little heat to the smooth, rolling glide.

"How did you learn to dance?" Penn asked, surprised. Very few women these days could manage more than a muddled two-step.

"One of my mother's boyfriends loved ballroom. She was usually too drunk to partner him, so he taught me."

Penn wasn't sure what to say. Unity's file contained references to a deadbeat dad and an upbringing in a tough West Baltimore neighborhood. There was no mention of an alcoholic mother. She wanted to ask: *How in hell did you ever end up* here? But she said, "He did a good job."

"Thank you." The reply was almost quaint in its reserve. "I always wanted to learn swing, but Seth thought that was the kind of dance that would get me into the wrong crowd. He thinks I'm susceptible to bad influences."

Penn grinned. "God, I hope so." *Seth.* Also not mentioned in the file.

"Why are we at arm's length?" Unity asked as they completed a quarter turn.

"I'm dancing with my boss." Penn's clit was hard as stone, a constant tender reminder of another dialogue going on while she and Unity stuck to small talk. "I thought you wanted me to look like real security."

"And you do." Unity lowered her free hand to stroke Penn's lapel. "You're very handsome tonight. You should get out of your jeans more often."

"Just say the word."

"You know what I mean."

Penn gathered Unity close. She realized she felt weirdly exposed dancing this way, discomfited by the old-fashioned formality of the ritual with its courtship symbolism and cultural script. She was guiltily aware of holding a woman in a big dress, looking calm and proud like the kind of date right-thinking parents would choose for their lovely daughter. At least, those who dreamed of a lesbian wedding. Only Penn wasn't planning to walk Unity up the aisle. She was that other kind of date, every father's nightmare, the horny cad hoping to get laid—exactly the type "Seth" was worried about.

She leaned into Unity and tried to imagine what her own mom and dad would have thought. They'd died before Penn came out to them, but she had a feeling they knew who she was. They were good people, baby boomers who'd met in college and eventually traded their politics and peace activism for responsible jobs, two kids, and a house in the suburbs. Unity would have impressed them.

Her mom had inherited a tidy sum after Penn's grandmother passed on. She and Penn's dad paid off the mortgage and bought a yacht. They'd dreamed of sailing around the world with Penn and her brother but she got so seasick, they gave up on the idea after a few attempts. Penn still had trouble with activities that involved spinning and turning. Even meandering around the dance floor with Unity required concentration on fixed points. Unity's ripe-pomegranate lips. Her vivid gem blue eyes. The sheen of her eyelashes. The small black mole on her left shoulder. The shadow between her breasts.

"People are noticing," Unity said.

"Noticing what?"

"That you look like you want to eat me."

"I do." They were flirting, Penn thought, the way people did in the days before speed dating and sex as foreplay to conversation. Or the lack of it.

"They've also noticed that we're two women. I can almost smell the perturbation."

Penn laughed. "Hey, it's not like I'm tearing your dress off."

Unity moved sensuously against her. In her ear, she whispered, "And it's not like I'm unzipping you."

A shock of awareness impacted her spine. A hot liquification enveloped her core. It was over. She was lost. Any idea that she could keep herself together till the band hit their finale was a joke. Her nipples were glutted and so painful she wanted to whine as her shirt scraped across them. Her eyes watered. She licked her dry lips. In the asphyxiating silence, their bodies conversed in a restless Morse code of desire. Unity's fingertips explored Penn's nape. Her breasts pushed up against Penn's. The small of her back welcomed Penn's touch. Their thighs met. Their steps slowed. Penn's stomach churned. Hot and cold shivers seethed beneath her skin. She didn't know how she could stay standing if Unity let go of her now.

She let her head rest against Unity's and pressed her mouth to the tiny pulse at her temple. Wracked with need, she stumbled out of rhythm. "Do you have any idea how much I want you?" she whispered hoarsely.

Unity's eyes blazed a neon whirl of blue. Her mouth was kiss-shaped as she pushed out a soft, maddening "No."

Penn trod on a toe. She was sweating, sinking, stranded on a shore she didn't recognize, looking out at a vast ocean she could never hope to cross. Unnerved, she said, "I can't dance anymore."

Their feet stopped. A pair of tremulous hands pushed the bangs back off Unity's forehead and cradled her head. The hands were hers, Penn realized, and dropped them instantly. The encroachment of others was upsetting her. Their marble stares. Their bodies brushing by. The jarring sense of their censure, or curiosity. Or maybe she was just too raw and sensitive, and no one had even noticed what was happening between them.

What *was* happening? Penn searched Unity's face for the answer.

"You've gone pale," Unity said. "What's wrong?"

The truth echoed through the caverns of Penn's mind. *I'm falling in love with you.*

Flinching, she said, "I need some air."

"We could take a walk." The offer was cautiously made. Unity seemed confused.

"No." Penn tried to soften her tone, but her throat felt wounded. She had to gouge out every word. "Stay here. I'll be back soon."

She heard the faint, wet click of tongue and teeth, words about to be spoken.

"Penn?" Unity's hand collided with her as she retreated.

Penn pretended not to notice. In her headlong quest to get out the door, she passed Merrill and didn't even pause to wipe the smug superiority off her face. All she could think about was driving away as fast as she could.

As if escape were possible.

❖

The garden smelled woody and wet. Beyond the lamp-lit brick pathway to the back door of Unity's house, the dark shapes of the trees and shrubs loomed like sullen observers at a crime scene.

Penn located the spare key left carelessly "hidden" in the most obvious place imaginable, beneath a conspicuously kitschy statuette of a kneeling fawn. This garish Bambi was positioned in the kitchen herb garden near enough to the door to spare inconvenience to a burglar caught in a rain shower. Penn was thankful for that, since she'd left her coat in the M6, and the soft pitter-patter would soon be a deluge. She disabled the external alarm and unlocked the storm door. The internal door was supposed to be dead bolted, part of Unity's freshly installed home-security system.

Unity's cats greeted her with soppy congeniality. Her previous generosity with cold cuts from the fridge had gone over big. After she took care of the internal alarms, she poked around in the deli compartment and found some roast beef for the meowing pair. She rinsed and dried her hands, and pulled some latex gloves from her gym bag. Taking a bunch of paper towels, she patted the moisture from her shoes and eliminated the wet footprints she'd left on the kitchen floor. She stripped rapidly out of her black jacket and pants, and deposited these garments with her shoes and car keys on the armchair nearest the staircase. She went back for a toolkit and flashlight from her bag, then hurried up the stairs.

It took ten minutes to disable the cameras and recording devices in the bedroom, and another fifteen to remove the basic surveillance units from the downstairs level. Once she was done she jammed everything into her bag and called Gretsky.

"You have some news?" he asked.

"Not the kind you want to hear."

"More technical problems?"

"Sir, I'm opting out."

There was a pause. "What, she's not your type?"

"Personal reasons."

"I see."

"There has to be some other way. She's anxious about the latest bidder. I may be able to talk her around."

"You think you have that much influence?"

"Possibly."

He was slow to respond, but knew her too well to miss the obvious. "So, you're involved."

Penn wasn't going there. "I'll do what I can and keep you posted."

"Take some advice," her old friend and mentor said. "Enjoy it while you can."

He ended the call while Penn was still getting over her surprise. The last thing she'd expected was to be let off the hook without a struggle. She dressed again quickly and checked her reflection in the small guest bathroom. Her facial features seemed no different, yet something had changed. Her mother's smoky green eyes stared back at her with her father's insight. In their depths was a vulnerability Penn had rarely seen. She hovered in front of the bathroom mirror, inspecting herself closely as she willed the expression away.

When she finally saw the confident, even cocky chick magnet she knew, she smoothed her collar and lapels and did a slow half turn. Unity was right. She should definitely wear formal evening dress more often. Women with her straight-up-and-down build and ordinary features looked good in dark, stark colors. She had almost traded her charcoal shirt for a classic white but was relieved she hadn't, when she saw Merrill. It would have been creepy to find herself wearing virtually the same outfit as the ex, even in a room full of guests in identical combinations.

Penn checked her butt and belly for firmness. She'd slacked off after her summer vacation, hadn't worked out properly for a month, not counting sex. If she ever got Unity into bed, she didn't want her grabbing spongy love handles. Grimacing, Penn flicked off the light. Since when was she paranoid about her body? She'd packed on a few extra pounds during her summer vacation on Santorini, after trying out every café along the caldera for two weeks.

After that debauchery, she'd abandoned the laid-back charm of her favorite Greek isle for a houseboat in Amsterdam. The floating apartment was owned by a couple of retired spooks, one CIA and the other MI6, who fell in love during the joint false-flag operation that brought down the Indonesian government in 1965. Somehow, they'd kept their affair a secret for the next thirty years. They were in their seventies now and made a good living renting out their properties as safe houses and holiday accommodations. Penn had first met them during a uranium sting operation when she was based in Moscow in 2002. She'd used one of their Amsterdam safe houses and had been taking vacations there ever since. It was comforting to shoot the breeze with a couple of old hands, to know it was possible to get out alive and be happy.

She walked through the house one more time, making sure she hadn't left any signs of her presence, then let herself out.

She'd just slid the key back under Bambi, when a halogen beam blinded her and a female voice demanded, "Who the fuck are you and what are you doing here?"

Calmly, Penn replied, "Lower the gun, ma'am."

"You haven't answered my question." The woman advanced toward her, arms extended like a zombie, wielding both gun and flashlight. She wore a heavy yellow rain parka, leopard-pattern pants, and black boots with stiletto heels.

"My name is Penn Harte and I'm a friend of the owner. Now, please, put the gun down before someone gets hurt."

"I don't remember seeing you around here."

"Who are you?" Penn asked.

"I live here." On a triumphant note, she added, "Which is something you'd know if you were my daughter's boyfriend."

Wonderful. She was looking at Unity's mom. "I'm not her boyfriend, I'm—"

"Changing your story. Hah!"

Penn shielded her eyes. The gun was about a foot from her face and the hand holding it was unsteady at best. Unwilling to have her brains blown out before she got the chance to kiss Unity again, she gave reason one more try. "Let me have the gun, please, Mrs. Vaughan."

When there was no sign of compliance, she sidestepped to redirect the line of fire, snapped her hand up, and gripped the gun. Over a strangled protest, she twisted it free of Mrs. Vaughan's grip and hit the safety. As she checked to see if the weapon was loaded, Mrs. Vaughan emitted a howl.

"You broke my nail, sonny." She swung the flashlight like a baton.

Trying to avoid the wrathful blow, Penn fell over Bambi and landed in the herb garden.

"Towanda!" yelled Unity's mom, and dived on top of her.

CHAPTER THIRTEEN

"What on earth are you doing here?" Unity was incredulous. "I can't believe it. I'm waiting and waiting, and you don't come back. Then I get told by hotel reception that my mother has interrupted a burglary and I'm needed at home. I was supposed to be at Professor Maass's table for the closing address."

It had taken months of lobbying to secure that honor, and now Merrill, of all people, was sitting in her place, no doubt holding forth on Fortis's latest impressive research endowments.

She addressed her mother. "Have you been drinking?"

"No, certainly not. How was I supposed to know she's a woman? It was dark and she looks like a man."

"She looks nothing like a man."

"She's got a man's name." Ellen shoved a hand in front of Unity's face. "Look at this. Brand-new acrylics. Ruined."

"I said I'll pay for a manicure," Penn offered wearily. "In the meantime, I'm soaked and I need to get out of these clothes."

Ellen pursed her lips in disapproval. "She says she's a friend of yours, Unity."

"She's my new security chief for the company, Mom."

"Well, how was I supposed to know that?"

"When you shoot first and ask questions later, that's the risk you take, Mrs. Vaughan," Penn retorted, obviously at the end of her patience. She stood up. "I have a change of clothes in my gym bag. Is there a spare bathroom I can use?"

"I'll show you." Unity placed a hand on Ellen's shoulder to prevent her from seizing the moment to scuttle away and hide in her cabana. "Don't go anywhere. We need to talk."

"Can't it wait?" Her mother sagged forlornly against the sofa cushions. "I'm exhausted. You have no idea what it takes out of a person to listen to country music every goddamn hour of the day."

"I'll be back in ten minutes." Unity led Penn upstairs.

"And then there's the church services." Ellen's voice followed them. "That so-called pastor of hers. A used-car salesman banging a bible, but you try telling my sister that. She thinks he's the second coming."

"Your mother's an original," Penn said.

Unity admired her diplomacy. "You're seeing her on her best behavior."

"I have to admire a woman who can rumble in a pair of stilettos." Penn's tone was grave.

Despite herself, Unity smiled. The situation called for some humor. It spoke well of Penn that she could still see the funny side after being pulverized with a flashlight and held at gunpoint until Unity arrived. Evidently she'd disarmed Ellen once, but somehow dropped the gun and Ellen had recovered it in a wrestling match in the herb garden. Unity could only conclude Penn had let her win.

They reached the landing, and she faced Penn, bewildered at how the evening could have spiraled so quickly off-script. One minute they were dancing and flirting, and Unity was letting herself imagine them in bed; the next, Penn looked like she needed to throw up and had vanished out the door. An hour later, came the bizarre message from the hotel desk. Unity always left her weekly schedule pinned to a bulletin board in the kitchen so that Ellen could find her if there was ever an emergency, and her cell phone was turned off. She was grateful the police weren't involved in this escapade, a blessing she owed to Ellen's colorful past. Her mother would rather wrestle an alligator than call 911.

"So, why *were* you here?" she asked.

Penn peeled off her jacket and inspected it with a pained expression. "It was too cold to take a walk, so I went for a drive. I figured, since I was in the car, I could come check on your house. You thought someone broke in while you were at the banquet. I wanted to see if he came back."

Unity felt terrible. The suit was expensive-looking and probably ruined. Penn had simply been looking out for her when she had run foul of Ellen the Avenger. She now knew what kind of parent Unity had, usually a deterrent to anyone nursing domestic fantasies. Not that Penn was. Unity felt pretty sure Penn's fantasies came with a use-by date, probably tomorrow's. And that was okay, or it would have been if all had gone well.

Despondently, she pointed toward the guest room. "Please, shower. Enjoy."

She hesitated, confounded by a crushing disappointment. She met Penn's eyes and watched her pupils enlarge. Her near-black hair was wet and wanted to curl. Impulsively, Unity collected a corkscrew strand that had fallen forward over her forehead. She pushed it to the side and let her hand stay where it was.

"I'm sorry about this."

Penn's hand closed over hers. "I didn't tell you how beautiful you look," she said huskily.

And it was as if nothing had changed. They were still circling each other, drawing closer and closer, knowing there was only one way this could end. Unity slid her hand out from under Penn's and down her cheek to the open neck of her shirt. She closed her fist over a handful of fabric and tugged, drawing Penn in.

"Ah, my pretty dress. I thought you hadn't noticed."

Penn's eyes blazed with urgent, helpless desire "I noticed."

Her soft words licked across Unity's skin like a velvet tongue. A hot ripple of joy annihilated her doubts. "Can I be perfectly up-front with you?"

"By all means."

Their faces were just inches apart. Unity could see the fine lines that crept out around Penn's eyes and read the dark intent that carved them deeper. Desire weakened her legs and they buckled just slightly. She swayed forward, off-balance.

"I want to sleep with you."

Penn flushed. "Say it again." At Unity's faint start, she whispered, "I want to hear you." Her lips caressed Unity's. She tasted of tannin and honey. Her tongue transferred the flavor, roughly demanding acceptance. Between hard kisses, she urged, "Do you want me the way I want you?"

"Yes."

"Do you think about coming with your legs around me?"

Unity forgot to breathe. Shocks of pleasure peaked where each nipple rose. "Yes, I think about you inside me. All the time. I think about us in a mess, all sweaty and fucking till we're exhausted. I think about how you'll taste and what you'll want from me."

"Everything." Penn's arms closed around Unity and she filled her mouth. They kissed deeply, grinding into each other like two parts of a whole, unbound and desperate to be rejoined. Clothes were in the way. And there were practical concerns.

Panting, Unity pushed at Penn's shoulders. "I have to deal with Mom."

"Don't make me wait. I can't handle it."

Unity's heart thudded so loudly in her ears she could hardly hear herself speak. No one had ever looked at her the way Penn was. "That's my bedroom." She nodded toward the hallway. "The second door. I'll meet you there."

❖

Penn almost passed out when Unity walked away. She stumbled into the guest bathroom and showered like a clumsy automaton. Time moved too slowly. The grinding pressure in her groin was killing her. She wanted to rub against something before she exploded. The edge of the vanity counter looked promising. Or the door frame. On autopilot, her fingers zoomed in toward the problem, a stiff clit that needed taking care of. She stood with her hand glued to her crotch, not daring to move or breathe in case she came immediately. Then she thought about what she was about to do. What sort of wuss would get herself off *before* making love with the woman responsible for her horny condition?

Consumed with anticipation, she withdrew her poised fingers by slow degrees, then toweled the excess water from her body, dabbing pathetically at her painful nipples and slippery thighs. Part of her was appalled that any woman could affect her so much. She'd always been quick to arousal, but this hairpin-trigger thing was ridiculous. She needed to stop thinking about Unity before she dissolved into a puddle.

Easier said than done. She sagged back against the wall, intensely aware that she could feel every prickling pore, every quivering hair. The only time she ever felt like this was out in the field, in danger, gambling on her survival instincts. They hadn't let her down yet. Why doubt herself now?

She took the familiar route to Unity's bedroom and dropped her gym bag in the darkest corner. From her previous visits the layout and décor were familiar, as were the contents of Unity's drawers and closet. Penn hadn't paid close attention then; her goals were single-minded and specific. Film the subject. Close out the task.

As she waited, she took in her surroundings, interpreting the room as a shrine to Unity's inner self. Bedrooms usually mirrored the obsessions and contradictions of their inhabitants' natures. Unity's private space revealed a dislike of clutter that seemed compromised by a yearning for home-baked comfort. Several ornate boxes decorated the dressing table, each with a key beneath it, suggesting a treasure trove of secrets within. Explicit love letters tied with red satin ribbons. Gold rings. Locks of hair and mysterious mementos of nearly forgotten affairs. But no. The hidden objects were cash, a baby tooth in a tiny specimen tube, and a man's mug shot in an unmarked envelope. Unity had his eyebrows and high cheekbones.

A row of Amish quilted cushions decorated a bed that was otherwise unadorned. The cover was a plain ivory cotton quilt. Fine-quality bed linen added no additional color. The pillows were soft. At either side, unfussy lamps stood in solitude on night tables that would have sported all the usual crap people piled on them were these items not organized in the top drawers, ranked according to size and function. Kleenex. Lip balm. Water. Scissors. Ballpoints. Notepad. Address book. IPod. On one side, in the bottom drawer, lay the vibrator responsible for Penn's escape undetected a week earlier. There were no other sex toys. Penn hoped that didn't suggest an aversion.

Unity's bedroom was unshared by images of the beings she loved, but a large, flattering studio portrait of Mrs. Vaughan hung in the hallway, and photographs of the pets were in the adjoining room, her office. Books were filed in alphabetical order on bookcases all around the house. Unity's reading tastes were eclectic, everything from romance novels to vast bioscience tomes. The only book in her bedroom was a diary, housed in the other bottom drawer. Penn was tempted to peek inside, but didn't touch it. She lowered the lamps and turned back the bedding on the side nearest the French doors. Unity slept on the other side, from what she'd seen. Penn could play unawares about that, she supposed, but why bother? As it happened, their preferences were complementary.

Chilled, she slipped beneath the covers and propped herself up against a couple of pillows.

"Did you find everything you need?" Unity asked from the doorway.

Penn's body leapt at the sight of her. With her skirt gathered in her hands, and her flighty luminous stare, she looked like a truant fairy-tale heroine about to flee back to the dry pages of her prison.

"Yes. Thank you." Penn had already forgotten the question. Inanely, she added, "Your bed's comfortable."

Unity advanced into the room. She stared into the closet for a few seconds, then took a hanger from one of the rails and crossed to her side of the bed. Penn sensed a hesitance in her, perhaps the reservations of a woman whose impulses too often let her down. She seemed to collect herself, and her movements were resolute as she unzipped her dress and let it fall. She wore a sheer beige bra and panties edged in dark rose lace. She moved around the room in her sexy lingerie, putting away the dress and shoes, taking off her earrings, brushing her hair in front of the dressing table, the perfect-peach globes of her ass rising and falling with each stroke.

Penn's heart threatened a shutdown. She couldn't stand it anymore. She got out of bed and stalked over to her. "You're teasing me."

Unity cast an innocent upward look at her in the mirror. "What if I am?"

Penn could smell her. She wanted to taste her. She wanted her face smeared with Unity's juices. "Turn around," she said.

Unity obeyed, but in no big hurry. She looked Penn in the eye as if she hadn't noticed her nakedness or the body that cried out for touch. The creamy channel of her breasts narrowed with the rise of each breath. Her skin was as exquisitely smooth as a pearl's, a dulcet disguise for the flesh-and-blood woman within. Penn stared at their sidelong images in the mirror, the lissome female form a pale, graceful opposite of her darker, more powerfully built frame.

Her reaction to the sight was visceral. Her stomach muscles bunched and she couldn't stop her hands from shaking. There was something profoundly erotic in their differences. She realized she'd always sought that contrast in her lovers, and that there were fragments of Unity in almost every woman she'd ever slept with. It was as if she'd been hunting a ghost who'd haunted her unconscious from the very start. There was never a time when she felt her quest was over, never a woman who made her feel she'd finally arrived.

Awestruck by the idea, she asked, "May I?" and placed her hands over the thinly clad breasts that tempted her. Unity's nipples rose like lovers' knots against her palms.

Her gaze fell to Penn's breasts. On a fractured sigh, she asked, "Are yours this hard too?"

"You make me hard." Breathing erratically, Penn kneaded the lace-clad flesh she'd claimed. "I want to show you how much."

Unity didn't move a muscle to touch her. Her eyes gleamed with a trace of dark mischief and she stepped back, dislodging Penn's hands. "I don't know. Sleeping with the help. It seems... uncalled for."

Jesus. The words jabbed at a sensitive spot. An atavistic need reared up in response. Penn knew the game Unity was playing. It worked for her, too—dangerously so. "What makes you think you have a choice?"

"What makes you think you're irresistible?" Unity leaned in and lowered her mouth to Penn's shoulder. She dragged her tongue along the tensing muscle, kissing, biting, licking. When she found Penn's earlobe, she caught it gently between her teeth. In her ear, she whispered, "Let me guess. You only fuck girls who tell you how hot you are. They're not that smart, but you don't care what's going on between their *ears.*"

Unity's breath was warm and damp, and every teasing word made Penn coil tighter. Her clit had never been so hard, jutting from the rigid flesh drawn back on either side.

"What's your point?" she asked. "That you're too brainy to fuck?"

Unity's breathing changed. "You have a nerve talking to me that way."

The breasts in Penn's hands felt heavier, the nipples straining. She got rid of the bra and slid her knee between Unity's thighs.

"I know what you really want," she said. "You're not thinking about namby-pamby kisses and a lover who only wants to borrow your lipstick."

"Now, you're getting carried away," Unity murmured unevenly. "Maybe you should go home."

"I don't think so." Penn caught hold of her sloping shoulders and backed her toward the bed. She pushed her onto the covers and tore off the panties. "You've been playing with me all night. Now it's my turn."

She dragged Unity unceremoniously up the bed and shoved her legs apart. Unity resisted, wrenching an animal growl from the back of Penn's throat. A mindless, primal compulsion gathered deep within. Her blood rushed. The molten pressure at her core pulsed through every limb. She seized Unity's wrists and pinned them above her head. Using her weight, she forced her legs wider.

"Oh, fuck." She gazed down at the glistening folds splayed in readiness. "You're perfect."

She skimmed past the fine briar of trimmed fair hair, coated her fingers in heavy strands of fluid, and circled the rose-tight whorl of flesh. Old habit drove her toward a fast, hard entry, but that would never be enough. She wanted to know the body stretched out for her pleasure. She wanted to leave an indelible imprint, like planting a secret flower that would burst into bloom only for her mouth. Her touch.

She pushed in slowly, guided by the kiss and suck of the hot, wet flesh stretching to accept her. When her paired fingers were sheathed deep inside, she shifted her weight and rocked slowly and sensuously against Unity. The roll of their flesh made her groan and shiver. Wanting more options, she let go of Unity's wrists and balanced herself, keeping her fingers firmly buried. She closed her mouth over a nipple and bit softly, polishing the engorged tip with her tongue. Unity gasped. Penn responded with a slow withdrawal. Turning her hand upward, she dragged it back and forth, soaking her knuckles.

Spilling profusely, Unity drew back her knees and levered herself with her feet. Eyes glittering with fierce hunger, she begged, "Fuck me, Penn," and pushed down hard on the hand that eluded her.

Penn sucked the other nipple, drawing it against the roof of her mouth until she could feel a pulse. She bit and held, and slid her fingers a small way in.

Unity seized her shoulders, digging into the muscles. She whimpered, "Don't stop. Please."

Penn stroked her thumb down over Unity's clit, dragging the wrinkled hood firmly over the gleaming tip. Releasing Unity's nipple, she moved over her, aligning their faces so she could watch. Unity opened her eyes and stared up at her.

"Is this what you need?" Penn drove in hard.

"Yes."

Unity thrust her pelvis to meet the next stroke, taking her deeper inside. A sharp cry was drawn from her, and her features cramped in the naked rictus of lust. She shoved Penn, a hand slammed to her chest.

"Come on," she gasped.

The thick, panting plea shredded Penn's control. She threw her head back and let herself go. She could feel her own orgasm hammering its demand, making her throb and burn with every thrust. Her nerves screamed. She was going to come and she couldn't haul herself back from the brink. Desperately, she pounded into Unity. She wanted to wrench her climax from her. Make her scream. Watch her lose it.

"Yes." The harsh cry was hers.

Unity was so close. Penn could feel it in the lush tumescence of her inner walls. Her head bobbed on the pillow, her pale hair wetly feathered over her scalp. Her eyes were closed. Her face was pink and still. She was almost completely silent. All Penn could hear were small grunting sounds and rapid panting. She slowed her thrusts, jarred by a haphazard fear that she was hurting her. That Unity was enduring, not enjoying. Penn whispered her name.

Unity's eyes opened, welling with tears.

Penn froze, her worst fears confirmed. She couldn't speak. Her mouth trembled.

An odd little smile expelled the glazed calm from Unity's face. In a voice Penn hardly recognized, she said, "I never felt this way."

She arched up, imposing upon Penn a new rhythm of prolonged sensuous strokes. With each delving thrust she sighed and her eyes never left Penn's face. Tears rolled into her hairline. Their lips met and they kissed with the wonder of grown-up children claiming a secret adult rite. Time slowed down. They rolled onto their sides. Unity slid her leg over Penn's hip. She found Penn's free hand, nestled over her heart, and laced their fingers together.

"Are you okay?" Penn whispered.

"Yes. You?"

"Yes." Penn was disconcerted by a stinging at the back of her eyes.

Unity moved against her

Their languid fucking was exquisite torture. With her thighs together, the pressure on Penn's clit was unbearable. All she had to do was squeeze a little harder and she would be history. She waited, encoding her every move with a new script written by the woman in her arms. They undulated together like oceans merging at a continental divide. Everything that was unknown between them lay exposed in full view. They saw each other and could not look away.

A profound spasm sealed Unity's body over Penn's. Shuddering, sobbing, she came so beautifully Penn heaved a deep sigh. That was all it took. Her body caved on itself, convulsing in a hot, tearing climax. She could hear her cries mingling with Unity's across the lonely wilderness they now shared. They clung together, panting and trembling.

Penn had no idea how long they lay there, spent.

Eventually, the warm muscles around her fingers fluttered and unfolded like a cocoon. Carefully, by degrees, Penn withdrew, and her mouth closed on a thought she couldn't speak.

I love you.

They stared at each other for a long time.

Unity drew her into her arms and stroked her head. "I wish I'd met you a long time ago."

Penn kissed her again. She understood exactly what Unity meant.

Chapter Fourteen

"Where've you've been all weekend?" Nariko demanded.

"Lila knows," Penn said.

"I suppose you think it's perfectly fine to leave me in charge of everything while you malinger in a bed of lust."

"So, she did tell you." Penn grinned.

"She didn't have to. Anyone can see what you've been doing. Just look at yourself."

Penn hit the light switch behind the bar and peered in the mirror tiles. No visible hickeys. As usual, Nariko was messing with her. "Well, I'm here now, so what's up?"

Nariko clamped the sides of her sleekly groomed head, her body language for impending insanity. "Who is she? Not that dimwitted sister of Violette's, I hope."

"No, you met her. Unity Vaughan."

Nariko regarded her suspiciously. "And?"

"And what?" Penn was about ready to pour herself a double and it was only ten in the morning. "I'm seeing her. Okay?"

Nariko continued to stare like a big, hairy tarantula was crawling up Penn's shirt front. "You're saying Unity Vaughan is your girlfriend?"

"I guess I am." Penn didn't hold her breath for the high five.

"I saw this coming."

"That Eastern-wisdom thing finally kicking in?"

"Don't be facetious." Nariko pointed at the bottles lined up along the shelves behind Penn. "Make me that drink you make for Lila."

"I thought you said I'm a lousy cocktail mixer."

"You're paraphrasing. I said you never have to mix an adequate martini because the women who drink it are only thinking about your naked body."

"How could I forget a compliment like that?" Penn hauled out a bottle of Gordon's sloe gin and found the Marie Brizard apricot brandy. As she squeezed a few limes and mixed the Charlie Chaplin recipe she'd learned from a bartender in Shanghai, she said, "Kind of early for the hard stuff, isn't it?"

"Thanks to you, I need stress relief."

Nariko sat down on a leather loveseat and produced one of her slender Cuban panatelas. She deftly removed the cap, lit a match, waited for the fizzle to die, then rotated the cigar tip over the flame. When it seemed to be burning she took a slow draw. She never lit up around Lila, so Penn seldom got to enjoy the aromatic ritual. Sometimes they smoked together on the roof after a rough night in the club.

"I thought Lila was doing better," Penn said. The good news had given her dear friend a burst of optimism and energy. She'd insisted Penn take the weekend off when she checked in on Saturday.

"The problem is Violette. She threw herself at Mistress Colette in a manner most rare for her."

"Well, I don't see what that has to do with you or me." Penn placed her masterpiece on a cocktail napkin in front of Nariko and joined her on the small sofa. "Anyway, Colette's a step up from the last piece of work."

Nariko sampled the drink carefully before concluding, "Making love with your new girlfriend has improved your flair."

Making love? Rare terminology from her harshest critic. "That's not how it seemed when I was parking my car this morning."

Incredibly, Nariko laughed. "Yes, we noticed. Felix says he can hardly wait to see you installing the new suspension bars this afternoon."

"Oh, they've arrived? That was quick."

Penn had been anxious about several of the ceiling-mounted tracks in the dungeon ever since a private event three weeks earlier. Several of the participants were big guys. They'd brought their own custom slings and treated the equipment with respect, but Inner Sanctum's system wasn't exactly state of the art. After the chubs departed, Penn had examined the fittings closely for metal fatigue and decided to order new units.

Nariko took another thoughtful puff. "I have a genuine concern about Violette. However, I wonder if I am merely prone to a dark perspective."

A loud *Duh!* seemed in order, but Penn was reluctant to nip Nariko's newfound camaraderie in the bud. "Violette's always low after her relationships tank."

"She says she wishes to end her life."

"Shit, she's not serious, is she?"

"Have you found her to be melodramatic in the past?"

Penn decided this wasn't a trick question. "No."

"Then you will understand why I am anxious."

"What does Lila think?"

"I've not yet spoken to her about this matter."

World first: Nariko lays her troubled brow in the lap of the unworthy clod, Penn, before confiding in Lila.

Duly honored, Penn said, "This sounds serious. What exactly happened with Colette?"

"Violette asked to be considered. But Mistress Colette says her self-esteem is not high enough."

"Hard to argue with that."

"She feels rejected—"

"Because, in fact, she suffers from low self-esteem," Penn pointed out.

"And because Mistress Colette is taking Thalia to the celebration party this Saturday." Nariko set her cigar down and sipped the cocktail. "Really, Penn, that girl is such a blabbermouth."

Penn had known this lecture was coming. She borrowed the cigar and puffed. Nariko routinely allowed this liberty out of self-interest; Penn kept her humidor stocked with contraband Cubans.

"I tried to warn you that night, when you were chewing on her ear," Nariko continued.

"Yeah, I remember the look."

"She took a commemorative video."

"Oh, my God," Penn yelped.

"I don't think she had time to e-mail it to her friends before I destroyed her cell phone."

"You what?"

"As soon as Violette told me, I took it from Thalia's bag and smashed it to pieces with a fire extinguisher."

"Well, aren't you full of surprises?" Penn was not so much taken aback as touched.

Nariko quashed any illusions. "Lila would have been very upset on your behalf. I could not allow that."

"Of course not." Penn slid over, took Nariko's narrow face between her hands, and placed a single sweet kiss on her mouth.

Nariko explored her lips with a couple of fingers. In a high, abraded voice, she said, "I hope you didn't smudge my lipstick."

Penn shook her head solemnly.

After a long pause, in which Nariko seemed to be weighing pros and cons, she said, "Violette found the video...exciting. If you asked her, she would probably sleep with you."

This long-sought-after news left Penn strangely unmoved. "Good to know."

"Presumably you have not embraced monogamy yet."

"No. It's kind of premature to be negotiating stuff like that."

"So Unity is also free to see others?"

Penn recoiled in dismay.

"That's what I thought." Nariko tugged up her white kneesocks and arranged the knife pleats in her plaid skirt. "Like all butches you apply a double standard."

"Hey, I've *never* asked a woman to be exclusive."

With a pert little sniff, Nariko declared, "I would not have requested fidelity from any of your women, either."

"Getting a tad judgmental," Penn warned softly.

Nariko gave her a long, sober look. "I still have that poem you wrote."

"You're a closet sentimentalist. I knew it."

Pausing for a sigh and an eloquent eye roll, Nariko took a mangled slip of paper from her breast pocket. "There is a line I wish to quote to you."

"Oh, dear God. Haven't I been punished enough?"

Pitilessly, Nariko read aloud, "I was a fool. I sought a gift I wouldn't cherish, instead of cherishing a gift unsought."

Penn grimaced. "And your point?"

"They're *your* words, and you want *me* to explain them to you." Nariko left the mordant statement dangling.

It was far too early in the day for cerebral jousting, and Penn had hardly slept since Friday night. Looking for a way out, she said, "I should go talk with Violette. Do you know where she lives?"

"She's handcuffed to my bed at this time," Nariko replied. "Under the circumstances, it seemed wise."

❖

"I don't understand the point of this meeting." Unity sat down at the conference table in her attorney's office. "I'm not taking their offer and that's final. I don't care how much they've increased it."

"You might want to reconsider when you see this." Jacob Stein opened his laptop in front of her.

Unity stared at the screen for several seconds, then closed the lid. "Where did this come from?"

"It arrived by Fedex. The sender doesn't exist." Jacob slid a single sheet of paper toward her. It read: *People who sell their amateur sex videos on XTube lose their TS clearances. Do the deal with Fortis and this goes away.*

"That's blackmail," Unity said. "Can't we just turn everything over to the police?"

"The note's in my handwriting," Jacob said. "The message came by phone. I wrote down what the guy said. Think carefully. Do you really want months of police investigation while this material is all over the Internet? By the time our friends in the Metropolitan Police Department figure out who to arrest, the damage will be done."

"Oh, my God." Unity rested her head in her hands.

"So, the video is authentic?" Jacob's face was completely dispassionate.

He was a clean-shaven man with a movie-star smile and thick, wavy black hair he kept ruthlessly coiffed. Unity found him to be professional and competent. Ellen said she could never trust a man with wax lips.

"I just got a new alarm system on Friday," Unity said in disbelief. "How could this happen?"

She finally understood what was going on two weeks ago when her house was broken into. The intruders hadn't taken anything because they were there to install a hidden camera. Maybe they'd come back the second time to add more equipment. She thought about the white dust in her closet. In her search for the source, she hadn't even thought to look up. Someone had obviously drilled into the ceiling that night.

"When did the...events occur?"

"On Friday. And during the weekend."

It was a miracle she'd been able to walk from the parking lot to the elevator, Unity thought. And remaining seated was a pain-threshold challenge. A terrible sick feeling came over her. Penn was on the video, easily identifiable. Not only would Unity be exposed and humiliated if she called the blackmailers' bluff; Penn would also be dragged into this through no fault of her own.

Horrified, she said, "There has to be some way we can stop this. Can we get an injunction against Internet sites to stop the video being aired?"

"Short answer, no. If whoever has this video wants to put it out there, we can't do a thing to stop them." He inspected his Mont Blanc pen. "If you were just Mrs. Smith, a Jersey housewife whose ex-husband thinks it's cool to post their personal sex videos online in revenge for the divorce, I would advise you to ignore the problem. Unfortunately you have more to lose. Can you work without your clearance?"

"Not in my present area of research. The DoD has us involved in classified projects."

Jacob extracted a folder from the pile at his elbow. "I received the best and final offer from Fortis. Seventy million for fifty-one percent. You'll be the executive vice-president of research, and you can keep your team intact." He paused. "Unity, as your attorney, I'm advising you to make the deal."

Seventy million was chump change for a multibillion-dollar corporation like Fortis, but in a sector where most start-ups failed within their first year, and small companies like hers seldom showed a profit, the offer was generous.

In case she still wasn't convinced, Jacob said, "Do the math. You seeded Vaughan with two million of your own. According to Fortis your forty-nine percent is now worth over sixty-seven million. That's a tidy profit for a few years of your time."

"It's all on paper," Unity said.

"Don't knock it." Jacob leafed through the contract document and tapped a clause. "Here's your option to exchange your forty-nine percent for a piece of Fortis anytime you want. That's your retirement fund, locked in no matter what."

"You're the best." Unity forced a smile.

Jacob had continued negotiations with Fortis even after she backed off. His theory coincided with old man Brady's: that there was no such thing as "no" when an offer was on the table. The clause was a new addition, one she guessed he'd fought for. She glanced at the laptop again.

"Is Fortis responsible for the sex video?"

"Definitely not," Jacob said with conviction. "It's not Sullivan Brady's style. The old man has too much class."

"Then who?"

"This has government dirty tricks written all over it. The DoD wants you to sell to Fortis. What else do we need to know?"

"We can't fight the DoD."

"No," Jacob said levelly. "They make the rules."

❖

Unity turned on her cell phone when she reached the Lexus. Penn had left two messages. The first was brief and husky: *Just thinking about you. I can't wait to see you again.* The second made Unity weak with longing: *Tomorrow seems so far away. I need you sooner. If you can't handle being fucked, I could just lick you. I love the way you taste.*

She agonized over what to do. She could tell Penn about the video immediately and ask her to try to trace the source. But what would be the point? Penn would feel just as helpless and infuriated as Unity did. And even if she found out who was responsible, they would never get the original back, if the DoD was behind the blackmail.

There was only one choice. And if she acted quickly enough, Penn would never need to know what had happened. The offer was fair and the more Unity thought about it, the more obvious the truth became. The only way she would stay in business was if she accepted the Fortis takeover.

Resigning herself, Unity located Brady Sullivan's card and called the number.

When his secretary patched her through, she said, "You've made me an offer I can't refuse, Mr. Sullivan."

"I was hoping you'd see it that way."

"I'll be honest with you, I feel like I'm in a corner."

There was a long pause, and then her future boss said, "I've always admired independent women. My mother was a fighter all her life. My sister still terrifies me. And I never had a daughter. If I did, and she accomplished all you've accomplished in a few short years, I would be very proud of her."

"Well, thank you." Unity was pleasantly surprised. She supposed, having got his way, Mr. Brady was trying to soften the blow.

"I guess what I'm trying to say is that you have my respect," he went on. "Words like loyalty and respect aren't in fashion anymore, in business. But while I'm chairman of Fortis, they still count for something. If you give me your loyalty, you'll find it's a two-way street."

"I appreciate hearing that." Unity mustered what good grace she could. Things could be worse. She could be selling to an asshole. Or the Mafia.

"Merrill told me you're our kind of material," he said. "You'll be working closely with her. The Unity Protein could be a very big deal for us, so she's taking a special oversight role."

I'll just bet she is, Unity thought bitterly. There was nothing Merrill loved more than a boardroom triumph. It stung to think she'd just delivered the next in a long line. Merrill would be unbearable.

"I'm curious about something," Unity said. "The Unity Protein wasn't named in any materials available to Fortis. How do you know about it?"

"You can't keep secrets for long in our business. All I can tell you is that Merrill obtained the information. She didn't mention her source."

Unity let the subject drop. It no longer mattered what Merrill knew or how she'd come by the information; the deal was virtually done. "Well, I guess what happens now is that my people call your people and we sit in a big room with a lot of men in suits."

Sullivan Brady chuckled. "A spit handshake works for me but attorneys charge by the hour. If you're really keen to avoid the circus, I could just send everything over for your signature. But Merrill will peg me out for a buzzard banquet if we don't go the whole nine yards." He paused. "I can live with that if you ask me to."

Unity warmed to him despite her dull spirits. "There's no need. I'm free this afternoon, as a matter of fact." The sooner, the better.

"Talk followed by action. I like your style."

"I'll see you downtown," Unity said. "How's three p.m.?"

"You have yourself a deal."

CHAPTER FIFTEEN

The average person on the street was still worried about genetically modified foods. The public had no idea what was brewing in labs around the world. Scientists were already injecting human embryonic stem cells into animal eggs, dreaming of a new breed of subjects for their experiments. Human-animal hybrids were bereft of rights. They could be harvested like cattle or corn, stripped of their organs as demand required. The public wouldn't want to think about thousands of "subhumans"—babies, children, adults—engineered for spare parts. Living in abject misery. Debased and abused. Plausible deniability was important for elected officials, so the truth about this emerging nightmare was kept very quiet, couched in euphemism, filtered carefully for public consumption.

And the nearly human chimera was just the tip of the iceberg.

Unity rested her head on her arms and listened to the wall clock in her office count down the minutes to her surrender. One holdout would make no difference in the end, she reasoned mournfully; the die was already cast. The genetic blueprints for numerous pathogens were available on the Internet. Anyone could buy DNA fragments manufactured to specification by American companies. These oglionucleotides, as they were known, could be fused and spliced to create a full sequence, which would then be brought to life in an organic gel, where it would suddenly start making proteins.

It was too late to reverse the inevitable. Since Eckard Wimmer built the first synthetic virus in his Long Island laboratory in 2002, new techniques had simplified the process, making it faster and easier even for amateurs to dabble in synthetic biology. The race was on to engineer synthetic building blocks—amino acids that could form proteins unknown to nature. These could bind to human DNA and dictate the way genes functioned. The ramifications were almost unimaginable. An entirely new approach to curing disease. Defeating the ageing process. Making people smarter, stronger, more or less similar.

Unity had made it over the line with the first genuine *de novo* protein The same biotechnology could also produce a terrifying new generation of weapons—not only superviruses that would mutate as scientists chose, but those that could target one gender or the other, or specific races. The possibilities would strike most people as rabid science fiction, but fifty years ago cell phones and GPS devices were unthinkable. Advances in biotechnology were occurring so rapidly even scientists could barely keep up.

When the phone rang, Unity ignored it for a few seconds, then sluggishly picked up. Merrill's voice poured into her ear like warm oil.

"We're ready for you."

"It's not three o'clock yet."

"I'm parked below. Want a ride into the city?"

"I'll take my own car, thanks."

"Suit yourself." Merrill couldn't just say good-bye. "I'm sorry it came to this."

"No, you're not. You got what you wanted."

"Unity, I'm going to say this once and then we never have to speak about it again. The video wasn't my idea."

Unity dragged herself completely upright, stiff-backed with shock. "You know about it?"

"I do now." Her tone was sympathetic. "I wish it had never happened."

Incensed, Unity demanded, "How *did* it happen?"

Merrill took a long time to answer. "I don't want to have to say this, but you placed your trust in the wrong person."

Unity's heart reacted with a strident thump. "What are you talking about?"

"Think carefully. You don't have anyone in your life, then all of a sudden—"

"Don't be coy," Unity said coldly. "It's not who you are."

"Penn Harte." Merrill delivered the name like a knockout punch. "She's the one they hired."

A cold jolt slammed the breath from Unity's lungs. "Penn?"

"I was in a meeting at the DoD this morning and I can't name names, but I was given a heads-up. Then I spoke with Sullivan and…"

Something crawled up from the pit of Unity's stomach to lodge in her throat. "I don't believe you."

"Of course you don't. You never were much good at seeing what's right under your nose." Merrill's exasperated sigh reverberated through the phone. "As of today, she's not on your staff anymore."

"I choose Vaughan employees." Unity flared. "That's what the deal says."

"Provided I have no objection. Read the contract." Merrill paused. "I will not have a spy inside Fortis. End of story. If you don't want to tell her, I will."

Shaking, Unity said, "She's not a spy. And she would never do this."

Even as the heated retort left her lips, her mind processed the facts. Penn had walked into her life a week after the break-in when the secret camera must have been installed. Coincidence? Ellen had found her outside the house the night of the ball. What was she doing there? Checking her equipment in preparation for a planned seduction scene?

The more Unity combed through their unlikely meeting the more naïve she felt. Common sense was inversely proportionate to passion, and she was walking proof. After a year without a lover, all of a sudden the ideal woman shows up and it just so happens she is some kind of freelance female James Bond. They then have the bad luck to hook up just in time for someone to make a sex video.

She thought about that evening in the parking garage when Penn just happened to be there to change her tire. Another inexplicable coincidence, or was Penn already following her, waiting for the right opportunity? No wonder she'd been shocked when Unity showed up at Inner Sanctum that day. Getting herself hired wasn't part of the plan, but she'd taken it in stride. She must have been laughing. All the way to the bank.

Merrill was still breathing calmly at the other end of the phone.

"I'll tell her," Unity said, as if from far away. Tears made the phone slippery where it was pressed to her cheek. She hunched over her desk, muting a howl of betrayal.

"It can wait till after the meeting." In a soft, conciliatory tone, Merrill coaxed, "Go wash your face and come on down. I don't want you driving when you're upset like this."

"Okay." Unity dropped the phone into its cradle.

Dry sobbing, she got up and ran blindly to the bathroom. Clutching herself like an arrow was embedded between her ribs, she rested her forehead on the cool, tiled wall and closed her eyes against the glare of the truth. She had imagined there was magic at work. She should have guessed it was too good to be true.

Penn had been paid to have sex with her and betray her. And she had done her job. Really, really well.

❖

The face was all wrong. Pinched. Taut. Branded with something ugly and painful. Her eyes were a mess from crying.

She grabbed the front of Penn's jacket and shook her. "How could you?"

Not content, she slapped her face. Penn caught her by the wrist before she could do it again and hustled her off the set, away from the flabbergasted onlookers.

"Let go of me." Unity thumped at Penn's arm with her free hand.

"What the fuck is wrong with you?" Penn dragged her into one of the downstairs offices and locked the door behind them.

Unity backed away like Penn was juggling plutonium. Her chest heaved. Her eyes swung wildly this way and that as though searching for a weapon. Penn could do without the excitement of a stapler attached to her head, so she yelled, "Sit down."

"Don't you dare yell at me." Unity picked up the nearest object and hurled it at her.

Felix's latest copy of *Honcho* landed at Penn's feet in a flurry of glossy pages, the centerfold hunk torn in two.

"Darling, calm down."

"Darling? Hey, you can stop acting now." Unity edged around the perimeter of the small room, clearly planning her escape. "I signed the deal. Okay?"

"What are you talking about?"

"Must we go through this farce—you pretending you're innocent and me having to lay it all out there?" Her shoulders sagged. "It's done. I sold to Fortis. Signed the deal an hour ago."

Penn felt disoriented. She knew she should have a handle on what was happening, but she didn't. Unity extracted a DVD from her purse and marched toward her.

Instinctively shielding her face, Penn asked stupidly, "What's that?"

She knew the answer almost before the question popped out. She just couldn't believe it.

Unity studied her closely, registering every giveaway facial tic. "Yes, it's all coming back now, isn't it?"

Her clothes were crumpled, nothing left of her usual immaculate presentation. A smear of lipstick marred the sleeve of her shirt. The blotches on her face were losing their color. She looked close to fainting.

Repeating, "Sit down," Penn took the DVD and slid it into the nearest computer.

Unity remained where she was, panting like a cornered animal. As the image consumed the screen, she lifted both hands to her face and started to weep.

Penn stared in stunned horror at computer, then closed the distance to Unity and grabbed her by the shoulders. "This isn't what you think."

"Liar." Unity's eyes blazed blue light into hers. "How can I believe a word you say?"

They both fell silent, riveted by the love-making on the screen. Unity's body filled the frame, rising and falling astride Penn's. The memory of that moment was so powerful Penn felt herself flood and swell. Cold fury seeped through her veins almost as fast. She needed answers before she could say anything else. She couldn't afford to lie. The ice was too thin.

Quietly, trying not to panic, she said, "Whatever you think you know, I can promise you, it's only half the story."

"Then let me cut to the chase," Unity said. "Were you or were you not hired to have sex with me and get a recording?"

The ice in her voice shouldn't have come as any surprise, but Penn flinched anyway. She considered lying outright and concluded that would be a bad idea. She didn't want to deceive Unity any more than she already had, and she needed to find out how much Unity knew. Someone was pulling strings. Hers. Unity's. She was pretty certain she knew the culprit, but until she spoke to Gretsky she couldn't name names.

Ejecting the DVD, she said, "Yes, I was hired to seduce you."

Watching each word sting as it landed, she felt like she was seeing her future smash into pieces before her eyes.

"That's all I needed to hear." With the candor of a woman who has nothing to lose, Unity said, "You know something, you were almost worth it."

Penn stepped in front of her. "Don't go."

"Say whatever you need to say." Unity stared through her. "After this, we'll never see each other again."

Penn couldn't stop herself from shaking. If the worst happened, and tomorrow failed in its promise of a new day and a fresh chance, there was one thing she wanted Unity to know. Leaving herself wide open for mockery, she said, "I'm in love with you."

A silence stretched between them unsullied by all that had led up to it, a pause between possibilities. There was only the present, a moment innocent of dogged resolve. Anything could happen. This was the fork in the road people talked about. The *What If?*

Penn said, "Don't throw this away."

Unity's face was stricken. She didn't bother to hide her tears. "I don't need you anymore, obviously. The Mafia called. They were pleasant. Even seemed to think we might do business one day."

Penn covered her hand. In the vast universe of dreams and destiny, the chance of their paths crossing was so improbable, she couldn't accept finality. A total loss. She tried to find words. "Please, I'll do anything you want."

Raw emotion made her voice quake. She knew Unity had heard it, too, because she steeled herself visibly. Her eyes held Penn at a distance.

With quiet sorrow, she said, "Penn, some things can't be forgiven. To do so means giving away little pieces of oneself. And soon there's nothing left. It's like inventing a new self, but in reverse. I can't do that again."

Penn drew in her scent. *Bliss.* Her legs felt weak. "I'm not asking you to."

"Yes, you are." Unity pushed the door open.

These things didn't happen in movies, Penn thought in desperation. There were better endings. People took chances. At the mere inkling of love, the heavens conspired to deliver rhapsodic sunsets into which trusting couples could ride. Self-respecting heroes did not give up without a fight. Heroines relented and swooned against firm chests. Penn had one. Unity ignored it. She hadn't read the happy-endings script.

She walked away. Penn didn't stop her.

❖

Gretsky grumbled about having to meet. He had things to do.

Penn dumped a backpack full of cash behind his seat and closed the passenger door. She dropped the DVD on his lap. "An explanation would be a good start."

He said, "Did you really expect me to have no Plan B?"

"I thought I was the Plan B, after the gigolo struck out."

The colonel wet his thin lips. "You can keep the money. You did the vigorous half of the job."

"I should punch you for that comment." Penn slapped her fist into her palm to illustrate. "I thought we had a deal."

"We did. You're the one who reneged."

"You knew I was involved with her." Idiotically, Penn felt betrayed. Gretsky wasn't her shrink. He wasn't paid to give a shit what his officers went through in their personal lives.

In timely acknowledgment of this fact of life, he said, "KR loves it, by the way."

"One day I'm going to kill that little bastard."

"Before you do, let me know," her boss said gravely. "I can probably sell about fifty contracts on him."

"Very funny."

The trouble with dealing with Gretsky was that they knew one another too well for bullshit. Neither of them could play chicken. They had the measure of each other.

"She'll never forgive me," Penn said.

"It was in her best interests to do the deal."

"That's beside the point. I'm crazy about her, do you know that?"

"Shit happens."

Caustically, Penn said, "Not to you, pal."

That one seemed to land. Gretsky said, "I've had my moments."

"How did you pull it off?"

He gave a world-weary sigh. "That new alarm system for her house, the one installed on Friday before the ball? I sent in a team to back up your equipment in case of another...technical glitch."

"You eliminated the real security company?"

"Christ, we're not the FBI." Gretsky smiled at his own testy joke. "There's something to be said for workers' solidarity. When our guys arrived to clean the vents, the alarm technician went on his lunch break. Highly serendipitous?"

Penn leaned back against the uncomfortable headrest and stared up at the padded vinyl ceiling. "You covered my ass?"

She hated owing Gretsky. Payback was always a bitch.

"Nobody needs to know which camera shot the footage," Gretsky said.

"You're telling everyone I delivered?"

"Everyone who matters." He experimented with the windshield-wiper controls. It was raining again and the car was getting fogged up. "You made quite an impression on KR. He got himself rather worked up over your...dexterity and varying techniques. I believe his actual words were 'What's a normal guy supposed to do?'"

"Scary to think what 'normal' means to him," Penn muttered. She held back on the obvious Viagra jokes just in case Gretsky was, himself, a beneficiary.

Her mentor responded, "For KR, happiness is a big, fat bonus payment."

"Well, that makes my day complete." They shared a beat of empathetic resignation, then she said, "I told her."

"About our operation?"

"No, I told her I'm in love with her."

Gretsky took a moment. Eventually the magnitude of this revelation sank in and he arrived at the inevitable conclusion. "And here you are."

What else was there to say?

"Want some free advice?" he offered.

"Why not?" How much worse could her prospects get?

"Simmons expects to hear from you tomorrow. Make the call."

Chapter Sixteen

The suicide blonde bent over the restroom counter offered her a line. Penn shook her head.

An up-down assessment followed. "You're Penn, aren't you?"

Penn thought: *Oh, Christ.*

"I'm a friend of Thalia's."

Yep, she saw that coming.

"You're hot."

With a flippant shrug, Penn said, "The fluorescent lighting in women's restrooms flatters me. Out there, on the dance floor, I can promise you, it's a different story."

The girl snorted, then burst out laughing. "Want to fuck?"

Her lipstick was candy apple and her breasts were small and high. She sidled up and zoomed in for a wet kiss. Penn stepped aside, not in the mood. Three days without a word from Unity and she was ready to do damage. Strangers who hit on her were taking lunatic chances.

Penn warned this one off. "Listen, you're very sweet, and there's a whole room full of cute chicks out there. Go enjoy."

A pout. "You don't want to party tonight?"

Someone else came in the door. Penn felt like she was suffocating. She was only in here looking for a clubber Felix said was losing it.

The new arrival was a regular. She said, "Hey, it's great news about Lila."

"Sure is. Don't forget the celebration party."

"This Saturday?"

"You bet." Penn seized the opportunity to glance at her wristwatch. "That reminds me. I need to go find her." She added the standard club salutation, "Keep it sane, people."

She almost smashed down the "Staff Only" door in her haste to escape. Nariko nailed her on the way up the staircase. "You can't go hide in your room."

"I think I'm having a panic attack."

"That's no excuse. Lila's looking for you."

"I can't go out there right now." Penn made it up as she went along. "I'm going to go have a drink with Chloe and Colette."

"They're in the dungeon."

It crossed Penn's mind to offer herself for a whipping that might clear her head. She said, "Leave me alone, Nariko."

"Leave you to your pity party?" Nariko struck a pose, hands on her nonexistent hips. "I don't think so."

"I just need some space. Okay? I'll come down later."

Unimpressed, Nariko said, "I can't believe you're going overseas. Anything could happen. What if she gets worse?"

"Then I'll come back."

"Why are you going?"

"I told you, I took an assignment in Amsterdam. For my real job. You know, the one that pays the bills."

Nariko slouched against the wall. She was wearing a red party dress with little white puffy sleeves, white stockings, and black Mary Janes. Penn thought if she tried looking her age she would have a better chance of getting a girlfriend. Maybe she would mention this tactic, just not tonight.

"It's funny," Nariko mused aloud. "When I first realized you and Unity were in love I thought you would be the one who got hurt."

"Congratulations. Right again."

Nariko looked at her like she was crazy. "You are so typical."

She flounced off with her pigtails swinging and her hands involved in a tense private sign language entirely of her own.

Penn yelled, "I begged her. I don't beg anyone."

Nariko spun around at the bottom of the staircase. "Talk is cheap. What do your actions say?"

"What am I supposed to do? Drag her to my cave?"

"Of course not," Nariko retorted sweetly. "You can't do any such thing, can you? Because you won't *be here*. You're *leaving*. Cutting and running."

She swung the door open and slammed it hard.

"Way to end on a high note," Penn shouted after her.

She plopped down on a grimy stair, confounded by her own bitter resignation. She wasn't a quitter; she had a choice in her own destiny. It was easy to blame Unity for her weepy sleeplessness, and for the decision to return to the life she knew best. The truth was more complicated. Feeling the way she did was like being a moving target within her own life, just waiting for the next shot to her heart. She'd already lost her family. When she left the CIA she felt like she'd lost her identity. Now she was terrified of losing Lila. And there was Unity. The loss of what might have been. Did that even qualify?

Penn felt hollow. At that continental divide, Unity's body had altered hers as the ocean alters a shore. Its absence left her incomplete, forlornly parched, dry where she could be wet, so incredibly wet. In her most abject moments, she thought she would never be the same again. Other bodies would make no impression. Other hands would touch, but not feel. Even in her own embrace, she would be forever foreign. Unable to come home.

Loss was not the right word. She felt stripped.

❖

"Who was the client?" Penn asked Gretsky.

"Three words," he said predictably. "*Need to know.*"

"I need to know."

"I told you, the original footage has been destroyed." There was a faint echo on the phone line. Gretsky sounded like a robot. "I did it myself."

"That's not good enough. In another week I'll be back in the field with that video hanging over me. I could be compromised."

"You have my personal guarantee that will never happen."

"Sir, I trust you with my life," Penn said. "But KR has the conscience of a reptile. How can you be sure he didn't make multiple copies?"

"I can't. But he knows if he shafts me there'll be consequences. I didn't spend the last thirty years in this trade without getting dirt on him."

Reasonable. "So, who has copies?"

"I had one, but I've destroyed it. KR has one, the client has one, and the last copy went to Vaughan's attorney."

"And I now have that one." Unity had stalked off without it that day. Penn had left a voice mail about dropping the DVD in to her. Unity hadn't returned the call. "So, the only time bomb worth worrying about is with the client."

"Correct," Gretsky said. "When are you leaving, by the way?"

"Next Monday. I'll be with our friends in Amsterdam for a week before I start work."

"Give them my regards." Gretsky paused. "Did it ever cross your mind that sometimes the people we work for have only banal motivations? Ambition. Greed. Revenge. Jealousy."

"Are you dropping a hint?"

"Just shooting the breeze. You have my London number?"

Penn smiled. Gretsky still operated by the same protocols they'd used in the field. "I hope I'll never need it. And, sir, about the hint. Thanks."

❖

Unity folded her napkin and placed it beside her plate. "Thank you, that was excellent."

"You hardly touched your filet." Merrill gave the fine steak a poke with her fork. "Too rare?"

"No, it's perfect. I have a lot on my mind, that's all. With the changes."

"Well, you can stop worrying about running your company from now on. That's my job. You'll have all the time and support you need to stick to what you're good at. In the lab."

This backhanded compliment was Merrill's idea of reassurance. Unity drummed up a tepid smile. Not that Merrill needed approval. Tonight's meal was a personal victory lap for her, in preparation for next week's dinner party. The board members of Fortis would assemble to meet the new vice president of research and congratulate Merrill on beating out the Chinese for the coveted acquisition.

Sullivan Brady was supposed to have been here. Unity would have begged off if she'd known he had to change his plans. But Merrill only gave his apologies after Unity was seated and they'd ordered wine. Good manners prevented her from leaving on the spot. She also wanted to show that she couldn't be intimidated. If they were going to be working together, she needed to assert herself now.

"I meant to ask, how's it coming with the peer-review process?" Merrill asked while they were waiting for the check.

"Neil's organizing everything. He's been great." To keep Merrill on her side, she said, "He's excited about the takeover. He always wanted me to accept your bid."

"Smart guy," Merrill said. "We talked some at the convention that night. He's wildly impressed with you. I was almost jealous."

Merrill seemed to think she'd said something funny. She cast an expectant look at Unity, who pretended to have her mind elsewhere.

"I'm going to have him head up a division. That'll free me to devote all my time to protein folding."

"Good idea." Merrill signed the check and left a fifty-dollar tip. "His technician has to go. The redhead. She's indiscreet."

"What are you talking about?"

"I can't remember her name, but she's the one who let it slip about the Unity Protein. Apparently she heard you and Neil talking."

"And she told *you*?" How would that have come about?

"No, she e-mailed a girlfriend of hers in Hong Kong. Bragging rights. The rest is history."

"I'm not going to sack her for that."

"Have it your way. I'll give her a warning if you need someone else to be the bad guy."

Unity wished Merrill would stop telling her how to run her team. So far, she'd done okay. She rose and picked up her purse. When they reached the lobby, Merrill helped her into her coat.

"It's snowing," she said. "I'll drive you home."

"There's no need. I had the snow tires put on this week."

Merrill's arms closed around her. "I think you know what I'm asking."

In disbelief, Unity ventured, "You want to spend the night with me?"

"It's about time, don't you think?" Before Unity could set her straight, she said, "I can't promise sexual gymnastics, but at least we won't be immortalized on a porn tape."

Sexual gymnastics? The intentional barb deserved a response, but a face slap probably wasn't the right move, since Merrill was now her boss. Shaking free of her grip, she said, "I think you've had too much to drink."

"Give me some credit. You're a very beautiful woman, and I'm only human."

Unity choked slightly as she pulled on her gloves. "We're professional colleagues and this conversation is inappropriate. I'll see you next week." She turned toward the door.

Merrill came after her. Eyes narrowed, she asked, "Why her?"

Blood coursed hotly to Unity's cheeks. Her heart raced. Her knees felt wobbly. She'd managed to lock Penn Harte out of her thoughts for the past three days and had no intention of letting her back in. Her body had other ideas. Desire settled low in her belly, teasing the starving part of her Penn had brought to life.

Instantly wet, her nipples getting harder by the second, she informed Merrill, "As you know, I like having sex, and Penn is extremely capable in that department."

"If that DVD's any indication, she certainly earned her fee."

Unity stifled her instinctive reaction. She couldn't allow Merrill the faintest idea of her feelings for Penn, or she would be tortured endlessly. "I thought you didn't watch it."

In fact Merrill had implied she heard of the DVD at a Defense meeting. Was she trying to protect Unity from a more egregious truth—that countless people had seen it, herself included?

Merrill didn't seem troubled by any inconsistency. "I hit fast-forward a few times, verifying that it appeared to be authentic. I can't imagine anyone sitting through the whole thing."

Goaded, and wanting to land a punch, Unity asked, "Did it turn you on to watch someone fucking me?"

"If you must know, I was disgusted to see you used that way by a virtual stranger. How could you allow that?"

The scathing indictment cut to the core of all that had doomed their relationship. Merrill was less interested in sex than most people, but because she considered herself superior, she would not accept that she had a problem. In her world, a desire deficiency was the norm, and Unity was "abnormal" by definition. Merrill refused to explore the possibility of an underlying medical or psychological issue, and Unity had given up trying to reason with her. She realized she'd even started to adopt Merrill's perspective, feeling ashamed of her desires and trying to detach herself from her physical needs.

Making love with Penn could not have been more different.

For the first time in years Unity had felt completely at home in her body, intensely herself, valued for who she was. She'd never had a partner in passion, a sexual companion with whom she didn't have to explain herself. She'd never felt free to explore who she was, sexually. Unity didn't know if everyone else in the world took for granted that they could simply be themselves in their most intimate moments, and whether she had been unlucky in her choices of lover. She had always imagined trust had to be built up over years of familiarity, yet with Penn it was a given. Unity held nothing back. She didn't need to hide what she thought or second-guess her own desires.

That was why she was so hurt. She'd offered Penn her most naked self and was certain the same gift was given in return. Strangely, despite all that had happened since, she could not believe her impression had no basis. The connection she felt during the time they spent together defied explanation. For as long as she lived, she knew she would always return to those hours as a touchstone. Whatever Penn's motives or flaws, however painful her betrayal, she had redefined for Unity all that a lover could be and rescued the woman Unity had let slip away. For that, Unity would always be in her debt.

Stirred by a vivid flash of Penn kneeling over her while Unity sucked and stroked and made her come, she said, "I loved every minute with her. And even knowing what I know now, I'd do it all over again."

Tension seized Merrill's jaw. Speechless, for once, she didn't move as Unity walked out the door into the night.

The cold air was a welcome assault and she turned her face up to the falling snow. For a long while she stood there, listening to the hush. Then she plodded to her car, loathing the thought of driving home. In the worst way, she wanted Penn to be there waiting for her. She wanted her in her home, in her bed, and in her body. The thought of never seeing her again made her feel physically sick.

Trembling, Unity got in the Lexus and closed the door. She

gripped the steering wheel and willed herself to settle. But a huge, noisy sob erupted from her, dragging Penn's words with it.

I'm in love with you.

Why say that after the fact?

Unity wondered what Seth would tell her. Probably *Girl, don't be a fool.*

❖

Penn selected a thin metal strip from the pouch tucked in her back pocket. Squatting, listening, she worked it inside the keyhole until the mechanism gave way. She had expected home-alarm overkill, but Merrill's mini-mansion on the Potomac was guarded by unremarkable locks and several zealous schnauzers that snapped around her legs until Merrill made her peace offering, a pound of thinly sliced roast beef.

The dogs dined with the dedication of animals whose diets were rigidly supervised. Penn was just guessing, but she suspected their treats were rationed and their food holistic. If she'd planned better, and odor wasn't a factor, she could have brought McDonald's.

Light from the porch illuminated the hallway and the staircase directly ahead. Penn climbed swiftly, working the odds. When people hid something, most made predictable choices. Wealthy, organized individuals opted for a large downstairs safe. That was the exception, and Penn always started with the likeliest scenarios.

She found the master bedroom, flicked on her small flashlight, and worked methodically through the usual places. Under the pillows, the mattress, the box-spring base. Inside the comforter sleeve. Beneath clothing in drawers. Within a stack of magazines. She opened the closet and surveyed the orderly racks of clothing. Merrill ran with Armani, Gucci, and Ferragamo. Her shirts were Brooks Brothers.

Penn hesitated and let her flashlight travel the room once

more. A large television dominated one corner, perched on a tall unit. Penn approached it, smiling. The "hiding in plain sight" rule was another popular convention, and logically there was no reason why Merrill would need to conceal the DVD if she had it. Who else was going to see it? She lived alone.

Penn opened the player and popped out the disc inside. The face was unmarked, with one small exception. Gretsky had etched the identifier UV4of4 near the center. Penn used her cell phone to take a wide shot of the discovery, within the identifiable surroundings, and a few close- ups before slipping the DVD inside an empty case and poking it into her backpack. The schnauzers had joined her and were lined up inside the doorway, tails wagging. Dogs were so easy. Penn snapped pictures of the threesome, too, then located a pen and a piece of paper next to the telephone on Merrill's night table and composed a succinct note: *I have the DVD. If you ever hurt Unity, I'll be back to break your neck. Penn Harte.*

As she placed this prominently on Merrill's dresser, light bounced off the wall facing the bedroom windows. Penn crossed the carpeted floor and peeped out. A pair of headlights bobbed through the trees, and she heard the muffled whoosh of the garage door rolling open. Hastily, she retraced her path downstairs and waited at the front door for the vehicle to disappear. She slipped out and closed it quietly behind her as the garage door closed.

It didn't matter if she left footprints, but she didn't want to be caught, so she bolted across the yard, avoiding the well-lit driveway. She'd left the M6 parked in front of one of the other grandiose homes on Merrill's street. It took less than five minutes to make her getaway. As she headed for Unity's place, she grinned.

Right about now, Merrill would be turning on the lights in her bedroom. Penn wished she could see her face when she read the note.

CHAPTER SEVENTEEN

Penn was used to seeing Unity everywhere she looked. In the arch of a neck, the angle of head, the grace of a walk. Unity haunted the features and form of every woman in the gyrating sea of bodies on the dance floor. The music was disco, in Lila's honor, a blast from the past to remind the post-millennium crowd that serious partying was invented long before they discovered it. The pounding bass rolled in waves through Penn's chest, dictating her heartbeat and punching through the swinging doors of her mind. Felix had gone all-out with the fog and lasers, adding to her dazed lassitude.

That was okay. She wasn't here to get ahold of herself, she was here to party and get laid. Business as usual. The DJ switched to Yvonne Elliman's "If I Can't Have You" and Penn groaned out loud. Next up would be the inevitable "How Deep Is Your Love." Then it would all be downhill. How was she supposed to keep her flagging libido alive?

A hand slipped into hers and Lila's familiar honeyed citrus scent carried to her nostrils, instilling comfort the way cozy kitchen smells sooth hungry children. Penn lowered her head so Lila could shout in her ear.

"Life's too short."

"I've already heard it from Nariko."

"Did you invite your girlfriend?"

"Last time I checked, she wasn't my girlfriend. And I talked to her voice mail this morning."

Penn thought she might have received a polite reply, if only to acknowledge the package she'd left on Unity's doorstep two nights ago. But, no. Apparently she was unforgiven. She took Lila in her arms, stroked tonight's copper-brown hair, and kissed her best friend's forehead. She felt so fragile, Penn feared to hold her firmly. Noting the weariness edging out her smile, she guided them to one of the quieter pockets of the huge downstairs space.

"I miss being touched," Lila said as they slow-danced out of time with the beat.

"You mean sexually?"

"Yes. People are afraid."

"Well, you've lost a lot of weight."

"It's not just that." Lila sighed. "They feel death creeping up. Not exactly a turn-on."

Penn wasn't sure how to make an offer that didn't sound insensitive. "I'll make love to you, if you want. I can be tender."

Lila laughed. "Have you ever felt like ripping off my jeans?"

"No," Penn admitted. Lila was one of those off-limits women she preferred to adore fully clothed. "But this isn't about me."

"Sometimes I love you very dearly." Lila stroked her cheek. "But I'm probably the only woman in this room you can't tempt, and that includes the straight chicks."

"What about Nariko?" Penn wasn't quite ready to give up. If Lila wanted a hot body next to hers maybe it was time for a creative solution.

Nariko massaged her several times a week, and Penn joined in every so often. She'd taken a reflexology class so she could press magic spots on Lila's feet. Some people thought that eased the side-effects of chemo. She was never sure if her technique was any good. When she practiced on Nariko, her nemesis said her fingers felt like floppy cat paws. Less than ideal.

Nariko seemed to sense Lila's loneliness and her need for

physicality. She often massaged her in the nude, bringing their bodies together for long, slow caresses that spanned the gray area between sensual and erotic. Sometimes she got impatient with Penn during those sessions, accusing her of getting horny watching. Penn always denied such crassness. Mostly, she was lying. She didn't want to sleep with either of them, but she wasn't dead from the waist down. Two naked women sliding over each other, even good friends—what was not to like?

"Nariko and I are too close to have sex. It would change everything," Lila said. "Don't try to solve this for me. I feel alive tonight, that's all. So I keep noticing breasts I'd like to squeeze"

Penn cuddled her tightly. "That's a good thing."

"I'm going to miss you," Lila said. "Send pictures of your Amsterdam girls so I can live vicariously."

"You're twisted."

The music changed and Penn felt eyes on her body. There was always someone looking, and tonight she was at her bad-butch best in her black-and-chrome cruising outfit, with her muscles on show and her hair combed flat. She felt like a fraud, because all she really wanted to do was cry in her beer. She scanned the tangle of wraiths around her, trying to get a fix on the watcher. Bodies and faces split and converged in a nonstop erotic kaleidoscope. Penn caught hazy fragments. Expressionless stares. Juicy lips. Ripe breasts. Naked thighs. Leather and lace. Latex and spandex. Pale limbs and dark.

Her gaze struck another in a split-second collision. Gravity shifted. Penn's heart slammed against her chest. Heat gathered as dancers hemmed her in when she needed to get out. A bead of sweat rolled down her spine. Desire, like hot needles, pierced her nipples and clit.

Lila tapped her shoulder, pulling her back from the edge. "Go find her."

"I don't think she's here."

Lila looked at her. "She's here."

Penn caught another flash. Unity's ragged pixie hair, but

shorter. A fine-boned, heart-shaped face shielded by a dark head. The mouths danced close. Chloe. Or Colette. The women kissed. Penn couldn't tell if the blonde was Unity. She almost drowned in the sex-drenched air. She started walking, weaving awkwardly through a steamy obstacle course of limbs. A wave of new arrivals surged between her and the two bobbing heads. She followed, too far away to know if her eyes were lying, inventing another make-believe Unity to beckon her.

They left the dance floor through one of the side doors. Penn convinced herself that she was seeing Chloe with her dainty submissive. Needing proof, she followed them through the labyrinth of offices to the silent, shrouded soundstage. The darkness closed in on her, and she blinked, waiting for her eyes to adjust to the few weak night-lights. The music was a distant pulse. She could hear breathing. Rough and fast. Voices. She flattened herself in a shadowed recess watching the play of shadow and light across the women kissing fifteen feet away.

Penn's heart pounded as the blonde slid to the floor on her knees, her head tilted back. She reached around Chloe to unzip the back of her skirt. The garment came apart. There were no panties. Something was said in French. Penn relaxed her shoulder muscles and silently expelled the breath trapped in her lungs. The kneeling girl held Chloe's hips and buried her face. Chloe threw back her head, her mouth parted in pleasure. She arched her back and gripped the steel tube frame behind her with both hands.

Penn shivered. A steady pressure built at her groin. She caught the front of her jeans in a firm squeeze and jerked hard. The slurping and licking sounds worked every nerve in her pelvis. She closed her eyes. She could feel Unity's mouth on her, the hot insistence of her tongue. The relentless pressure. The suck and tug. The perfectly timed flicks and long, slow strokes. The muscles of her belly contracted. She pictured Unity kneeling next to her, inspecting her like a librarian making catalog entries. This scar. That jumpy muscle. A clit constantly engorged and visibly throbbing. Nipples that hadn't softened in days. An orgasm breaking across a kiss that never seemed to end.

Chloe was trembling. Wild color tinted her porcelain cheeks. One of her hands clamped down on the back of the girl's head. She seemed close to losing it, breathing hard and moaning deliciously. Penn opened her jeans and caught her clit between two fingers, sliding down until she bucked instinctively. At Chloe's harsh cry, she felt the pressure build. Yes, if she kept this up, she would come. Soon. And she sure needed that orgasm. It had been hovering for days, drawing her to the brink before returning her to her constant state of pent-up arousal.

Aching with frustration, she took a couple of deep breaths and worked her fingers diligently back and forth along her swollen, sensitive folds. She wasn't there. Maybe she would never get there again. Unity had ruined her. Filled with pitiable yearning, she almost sank to the floor.

Chloe did exactly that, panting and sighing from her effortless climax. She kissed the young blonde, both of them kneeling. They barely caught their breath before shifting with the fluid ease of familiarity into the next phase of their play. Chloe kneeled upright and shoved the girl onto all fours, exposing her ass and pussy for a long, languid appraisal. She stroked the smooth skin with both hands, testing, telling the girl how wet she was. Then she spanked her ass gently with the open flat of her hand, crooning to her in a voice that was anything but stern. Penn recognized occasional words from her own trysts with Frenchwomen. Taunts and slutty promises. The slaps were louder, drawing small shocked gasps and unconvincing struggles. Penn wondered if they could hear her breathing. Every moan of theirs, every sigh, every slap was amplified in the silent, sprawling space.

Chloe slid both thumbs along the cleft of the pretty ass and spread the cheeks. Penn couldn't drag her eyes away. Her legs lost strength. She repositioned her feet, trying to keep up the pressure on her stubborn clit as Chloe teased a glistening trail of moisture from one opening to the next. The girl made a throaty sound halfway between a groan and a growl and spread her legs wider. Penn could almost feel the silky glide of a fingertip along that tempting parting.

The sensuous torment continued, no relief in sight. Chloe was taking her time, arousing her plaything, making her whine and wiggle and beg in breathless, pretty French. When she finally buried her fingers in the girl's pussy and her thumb in her ass, Penn shuddered, thrilled by the sight. She dipped a couple of fingers and circled the head of her clit, gradually compressing until she had to let go.

She saw herself behind Unity, one hand flat on the small on her back, the other buried to the knuckles. She loved that sight. Unity with her head resting on a pillow. The flat, neatly muscled planes of her shoulders fluttering as her hands ball around the bed covers. Her narrow waist flaring to the most perfect rounded ass. Penn lost herself in memory, watching herself sliding in and out, drinking in the sight of that pink, ripe flesh stretched around her fingers. She could hear Unity's soft begging, "Now. Mmn. Tell me." And her reply, "You're mine. I can fuck you any way I want, any time I want."

She broke out in a sweat and pinched the thick folds that gathered across her clit. At last. She was rigid, throbbing, ready to burst. Penn pumped feverishly, caught up in the ragged rush of her own breathing and the moans coming from the other women in the room. She was right on the brink of unloading, when a strange metallic sound called her present, snapping her out of her erotic trance.

Before she could turn her head, a gorgeous scent flooded the air and an arm slid across hers, ruthlessly evicting her hand from her jeans.

"I've been looking for you," Unity whispered, biting her ear.

❖

She felt a tremor run through Penn. They faced each other slowly. Penn's face was in deep shadow, but a thin cradle of light tipped across one side. Her eyes gleamed wildly. The muscles worked in her jaw and neck.

"Unity." Her voice was so hoarse, her whisper sounded like tree bark against a window. "I need you."

"Right now, apparently." Unity explored the open front of Penn's jeans. The fabric was damp.

"Yes." Penn's fingers crushed hers. "But not here."

"Why not? Do you really think they'll notice?" Unity ran her tongue over Penn's lips and said, "You're very close to coming. I can smell it."

"Yes." Penn let go of Unity's fingers.

Unity took advantage and slid her hand in her open fly and inside the soaking briefs. "You always get so hard."

She milked Penn's clit, smearing thick juices.

"Fuck." Penn groaned.

"I missed you."

"Oh, baby. I missed you, too."

"But you almost came without me, didn't you?" Unity underscored each word with a tug. She loved the surge of power she felt as Penn's body seemed to sink and soft groans shook her.

"You're killing me. I can hardly stay standing." Penn bit down on Unity's throat and pulled her skirt up.

"Oh, no you don't." Unity shimmied free. "I haven't said you can touch me, yet."

She glanced sideways, briefly distracted by the noisy cries of the young blond woman on her knees a few yards away. Her partner, one of the beautiful twins, was fucking her so hard they were both sliding in increments across the floor. The sight and sound of them and the feel of Penn pulsing wetly in her hand made Unity gush.

Penn worked against her fingers, eyes closed, her face lost in abandon. "Oh, yeah." She jerked hard, thrusting, swelling even more. Her hands closed over Unity's shoulders. Propping herself she leaned back, the arc of her pelvis lifting her until she filled Unity's hand.

Stroking along the hot, wet seam, rolling her thumb up and down, Unity said, "You better come soon. I need to be fucked."

Penn quivered and convulsed. A hoarse howl of joy broke free of her clenched teeth. Unity could feel her clit twitching in release. Easing her fingers open, she gently cupped the supersensitive area.

Penn sagged into her and took several deep, shaky breaths. "What are you doing to me?"

Unity carefully withdrew her hand. "Making you lose control. Letting you know who's in charge."

She loved the way Penn reacted when she was challenged. Her expression was instantly wolfish and dangerous. "I have to be inside you."

"I'm very wet." Unity's body renewed its relentless hollow ache. "I was thinking about choosing one of those women out there. Someone kissed me."

"Are you trying to make me crazy?"

"She was hot," Unity teased. "I let her touch my nipples."

"Really?" Penn cast a cursory look at the other women, who were in a panting post-orgasmic heap. They didn't seem to care that they had an audience.

"Well, you weren't there," Unity said. "And Nariko told me you were with two other women. What was I supposed to think?"

"I was trying to find you."

"Before or after you watched them fucking?"

On a low whine, Penn grabbed her elbow. "You're coming with me."

Unity didn't resist. She'd shared their intimate space long enough. "Where are we going?"

Penn fastened her jeans. "Upstairs to my room."

Unity walked faster. Her thighs slid together. All she could think about was tearing off her clothes and wrapping her legs around Penn's waist.

The door slammed shut behind her and they were in a small bedroom with a single lamp burning. Unity loitered. Nerves fluttered in the pit of her stomach. She inhaled Penn's scent, a clean tang laced with salt and sex. She looked incredible, solid and sinewy with her powerful shoulders shifting beneath the tight tank.

"Take off your clothes," she said.

Dry-mouthed, Unity unzipped her skirt and let it fall.

Penn drew the tank over her head and dropped it on the floor. Her dark nipples were stiff. Her eyes glinted with hungry intent. "I thought you wanted to be fucked."

Unity discarded her flimsy top and bra. Penn unbuckled her belt and opened her jeans. Unity hooked her thumb in her panties and pulled them down. Her heart beat so hard she felt light-headed. Something clicked inside her and she knew that, even without the package Penn had delivered to her door, she would still be here. She had already decided to ask Penn for the truth, and to believe her.

As Penn got rid of her boots and jeans, Unity said, "There's something I have to tell you."

She heard the swift intake of breath. "I'm listening."

"What you said...about being in love with me. I know it's true." Unity hesitated. "I always believed it."

Penn drew her close and walked her to the bed. "The last few days. Without you. It was ugly."

"Kiss me," Unity said, and with a stifled growl Penn pushed her down against the pillows and parted her lips in a searing kiss that made her flood in want.

She found Penn's hand and placed it between her legs. The kiss changed. Penn sucked her bottom lip gently, then eased back.

Caressing Unity's breasts, she said, "Let me see you."

Color warmed Unity's cheeks and she glanced down at her

nipples. They were rosier, too, and tightly bunched. Penn clamped them, one in each hand, trapped between thumb and index finger. As Unity opened her legs wider and parted herself, Penn twisted and pinched. She took in the sight of her, then bent down and ran her tongue once along the slippery groove.

"I just had to taste you," she said, and pinned Unity down.

She pushed in hard, stretching her open, sliding deeper with each thrust. Unity bore down, shaking with relief to be filled again. Over the past few days the impression of Penn's fingers had faded and she'd felt unbearably empty. She held Penn's gaze and lifted her hips, meeting each stroke with a sigh of joy. Her skin was damp and hot. Her breathing changed. She felt her flesh give, and swell.

"I love when you fuck me," she said.

Penn drove deeper. "Next time, I want you taking my cock."

The thought made Unity's shiver and moan. "I've never done that."

"Oh, God." Penn's rhythm changed. Her strokes were shorter and faster.

Unity steadied herself, clutching Penn's shoulders. She didn't know how Penn could make her come so fast, but a sharply spiraling tension grabbed her at her core and she knew she was only seconds from letting go. She dug her fingers in and pushed back, wanting more. All she could feel was Penn, hot and hard and pounding into her.

She arched up as the first deep tremors compressed her groin. Tensing, clamping down, she repeated Penn's name in fractured, inaudible mumbles. As she made the final push to climax, she whispered, "I love you."

Then she was surging inside, coming all over Penn's hand, moaning and begging, "Do me again."

Penn's mouth was on hers and she was shaking, too. And smiling. Between kisses, she said, "No one's ever asked me to do them again before they've even stopped coming."

Panting, Unity said, "No one ever wanted you like I do."

Penn hauled her into her arms and cradled her tenderly. "I can live with that."

❖

"When you didn't call, I thought you'd washed your hands of me," Penn said, the next morning.

Unity propped herself on an elbow, lying on her side. She trailed the back of her hand down Penn's cheek and throat, and let it come to rest over her heart. "I wanted to see you face-to-face, and I had a few other things to take care of yesterday."

"Such as?"

"Your map of camera locations was interesting. When did you disable everything?"

"That Friday night when your mom found me. My bag was full of recording devices. I spent the whole weekend terrified that you'd find them."

"Was that why you kept me on my back the whole time?"

Penn laughed. "I don't need an excuse."

"Why did you do it?"

"Because I felt like a jerk taking that job in the first place, and it only made matters worse when I fell in love with you."

"So, there was another camera you knew nothing about?"

"My boss organized back-up," Penn said. "I only found out after you saw that DVD."

Unity sighed. "I still can't believe Merrill did that. What was she thinking?"

"Do you want me to weigh in?"

"Sure, why not? She had your ass on film as well."

"She doesn't like losing and you slammed the door in her face twice. You dumped her, and you rejected the Fortis offer. She looked bad on both counts."

"It's hard to believe she could be so vindictive."

"I doubt she'd see it that way," Penn said. "My guess is that she truly thought the end justified the means, and it was just good luck that she got some personal revenge at the same time."

"I spoke with her," Unity said. "I think I was very reasonable, all things considered. I told her that if she wanted to keep this matter private, she'll need to keep her distance from me at work. No bullying. No hassling my staff."

"How do you think that'll pan out?"

"Well, Sullivan Brady is an old-fashioned kind of guy. I don't think he'd want to keep a CEO who did what Merrill did, no matter the justification."

"Tell me something, do you have any vacation time before you make the transition to Fortis?"

"I could find some."

"Have you ever been to Amsterdam?"

"No."

"I'd love to take you there, pun definitely intended." Penn grinned. "I have friends with a houseboat."

"That sounds very romantic."

"We could have a honeymoon."

"Are you asking me to marry you?"

"If I did, what would you say?"

"That I like the sound of living in sin better."

"How did I get so lucky?" Penn growled.

Unity dropped a fleeting kiss on one of her nipples. "You underestimate your charms."

"A rare accusation."

Laughing, Unity said, "Are you going to behave yourself in Europe for the next three months?"

"I may need help."

"What kind of help?"

Penn rolled her onto her back. Parting her thighs, she said, "You. Spread out like this. Waiting on my bed at least once a month, when I'm totally horny."

"I could work on that." Unity moaned softly as the weight of Penn's body settled over hers.

Penn sucked a nipple until Unity squirmed. "I've told my boss that I need a transfer back to DC when they can make it happen."

"Meanwhile, Fortis has a couple of European facilities. Perhaps I'll need to visit them. Often."

Unity gasped as Penn entered her almost too quickly. She was so tender, even the slightest movement sent waves of sensation radiating through her pelvis. A hot pulse beat relentlessly at her core, never letting her forget for a minute that she had a lover who used and pleasured her body.

A flush climbed Penn's face, making her look like an embarrassed kid. "God, I'm sorry. You must be...raw."

"Just slightly."

Instead of easing back, Penn pushed into her. "Get used to it."

A shock of delight raced from Unity's clit to her throat, emerging as a squeak. "I don't think I can come again," she whispered, wondering if there was such a thing as an orgasm limit.

"Trust me, you can." Penn slid irresistibly down her body and engulfed her clit.

Blowing, and delicately teasing, she summoned the sensitive head from its sanctuary. Alternating between exquisitely soft kisses and slow licks, she coaxed Unity back to the trembling edge of release. Every nerve in her body seemed to end in that dripping, aching ball of desire between her thighs. With every breath she took, the unbearable tension climbed.

"Yes," she cried, drawing Penn's fingers deeper. "Do it. Make me come. I want to come in your mouth."

A sharp spasm held every muscle captive as she finally imploded, spilling out all that was stored up in liquid, hot tears and choking words.

"I love you, Penn." She shivered uncontrollably and reached for Penn's hand to stop her withdrawing. "Stay."

Penn shifted so they could lie on their sides. Cupping Unity's face, she said, "I love you, too. I've waited my whole life for you."

They kissed and rocked together slowly, and Unity felt a pang as the warm, deeply buried fingers slid free of her.

Staring into Penn's eyes, she said, "Don't change. I love you exactly as you are, with your past, and your secrets, and your fantasies."

"Thank you," Penn whispered.

They lay still for a long time, absorbed in one another, and Unity felt something fragile form in the hollow cusp between them. A newborn, naked heart filled with hope and beating entirely out of love.